The
Unexpected
Love
of
Lexie
Byrne
(aged 39½)

The Unexpected Love Story of Lexie Byrne
(aged 39½)

Caroline Grace-Cassidy

BLACK & WHITE PUBLISHING

First published in the UK in 2021
This edition first published in 2022 by
Black & White Publishing Ltd
Nautical House, 104 Commercial Street, Edinburgh, EH6 6NF

A division of Bonnier Books UK
4th Floor, Victoria House, Bloomsbury Square, London, WC1B 4DA
Owned by Bonnier Books
Sveavägen 56, Stockholm, Sweden

A CIP catalogue record for this book is available from the British Library.

ISBN: 978 1 78530 385 2

1 3 5 7 9 10 8 6 4 2

Typeset by Iolaire, Newtonmore
Printed and bound in Great Britain by Clays Ltd, Elcograf S.p.A.

www.blackandwhitepublishing.com

My rock star Robert Grace and my rock Noeleen Grace,
for you both, Mam and Dad, with my greatest love and thanks.

1
Sliding Doors

RIGHT ON THE PART WHERE JOHNNY CASTLE informs Doctor Houseman that nobody puts Baby in the corner, my phone vibrates.

'Oh, no . . . here we go, Garfield.' I nudge the pudgy ginger cat sprawled across my thighs and hit pause. Without looking at the caller ID, I know who it is. With slight dread but determination, I answer.

'I'm not going to make it tonight.' I come straight to the point, stuff a handful of hot, salted microwave popcorn into my mouth. Garfield wobbles down and I tuck my sore feet under my backside.

'The bra's come off. I'm sorry, but I'm absolutely wrecked.' I shut one eye, wince and wait.

Glasses clatter. Voices are high. Traditional Irish music booms. A noisy pause.

'Eh . . . you are so too gonna make it tonight! Strap yer C cups back on, and get yer arse into town, Lexie Byrne!' Jackie screeches down the line, over a predictably boisterous bar. I snap my phone away from my ear, and it clanks against my earring. I'm dog tired, starving, my feet ache, I have dirty hair and the thought of having to get 'going-out-ready' to go back into town fills me with horror. All I want to do is eat my popcorn, see *Dirty Dancing* through to the end, stand under a steaming hot shower, and order a late supper of chicken tikka masala with pilau rice and naan bread.

'Heelloooo?' Jackie yells.

'Yes, I can hear you. The apartment above me can hear you! I'm not long home; the centre was jammed with lively tourists. You picked the right week to leave the job – myself and Annemarie were slammed.' I lick the tips of my salty fingers.

'The curse of working behind the information counter in a shopping mall, in Dublin city centre, on Paddy's Day, wha'!' Jackie roars as I stick my face into the bowl and gather a few half-popped kernels on the tip of my tongue.

'I guess so.' I release an anxious breath. Maybe she's going to give me a pass?

My very own Get Out of Town Free Card.

'Now. Get up. Get your glam on. Get them dancin' feet washed! D'ya hear me? Ahh! Will ya watch out, ya mad yolk!' she yelps.

'You all right?' I unhook my earring, balancing the phone between my neck and chin.

'Some lad just spilled half a pint of Guinness down me good top. We're like sardines in here.'

'You're really not selling it to me, Jackie.'

'No, it's all good, gives me a reason to go chat to him later, if I'm desperate, like. Not me cuppa Barry's now but wait till I've fitted me beer goggles in place, he'll be *Barry-Right-Now*! C'mon, Lexie, please – all the gang are here!'

'Seriously, Jackie, I haven't the energy.' I'm losing. She's not going to give up lightly. She's like a dog with a bone, or at the very least a dog with a phone.

'I've the good leather seat right by the old oak door. You'll see us as soon as you walk in.'

'But I'm –'

'Ahhhhhhh, please, Lexie! For me? We're just waitin' on you and Annemarie to get the party started, as Pink would say.' As Jackie breaks into a rather impressive rendition, singing about everybody waiting for me to arrive, I know she won't relent. I'll have to show my face.

'Oh, okay, okay.' Reluctantly I slide my best artisan bowl onto the low table. I know for a fact wild horses won't drag Annemarie back out tonight – she's seven months pregnant after a trojan two-year fertility battle and exceptionally careful of herself. Borderline obsessive, but don't tell her I said that. I squash the green button on the remote and my Patrick Swayze disappears. I stretch and yawn loudly.

'Atta girl!' Jackie's only delighted with me.

Us singletons rarely have enough excuses in our handbags to get out of going out. I can't cite boyfriend commitments or lack of babysitters. It's Jackie's leaving party – leaving from our workplace, Silverside Shopping Centre, and I did promise I'd be there. And I'm incredibly fond of her. Jackie has a heart of gold; she'd do anything for you. I just need a second wind. No. You know what I need? The door to burst open with an army of makeover people to 'do me up'. You know the ones? They look effortlessly stylish and bored stupid at the same time. Holding safety pins in between their teeth. Always have bulging bumbags. Don't tie their laces.

Wearily, I stomp into the kitchen with my new Bosch appliances, clad in only my navy gusset-enforced tights and white work shirt, and dump the bowl into the sink. Grumbling to myself about why people can't just leave me alone, I walk out and into my bedroom where I heave open the overspilling mirrored wardrobe. Hitting loudspeaker, I throw my phone onto my bed. 'The Irish Rover' blares out in the background as Jackie is still rambling on, the effects of a few early drinks resonating in her high-pitched voice.

'. . . a loada Scottish lads in here too, fine t'ings . . . and all in kilts! I'm debating dropping my powder compact under the table, opening it to the mirrored side and seeing what kinda jewels I can spot!'

'Stop being ridiculous.' I can't help but laugh as it's not beyond the realm of possibility.

'C'mon, Lexie, I've two Jägerbombs waitin' on ya and we're in a bar where the women actually wear the trousers! It's gonna be some craic tonight!'

I pull the clips from my high bun and shake out my hair; its curls twirl onto my shoulders.

'Jackie, Annemarie is not coming out, she's . . . gone to the cinema with Tom – don't call her,' I cover for my friend. 'And I have no intention of getting drunk or ogling up men's tartan skirts – well not tonight anyway. I'm in early tomorrow and it's into a late shift. So I'm having *one* glass of wine to bid you farewell because I'll miss you.' I soften. 'That's it. We can grab a toastie in Marco's before you leave next week?' I perch on the edge of my bed and release my feet from their nylon constraints. There's one thing about Jackie Brophy – that girl knows how to have a good time.

'Bid me *farewell*? Who'd'ya tink ya are? Camilla Parker Bowling Ball?'

'Let me get ready, ya loon.' I laugh, cross one leg over my knee and massage my bare foot.

'As you wish, Miss Byrne. As you wish,' she declares in a far too convincing received pronunciation accent, then hangs up. Tempestuous March rain drums against my second-floor window. It's dark outside and the only place I want to be is curled up on my sofa, but I order a taxi for half an hour via my app.

'Oh, there you are, Garfield.' My old cat slides back in through the door and curls up under my window, on my sheepskin rug. He purrs lowly. I inherited him when my granny passed away eighteen months ago.

'You're still missing Sir Patrick Dun's, aren't you?' He licks his paw. He lived in the leafy residential home with Granny for ten years.

'I guess you heard that call? I have to go out.' He rests his head on his silky paws, eyeballs me. Ever since Granny passed, I volunteer at the home almost every weekend I'm not on shift at work. I've given up on the dating scene so I've zero ties and I can't think of a more worthy way to spend my weekends.

'Believe you me, I'd much rather stay here with you! One hour and I'm out of there! I don't care what Jackie says. I'll order our supper in the taxi on the way home. Now, what the hell am I going to wear?'

I pull out a soft off-the-shoulder angora sweater that has been in a crumpled red ball and shake it out. Stretching up, I drag down my pleated skirt, the same one my ex, Dermot, used to tell me I was too old for – apparently made me look like a trying-too-hard has-been . . . Prince Charming, he was not. A cheating, Jack-the-Lad sort, let's just say he put a whacking great dent in my self-esteem, but ten months on, I'm getting myself sorted. I kicked him out on his love-rat arse and pressed the reset button on my life. It was grim, to be honest, but I'm contented with myself when I look in the mirror these days.

'Lexie, my girl, you need to jump in that shower and freshen up,' I tell myself, licking my index finger and running it under my smudged eyeliner. This morning's liquid over-eye is still winged into a thick flick above my green eyes.

'I can't be arsed applying a fresh face,' I say to a now-snoring Garfield as I take in my reflection. 'But I suppose I have to do a little preening. Quick fix-up, blast of the hair dryer, smudge of lip gloss and a spritz of my finest Chanel,' I tell him. 'The basics.'

I'm no raving beauty, and that's fine by me. I feel deeply sorry for raving beauties, truth told. Beauty's longevity isn't enough to render me jealous; falling in love with *The One*, now that renders me pea-green with envy. Hence my choice of movie as I curled up with my salty snack after work. I've been told by Annemarie I possess an unhealthy fixation with *The One*. It's true. I'm obsessed with finding true love, or no love at all. I can blame the movies. I'm besotted by all the romantic classics, *About Last Night, The Holiday, Dangerous Liaisons* but mainly *Dirty Dancing*. That's my romantic bible. I've kissed a lot of frogs in search of my 'Johnny', but it was not to be. I never found him. So, when I met Dermot at work and he chased me, I was flattered. He made me laugh and I enjoyed the security of being in a couple, but I know now I just settled for him. We were together five years, but like I said, he turned out to be a cockwomble.

So I made the decision that unless Johnny Castle merengues into my life and literally lifts me off my feet, I'm done with second bests. I'm thirty-nine and a half and I'm far better off on my own. Granted, they aren't beating the door down to woo me, but I'm fine with that. I'm quite happy in my single life. A bit like Garfield, who purrs in his sleep as I bend to rub his generous belly.

'Right, two-minute shower and patch-up job and I'll be straight back,' I whisper into Garfield's velvety ear. 'I'll scrape some sauce off my chicken tikka for you later.'

Content with my plan to get in and out of town as fast as humanly possible, I head for the hot jets.

2
Some Like It Hot

WHISKEY IN THE JAR' GREETS MY EARS before I even open the taxi door. The pavement is spilling over onto the busy road. The famous bench that rests between two wooden beer barrels is home to what seems like a hundred shades of green. The Brazen Head is physically heaving. Literally bulging. Green shamrocks are bouncing, projected all over the medieval brownstone building of Ireland's oldest pub. Bodies, dressed head to toe in green, are pressed against condensation-dripping windows. If the brick walls suddenly burst open and people spilled out on top of one another, it would not have surprised me in the least.

'Oh Lord.' I brace myself as I lean forward to pay the driver.

'Yer brave headin' in there sober, pet, at this hour on a Paddy's night.' He chuckles and tips his 'Kiss Me, I'm Irish' plastic hat at me, then, turning in his seat, hands me over my change. I unclick my seat belt.

'Believe you me, it's the last place on earth I want to be right now.' I tip him and, sighing, I get out and pick my way through the swaying smokers. As I step up, I pull open the heavy oak door to the left, just at the same time as someone pushes it with force from the other side, and we collide with a clash of heads. Stumbling, I miss the step and fall backward, flat on my back.

'Owwwwww! Fu–' I hit the ground hard, legs in the air, contents of my bag rolling everywhere. I grab my head, checking my fingers to see if there's blood.

'Oh! Bugger! Oh shit! Sorry! I do apologise . . . oh, I'm so sorry . . .' a voice echoes. An English accent apologises profusely over and over.

'Seriously, I – Could this day get any bloody wor–' I look up.

A vision stands above me. Things suddenly seem fuzzy. In and out of focus. I can't find a focal point. I'm not sure if it's the bang to my head or . . . *him*.

He reaches down for my bag, which has vomited all over the ground. Phone, tissues, loose batteries, keys, lip gloss, tampons, coins, a Subway wrapper – he gathers it all back into the bag and throws the brown leather strap over his shoulder. Then extends his hand. I pull my skirt down, thankful for the coverage of my tights and high boots.

'I think that's everything? Here, please take my hand?'

I'm almost afraid to.

'Oh, I'm so sorry, this pub is like a maze, so many doors. Are you sure you're okay? That was quite the tumble.'

It's like I'm experiencing some sort of déjà vu. I can't take my eyes off him. It's his dark messy hair, his thick stubble, his strong jaw, his black leather jacket. His voice penetrates my brain.

He repeats himself.

'Are you sure you're okay?' He tilts his magnificent face to look down at me. Never mind the fact he could run away with my bag, I still can't find my voice. I continue to stare. Eyes to drown in. The darkest brown. Melting. He's in jeans that hang off his hips like a Tom Ford model. A brown belt with a silver buckle. He's tall, broad, olive-skinned and he just has this . . . presence, like he never looks in the mirror. A real man. Not one of the Gym Robots that roam the plains.

'I . . . am – I . . . am –' I come around, take his warm hand and he pulls me up gently.

'Well . . . if you're sure. Again, I'm terribly sorry.' He touches his own head.

'No, don't be silly – it wasn't your fault.'

Then he smiles at me. Oh what a smile. My stomach does a double back somersault roundoff. An imaginary row of judges all hold up straight tens. I complete the scene with a neat curtsey. He really is a *vision*. I lick my lips, glossy with my best MAC and thank Christ for that basic wash-and-scrub-up under the shower earlier.

'I was too heavy handed with the door. If you're sure you're not hurt?' He slips my bag off his shoulder and over mine. It's a simple action that feels anything but.

'I didn't want to come out tonight; at least that's what I told my cat.' As soon as the words leave my mouth, I cringe so hard it hurts. It's my *I Carried a Watermelon* basic blunder.

'Is that a fact.' He laughs. Bites down on his bottom lip. Perfect teeth.

'I mean . . .' People push past us now on their way into the bar. I'm jostled. He reaches a hand to steady me. Delicious.

'You don't feel dizzy or anything, do you?'

'No.' A barefaced lie.

'Can I –' he starts.

'Adam! There you are, Coops!' A group of heavy-set, thick-necked lads surround him. 'Were you trying to escape while we were vaping, mate! Caught ya!' Riotous laughter. From within the scrum that's now carrying him away from me, he leans his head back and holds my eye.

'I was. But I'm staying now.'

They move away in the pack.

Holy shit, I think as I gather myself and this time slip in through the open door, incident free.

3
Brief Encounter

'LEXIE! LEXIE! LEXIE BYYYYRRRNNNNE! Over here! I'm here!' Jackie jumps up on the leather seat and waves wildly at me as though she's been clinging to a buoy in a rough sea all night, and I'm a lifeboat crew at first light.

'I knew ya wouldn't let me down, chicken!' She expertly flicks over her shoulder the two long clip-in green plaits that hide her own pixie haircut, currently nestling under a Viking hat.

'Hey.' I feel as though I'm walking on air. We double-cheek kiss and I squeeze in.

'I just got hit –' I begin to tell her.

'Did ya run out of hair product?'

Oh shit! Am I that looking that shite?

'Eh, I was in a hurry.'

'I'm only messin' with ya. Don't ya always say ya do a ponytail when you've no time to style yer hair? You always look fab, all those wild, blonde curls, them to-die-for cheekbones. Yer a little ride, Lexie Byrne, sure amen't I always tellin' ya how lucky ya are to have lips that natural but look done? Ya know everyone.' Jackie pinches my cheek then extends her hand. There are about eight people on the long leather seat. I know this seat well – the same seat where Annemarie met her now husband, Tom. Alas, no, I don't know any of the people sitting here tonight. Silverside Shopping Centre is huge – it's on four floors. Jackie tends to be out five nights a week, so she moves around the centre a lot meeting staff. Fresh blood. Her words not mine.

'Hi.' I give a mini wave. 'So are you all excited for this new journey?' I try to hold her attention, engage with her – that's why I'm here, for her. Try to put the man who's just floored me, literally knocked me off my feet, out of my racing mind.

'Go up an' get a drink. I drank yer Jägerbombs. Soz.' I can see the dark Guinness stain down the front of her yellow *Life Is Good* T-shirt.

'I've just sat down – the bar is teeming. I want to talk to *you*.' I slip off my denim jacket as Jackie takes my cold hands in hers. I wonder if she can feel how my heart is still beating like a pneumatic drill after that encounter.

'Lexie, I love ya, ya know I do . . . but I'm like Julie Andrews here, chicken.' Jackie leans right into me, holds her fake plaits back and nods at the others. 'I've all these Von Trapps to keep amused.' She flicks her thumb in their direction. 'Now I've no room to run around the bar and wrap meself in the curtains, or any brown paper bags to tie up with string, so I've suggested a drinking game. Now get in the queue and get yerself a beverage. Ya can't have me all ta yerself, pet.' She winks at me, crinkles her pierced nose.

Typical Jackie. 'Okay.' But I look around the pub from pillar to post to see if I can spot him.

'Whaddya doin'?' Jackie pokes me. 'Yer like a meerkat! Gerrup!'

'Well can I get you a goodbye pint?' I ask her.

'Ya cannot. Ya brought yerself and that's good enough for me.'

I get up. It's impossible to make out any individual in the throng of bodies. What are the bloody chances that the biggest ride I've ever seen would poleaxe me with a door on the night I'm not exactly at my Lexie Byrne best?

I squeeze through the mass of people, elbowing my way to the bar. U2's 'Pride (In the Name of Love)' plays out and the whole bar seems to be singing along.

'Excuse me.' I slither between a kissing leprechaun and a very short St Patrick, take my place and that's when I spot him again, right at the other end of the bar.

'Bingo!' I say to myself. I need to act on this. There was something about his voice that shook me. I don't think I've ever been attracted to a *voice* before. I know what I have to do. Annemarie and I used to call it the *orchestrated bar-bump*.

I shimmy across and find myself in the queue behind him. He's jostled in the crowd. I see two younger women poke one another. One juts her thumb upward behind his leather jacket, the other makes a circle with her finger and thumb and inserts her index finger in and out. They high five one another. He shouts his order of three Guinness. My heart starts to pound again. His pints are served. He turns with his drinks.

'Oh! You again! That's mad. Hi!' I strain my eyes, opening them so wide in fake surprise that the right one starts to water. I'm giving an Oscar-winning performance here.

His hands are full, trying to carry all three. But his brown eyes light up, laughter lines dance.

'Hey! Oh! Hi again!'

'Here, let me help you.' I prise a cold pint from his full hands.

'Why thank you! Oh, can I buy you a drink?' He does a double take from me to the bar.

'No, but thanks – I just got a full glass of wine.'

'This way.' He raises the other two pints above his head, and I follow him. When we reach his busy table, I rest the pint down and stand back. God, why didn't I style my hair and even out my complexion? I've made a bigger effort going to the bottle bank.

'I'm Adam by the way.' He wipes his hands on his jeans, extends his hand.

'Lexie.' Again, electricity shoots through my veins at our touch.

'Nice to meet you, Lexie.'

Oh, suddenly I'm tongue-tied.

'That was quite the *meet-cute* we had outside, I mean –'

'Oi! Adam! Found you, mate!' Another larger-than-life Englishman drapes himself across Adam's shoulder, oblivious to how rudely he's interrupting us. 'JJ! Michael! Over 'ere, lads!' He beckons.

'All right, Dominic,' Adam says.

'Yeah, mate, they really did turn the River Liffey green. You should have come with us, mate – looks class!'

'Sorry, we've a bit of a gang here.' Adam tries to untangle himself.

'Don't worry.' I tug my sweater down, revealing more bare shoulder, look up through my eyelashes. Adam seems to be holding this guy up.

'I'm sorry about this,' he says as he tries again, unsuccessfully, to free himself.

'Shots! Shots! Shots!' Dominic punches the air gleefully.

'Don't worry, I best be off. I'm over there with friends . . . at the long leather seat by the door. They'll wonder where I've got to.' Crash! Bang! Wallop! I drop my whereabouts. I don't want him to think I'm alone or just after a free drink. So, as casually as I can, I saunter off back to my seat, stomach sucked in so hard it pains, praying he's watching me go. When I get back to the table I have to squeeze into the corner. The drinking game is in full swing and I watch, amused but distracted. Wait until I tell Annemarie about this guy. She'll never believe it.

'C'mon, Lexie! Join in!' Jackie tries, six be-kilted Scottish men all standing around us now, a peeled beer mat stuck to her forehead with *Kim Kardashian* scrawled across it.

'Not tonight, Jackie – I'm in work early, remember.' I keep one eye on the game and one on the passers-by. *Come on.* I will Adam over.

'Here, neck this! We'll ease you into the night.' She pours me a glass of Prosecco from a newly appeared silver bucket in the middle of the table. Thanking her, I accept the chilled flute and put my mouth over the glass to slurp the excess she's poured.

'You have one question!' A man jams a finger at her, holding his pint precariously.

'Am I mega famous?' Jackie's asking the crowd around her.

'Yes!' another Scotsman roars.

'Am I Kim Kardashian?'

One-take Jackie. They all cheer and drink.

After about thirty minutes of increasingly daft and leery 'Who Am I?', I notice Adam approaching the table. *Finally.* Our eyes connect across the crowded room – he smiles, I swallow and try to keep my cool. How is he having this effect on me? He gets nearer, until he's only a few feet away. I cross one leg over the other, he smiles at me, then pulls the door carefully open, turns and exits. The door slams behind him.

Just like that my adrenaline disappears and I feel completely wiped out.

'Jackie!' I roar down the table from the corner I'm still stuck in. 'I'm gonna head in a few.'

Jackie nods, but it's clear she has no idea what I'm saying. In a pathetic attempt to forget the greatest clash of heads I've ever experienced, I swig back the last of my rapidly deflating bubbles. The taste is sour in my mouth. Time to call it a night.

4
Singing in the Rain

I'M STANDING BY THE SIDE OF THE ROAD, my hand out hailing a taxi, when he steps down off the path and moves towards me.

'Tell me you're not going home, Lexie?'

'Oh!' I say, startled. 'There ya are.' Jesus, this is madness. I thought he'd gone. 'Adam. Hi . . . yeah, yup . . . I am.' I throw my hands up as a taxi with his lights on spins right past me, thank God. Imagine if it had stopped? I'd been about to order a taxi on my app, only I was desperate for some fresh air.

'So annoying when they leave their lights on but have passengers in the car. I am . . . going . . . home . . . yup, indeed.' I click my tongue off the roof of my mouth as I desperately try to coax some saliva back.

'Well now, that's a real shame,' he says, looking like he means it, zipping up his leather jacket halfway, the breeze blowing his hair into his face. He brings his hands together to pull it back, making his high cheekbones even more pronounced. I smile at him curiously, my heart picking up the pace again behind my ribcage as I slowly drop my hand altogether. The last thing I need right now is for a taxi to take me home. Outside, on this noisy street, it feels like it's just the two of us. *Don't be an eejit*, I tell myself. *Pull yourself together. Be normal.*

'Are you over for St Patrick's Day, the rugby or a stag? Or all three?' I manage.

'Pardon? For what?' He gently tugs the lobe of his right ear and seems amused by my accent. His brown eyes crinkle at me with his well-set laughter lines. A man with laughter lines, it says everything.

'You know, a stag party, when the guys celebrate the last day of their friend's freedom before the ole ball and chain gets them.' I wiggle my wedding-ring finger and imitate the walk of one such.

'Oh, a stag!' He laughs, hard. 'Oh right, sorry . . . no, I just had a very unexpected week to myself. For a change! Thought I'd fly over seeing as it was St Patrick's Day, and I've never been to Dublin on this day. The lads always come. I've always wanted to but I've a . . .' He trails off.

'Hope you are finding us' – I find a flirt! – 'to your satisfaction.'

'A knockout.' Touché.

We both laugh. His friends are nearby, and we hear Adam's name on the wind and harmless, good-humoured, drunken sniggering, but he ignores them.

'I don't get to travel much anymore unfortunately. Deborah, my sister . . . lives in County Clare. She just got engaged. I'm going to visit her tomorrow, be nice to catch up with her before she comes home for her engagement party next weekend . . . it's been a while . . . well . . . families, you know.'

I notice a chain snug around his neck, a small silver feather dangling from it. The proximity of him makes my breath come fast. I seem to be speechless once again.

'I'm guessing you're from here?' he asks into my silence. 'This city, it's stunning, my God.'

'Yeah well, we like it here, it's eh, a grand place altogether so it is . . . so it is,' I manage, sounding very Oirish for some reason.

'Yeah, so beautiful.' His eyes connect with mine. 'I love your accent by the way,' he adds as if he's just read my mind.

'Do you?' I back-heel the kerb with my boots.

'I do.'

I blush, drop my head, smooth my fringe down with my hands then look up at him. The earlier rain starts to pitter-patter in fat droplets again.

'I don't know if this sounds crazy . . . you're heading home and all . . . and in light of the fact you've already told your cat you didn't want to come out at all this evening.' His eyes dance. 'But is there any chance I can persuade you to stay out a little longer and let me buy you a nightcap?' He nods to the oak door where two beefy bouncers now stand, arms folded, impatiently waiting for chucking-out time, a hard-earned can of Coke and doner kebab.

'Funny.' I laugh. 'I'll have you know Garfield is a very good listener.'

'And a lasagne lover, I hope?' He raises an eyebrow.

'Of course.'

'Garfield sounds like my kinda cat.'

Yes. Yes. Yes.

'So what do you say? We're getting wet here.' He holds his hands up as if to catch the night rain.

'To a nightcap? I say go on then, old chap, how very kind of you to offer!' Adam laughs and I feel pathetically elated. In fact, I'm performing the Gene Kelly dance from *Singing in the Rain* in my head.

'But weren't you leaving too?' I wonder, looking across at his gang of friends still vaping away as I hold my leather bag over my head as a makeshift umbrella.

'The Great Tew rugby lads are heading off to a club. I was sneaking out earlier when . . . well . . . I'm up early on the bus down to Clare. I'm going to see the Cliffs of Moher before I land in on my sister. I'm a bit of a lightweight these days, so I was just going to say goodbye to the lads and head back inside to have one for the road, see perhaps if I could persuade the beautiful girl I hit in the face with a door to join me.' He grins, zips his leather jacket to the very top, against the freezing March night that's now pouring down on us.

Excuse me? Did he just call me beautiful?

'Well thank you, sir, I'd be very pleased to join you.' I salute. He laughs again, and I'm pleased my voice doesn't reflect the chipmunk-like pitch of excitement I feel about sharing a drink alone with him.

'Great.' His eyes sparkle with what looks like genuine pleasure.

'Great.' I'm fit to burst but try to keep playing it cool.

'This time allow me to open the door?'

Then he puts his hand on the small of my back and, although I know my feet are on the ground, I feel like I'm about to float back into the bar.

'After you, m'lady?' He holds the heavy oak door, nods at me in a mock bow and I giggle.

Keep calm, Lexie, keep calm . . . keep calm. This is really happening, I chant in my head as we enter.

Inside is emptying out now; tables are cluttered with ripped beer mats, flat crisp packets and empties, the floor glue-like beneath my feet. 'Nothing Compares To You' is playing over the speakers. St Patrick and the leprechaun are slow dancing outside the toilets. I wave at Jackie who looks like she doesn't even know her own name by this stage, never mind the name of someone else on a ripped beer mat. She might not always know when to call it quits, but by God, I'll miss her – she's one of a kind.

'Is here okay?'

I nod. We take the two recently vacated high-backed stools up at the bar.

'What can I get you then?' he asks, pushing a load of half-empty pint glasses and long-necked bottles up the bar out of our way.

'I'll have a glass of Pinot Grigio, or any dry white, but here let me.' I rummage in my bag for my purse, feeling absurdly, acutely alive but also like I'm watching myself play out a scene on a film set.

'Oh no, no . . . I invited you. I've got this, please?' Again he runs his hand through his slightly wet hair and yet again my mouth goes completely dry. A younger woman struts past, tanned, in her cut-offs and scoop neck T-shirt. Her blonde ponytail sticking out of a green Ireland baseball cap; a pair of generous, bought lips. She stops, takes a step back and leans into the bar counter beside him. To my astonishment he doesn't give her as much as a glance. Dermot was a pig for 'admiring' other women – it used to drive me demented.

'Okay, thanks a million.' I cross my legs, noting his double take to the little flash of upper thigh under my pleated skirt.

'It's my pleasure.' He holds his gaze on my thigh for a fraction too long, then grins cheekily, as Miss Baseball Hat Wearer of the Year sashays away.

I inch my skirt down a touch. 'So where are you staying in Dublin?' I ask, clocking the dark hairs on his arms now visible as he removes his leather jacket and rolls up the sleeves on a light blue shirt. Not a whole lot of give in the material on those sleeves, I note. His physical presence thrills me. Just as well I left a full saucer of tuna for Garfield and decided against pre-ordering our tikka masala.

'Jury's Inn, Christchurch.'

'Good location,' I say, like he wouldn't know that for himself. 'How is it? Okay?'

'It's perfect . . . might I grab a Guinness and a glass of dry white wine please?' He leans on one elbow at the bar, and I notice that he's not wearing a wedding ring. I probably should have checked before I agreed to this nightcap. Meanwhile, the bartender looks like she might need an army of doctors to help fold her tongue back in her mouth.

'Coming right up!' she flirts. Can't say I blame her. She's only human.

'Thanks.' He smiles but again, no obvious extra attention on her. None of those I-would-if-I-could-but-I-can't eyes which Dermot had never bothered to hide.

He peels open his wallet. There's a photo behind the clear plastic that I can't make out as he pulls out a twenty-euro note.

'There ya go now – enjoy!' The bar girl beams at him as she delivers the drinks and his change, an off-white tea towel slung over her shoulder. She only just stops herself winking at me as she reaches over and wipes down the wet bar for us.

We clink glasses. 'Sláinte!' he says.

'Sláinte!' I say back. A feeling of being profoundly alive floods my entire body. Every sense on high alert. And to think I nearly stayed in for another night on the sofa in my jammies! To think I might have missed this. Missed *him*.

'So . . .' He glances about dramatically, a smirk on his perfect face. 'Is there a jealous boyfriend about to pounce on me?'

'Nope,' I say with a lift of my eyebrows. 'How about a jealous girlfriend-wife type storming the bar to throw the slut bomb at me?' I tilt my head at him as I take a long welcome sip of wine, which is surprisingly chilled for the time of night.

'None of the above.' We balance our drinks back on the bar.

'Lovely.'

'Lovely.'

'So why no boyfriend?'

'Oh, don't ask me that!' I laugh, trying not to stare as he crosses his legs on the high stool, his thighs muscular in the faded denim of well-worn jeans.

'Why?'

'It implies there's something wrong with me!'

'Well that's not what I meant at all!' He grins and holds his hand up.

'I've been in a few relationships; they didn't work out. You know, the usual.'

'What's the usual?'

'Infidelity.'

'Oh no.'

'Uh-huh, oh yes. But not on my part.' I look away, off down the bar where the girl is loading glasses into the dishwasher. 'One in particular, and often,' I sigh, 'by all accounts.'

'I'm sorry.' His jaw tenses; he scratches at his stubble.

'Don't be. You know what, I had a lucky escape.'

'Still, it's an awful thing to . . .' He trails off.

'Worse things happen at sea.' I try a joke, wanting to lighten the mood.

'At least you weren't married, I guess, so that's good.'

'That it didn't work out?'

'Yeah. I'm very glad about that.'

'Are you now?' I change the direction of this conversation with a flirty line. The wine is reaching my sucked-in-for-dear-life belly and a surge of alcohol washes over me.

'I am.'

'So you want me to be lonely?'

'Are you?'

'No, not at all.' I twirl the glass by its delicate stem, take a sip.

'I didn't think so.' His eyes take me all in. 'You look like a woman who can be on her own.'

'Is that right? I'm curious . . . you reckon that's a good thing?'

'It's an imperative thing.' He pauses, smiles. 'You know, my parents were fifty years married last month. They're both very independent-spirited . . . but also like lobsters. Fifty years! It blows my mind.'

'Amazing,' I agree. 'But – lobsters?'

'They mate for life.'

'Aha, so is that the dream for you? A fishy fifty-year love story?' I ask and he grins, thinks about it.

'Maybe, with the right person . . . yeah, I suppose . . . but you can't really know that starting out, right? We all have the best of intentions.'

'The idea of it is beautiful though, I'd say. Unlike lobsters.'

'Right?' Raised eyebrows.

'I've a busy life; it's all good.' I hold his gaze. 'Although I have to ask. Are you by any chance a swiper?'

His eyes narrow in puzzlement for a moment. 'Tinder? Christ no! All that starts on a lie. Lies about what they look like, how old they are, what their interests are. And then they want you to take them out for dinner, just so you can find out how many lies they've told? No swiping for me. I don't get it.'

'Truth!' I raise my glass in a toast. 'So tell me, why are you single?' I ask, trying to keep the disbelief out of my voice.

'Why am I single?' He picks up his pint and swirls it. The black and cream mixing. No bubbles floating merrily to the top. It settles deadly still, unlike my fluttering heart. He takes a long, appreciative sip.

'It's complicated.'

Curiouser and curiouser.

He wipes the cream from his upper lip with the back of his hand.

'Life's very complicated.' My words come out lightly, afraid to push him in case I burst this magical bubble.

'Ain't that the truth!' he says, and we hold eye contact again. For two complete strangers it's eerie. Intimate. Like we each know exactly what the other is thinking. This has never happened to me before. I break away first, my eyes drawn by the slight lift and fall of the small silver feather around his neck.

Then Adam makes this sound. A sound one might make when devouring the most delectable bacon double cheeseburger after a week-long celery-juice detox.

'You okay?' I've never encountered such a sound directed at me before.

'I'm not sure.' He uncrosses his legs. 'This is . . . I mean . . . Can I just say . . .'

'Well fuck me sideways with a non-organic cucumber! Where'd ya find this magnificent species, Lexie, ya bleedin' wagon ya?'

Jackie drapes herself over my shoulder like a sack of spuds and hiccups a miasma of alcohol fumes in my face.

The bubble is well and truly burst.

5

It Happened One Night

'HEY, JACKIE!' I manoeuvre her to stand beside me.

'There ya are, Lexie!' she exclaims, clinging on to the bar top. 'I thought ya said ya were going to the loo?'

'I said I was going to head in a *few* . . . but then –'

'Ya said ya were going to the loo but I thought ya must have fallen down the pan or something yer gone missin' that long . . . then I seen ya walk back in the door with Cillian Fucking Murphy! No way, says I. Jammy bitch. Yer hair's mad long, Cillian!' And then she reaches over and strokes Adam's hair admiringly. I resist the temptation to lightly slap her hand away, but somehow she gets the message and starts to twirl her oversized gold hoop earring through her ear over and over.

She hiccups again, then slurs at him, 'Are-ya-no' married to'a Cork girl but?'

'He isn't *actually* Cillian Murphy, Jackie. Listen, will I order you a taxi? It's crazy busy on the road out there.'

'Ya will in yer hole! Yer still out so you've no excuse now, you'll have a shot wit' me . . . I'm going to Dubai, baby!' As if in mad celebration, and completely unaware of her surroundings, Jackie begins to do the floss. I start to laugh – I can't help it. She's like a kid, one who's just spent all her communion money at Krispy Kreme.

'Three tequilas, hun!' She steadies her Viking hat and holds up four fingers to the bar girl.

'Oh no, please!' I protest, shifting forward on the high stool.

'Can't drink tequila.' Adam holds his hand up.

'Sambuca?' we both say at the exact same time.

'Freaky.' Adam wiggles his fingers, magician like.

'Freaky Blinders wha'? Yis are well suited an–anyways. Three sambucas hun when yer ready please!' Helpful, as ever, she holds up two fingers.

'Dubai?' Adam draws her attention, engages with her.

'Du-bleedin'-bai . . . I've a load of mates over there from me ma's road, brew their own like. I've a lotta livin' ta do; I'm not an aul' wan like Lexie here!' Jackie slams her hip into me, and I nearly fall off the stool. Adam grabs me and sets me right.

The shots come and Jackie shouts, 'One, two, three,' and we knock them back.

'Hope you won't be too wrecked in the morning, Lexie.' Jackie teases me playfully as I compose myself after the acerbic liquid. 'C'mere, I can't find a sign of *Barry-Right-Now* who spilled the drink down me. And c'mere, the Scots all left but that lad from Café Tree arrived and he fancies me but . . .' She hiccups again, tugs on her green plaits. 'And c'mere, he seems to only have the one brown jumper and he never wears any socks. Like can ya imagine the bang offa his mincemeat?' At which thought, she sways slightly.

'Feet,' I translate for Adam. He nods. Bites his bottom lip.

'I don't know him very well, but he seems so lovely,' I offer.

'Hmmm. He's also over from a different religion, and I've no interest in listening to his religion – why should I when I don't listen to me own? And he doesn't even drink! Like what's that about?' Her shoulders hit her ears she hunches that high. 'And we've nothin' in common . . . bu' I leave soon so I suppose if I tell him to keep his moccasins on . . . I won't smell his mincemeat, will I? Ah shite, I forgot me purse. See yiz!' Jackie takes my face and squeezes it between her two sticky hands and kisses me on the mouth.

'And c'mere, I love you, Lexie Byrne. I'll never forget you, chicken . . . all right?' I nod. 'I'll WhatsApp ya from Dubai . . . yer always in here.' She makes a fist and thumps herself hard on the chest through her Guinness-stained top. Actually winds herself. She momentarily puts her head between her legs and when she comes up, surfacing like a pearl diver, she says, 'We had the best of craic in Silverside, didn't we?'

'We did.' I smile fondly at her. 'We really did.'

'I won't kissa you, Cillian, in case it goes in the papers, hun.' She winks at him and wobbles away. I watch what's left of the crowd as it disperses to let her pass through and see kind-hearted Nnamdi, the barista from Café Tree, wrap his arms around her, then help her put one of her arms into her bubble coat. When I turn back to Adam, he's paying for the shots.

'Ah no, sorry about that – she's a terrible woman.'

'I thought she was brilliant!' He laughs, licking the sticky remains from his long fingers. 'Her own woman, right?'

'Oh, that she is!' I grin openly at him – that sambuca hit the spot. 'So, in her honour, like – she's one for the drinking games – want to play twenty questions?' I ask him.

'Sure.' He looks intrigued.

I don't miss a beat. 'What age are you?'

'Forty-two.'

'Star sign?'

'Capricorn.'

'Did you watch *Normal People*?'

'Didn't everyone?'

'What's your favourite film?'

26

'Oh. Just one?'

'Yep.'

'Uhm, *Lost in Translation*.'

'What do you think Bill Murray whispered to Scarlett Johansson at the end of the film?'

'I have had sleepless nights over it . . . I do not know.' He face-palms gently.

I don't want him to ever try and leave so I keep it going with more random questions.

'Are you a beach bum or mountain-climbing type guy?'

'Beach bum.'

'Do you count your weekly alcohol units.'

'Never.'

'Death row meal.'

'Fish, chips and mushy peas.'

'Best trait?'

'Good-natured.'

'Worst trait?'

'I can't tell you that, I'm trying to impress you.'

You are? I think. But instead I say: 'Your turn.' I fix my sweater, revealing my right shoulder. His eyes dart. I swish my ponytail and can't help smirking to myself.

'Favourite movie.'

'*Dirty Dancing*.'

'Pet peeve.'

'Meanness.'

'Morning lark or night owl.'

'Night owl.'

'Favourite pastime.'

'Drinking wine and eating cheese.'

'Type?'

'Of what?'

'Man.'

'Oh, I thought you meant cheese.'

'No.'

'Loyal.'

'If you could have one wish, what would it be?'

I'll tell him the truth, that there is only one answer to that question, and at the same time we both say: 'I wish for all the wishes I want.'

Verbatim.

'Superpower?' he asks me.

'Invisibility.' No need to think twice.

'Me too!' We high-five. Game over.

I reach for my wine.

'I've the makings of a wine cellar at home,' he says. 'Bit of a work in progress.'

'My favourite type of cellar.' I raise my glass. In the night's last dregs, surrounded by the abandoned green detritus of another St Patrick's Day, still that magical-bubble feeling envelops me.

'So *Dirty Dancing* yeah?'

'Yeah. I saw it at Tara Durkin's sweet sixteenth birthday party – there was a rerun in the local cinema. It kinda had a profound impact on me.'

'Nobody puts Baby in the corner, right? A metaphor for how every woman should be treated?'

'Right. That . . . and the visceral love they shared on-screen . . . that connection through lust, the evocative music over the backdrop of steamy Latin dance. It all felt other-worldly when I was sixteen. I couldn't wait for it to happen to me. True love filled my dreams. But then I grew up.' I laugh.

'I'll remember that.' He smiles, shimmies his shoulders.

'Do you believe that things happen for a reason?' I have to ask.

He nods. 'In so far as I believe in taking responsibility for your own life, your own mistakes and righting them as best you can.'

Profound, I think, only a little sarcastically. But nice to hear.

'Ladies and gentlemen, last orders now please!' the young lounge boy calls out as he walks past us, his dicky bow undone, a dripping wet tray tucked under his arm.

'It's not one o'clock already?' I gasp with a shocked look at my watch. Not a great sign that I know the time of last orders.

'It's never?' His dark eyes dance, and with every flash of the house lights I can see now that he's a little merry. He reaches into his inside jacket pocket on the back of the stool for his phone and I glance at his screensaver – all I can see is a big white Fedora hat, but I look away quickly, not wanting to appear nosy as he checks his messages.

'So what is it you do across the pond?' I ask as I stand a little shakily, on the slim back bar of the high stool, to get the bartender's attention. I'm not asking if he wants another drink – I'm just getting it. My round. No one can disagree with that. It's an unofficial Irish law. It's written somewhere in the constitution I'm sure.

'Hey let me.' He pulls his wallet out again.

'No chance!' I take the opportunity thanks to the bite of Dutch courage I now have to put my hand on his shoulder. It's sculpted, rock hard.

'It's my round!' I wave my credit card at the bar girl, who sees me and gives me that *Jesus, you're one lucky wagon* look again. I grimace at her by way of apology. I'm getting the feeling every straight woman in Dublin would gladly trade places with me.

'So what do you do?' I ask again, my voice coming out in a higher pitch as though he'd answered and I hadn't heard him.

'Um. I . . . well lately?'

'Anytime?'

'A lot of painting and decorating. You?'

'I'm in customer service, at a shopping centre here in town.'
But, as I tap my credit card, then carefully lift the drinks, I sense
he's not really listening.

'It's getting late, so I have to say this.' He stops and inhales.
'I really do think you're beautiful, funny, smart and witty – and,
well, the second I saw you . . .'

I realise I'm holding my breath.

'Or should I say, hit you with a door, well . . . I couldn't take
my eyes off you . . . it was a bit like a déjà vu.'

I thought the same. Still speechless. I'm guessing it's my turn
to speak but I can't.

'What I'm trying to say is this feels different and I don't want
the night to end.' The words spill out of his mouth and I can't be
sure I've heard him right.

'W-What?' I stand his pint half on, half off a soggy beer mat.

'Oh, jeez. I'm sorry!' He pulls at the chain around his neck,
twists the feather, then reaches for my hand.

'No! No! Don't be – I –' I put my free hand on his shoulder
again as he leans into me.

'It's just that I haven't met anyone like you before. It feels
so *good* to be hanging out with you. Totally brand new and . . .
intoxicating.' His gaze never leaves mine, only intensifying the
urgency of the eye contact between us that's been building all
night. 'Do I sound mad?'

'No,' I spurt. 'You don't.' I swallow a large gulp of wine. 'I can
live with that.'

'Not too heavy considering we only met a few hours ago?' He
narrows his eyes.

'Honestly?'

He nods. I have to go for it.

'I fancy you like crazy. It's almost too much for me.' I did not
just say that! The blood rushes to my face and my cheeks turn

30

crimson. I feel them sting as I plunge back into the wine glass.

'Really?' A gigantic smile spreads across his perfect, chiselled features. 'Do you . . . well . . . would you? I mean, do you want to keep the night going, Lexie?' He leans even closer on his stool, that face inches from mine. I can smell his skin, minty wash mixed with musky aftershave, spiced and sage undertones, and I can see the different shades of hair in his stubble.

'I do.' Never has a woman meant those two words as much.

He stands. Pulls on his leather jacket. 'But . . .'

He looks like he wants to say something. I give him no chance. 'But nothing!' Downing my wine, I slam my glass onto the bar. It's all a little too Shane MacGowany, but then he reaches for my hand again.

We are physically connected. A million watts run through my body.

Hand in hand, I walk two paces behind him, conscious of looks of envy from the remaining punters, men and women, as we float outside. Miraculously a taxi is passing and stops. The stars have aligned. Adam holds the door open for me, I slide in, he closes the door, walks around the back and folds himself in beside me.

'Thanks, driver.' With a sideways, cheeky glance at me, he adds, 'Jury's Inn, Christchurch.'

6
About Last Night . . .

CALM DOWN, LEXIE! CHEW YOUR FOOD.' Annemarie, best friend and work colleague, hands me a napkin from across the table as we take our Friday lunch hour together. 'Now, was this guy at Jackie's goodbye party last night?'

I nod. 'He's English!' I cover my mouth with my hand, so exhilarated I can't get the words out fast enough.

Annemarie holds her palm up. 'Chew faster.'

'From the Cots–' Accidently, I spray some hot chicken baguette as Annemarie ducks out of my line of fire.

'Oh, Lexie, come on!' Annemarie wipes her freckled cheek.

I swallow hard.

'Sorry.' Using the napkin, I dab my chin, pick up my Americano. 'Yeah, I met him in the Brazen Head last night – he's from the Cotswolds!'

'The Cots*what*?' Annemarie swipes a sweet potato fry through a mound of mustard.

'The Cots*wolds*!' I repeat. 'Seriously, want a chip with that mustard?'

'Whatevs.' She pops it in and chews slowly.

'He's unbelievable. Truly, my leading man – I found him! I can't tell you! I've been dying for lunch hour to tell you!'

Annemarie sits back in her chair, eyeballs me.

'I had a feeling I wasn't just going to get the dirt on Jackie's leaving do. Okay, Lexie Byrne, you look very . . . flushed. So let me get this straight – he was in the Brazen Head last night, he's English but he lives here, in Dublin, right?'

'Nope.' I shake my head. 'He's nothing to do with Jackie. She actually thought he was Cillian Murphy! He's here on a week's holiday but he left for Clare this morning, to visit his sister, and go sightseeing around the Aillwee Cave and Cliffs of Moher. He's coming back to Dublin tomorrow!'

She curls her lip. 'Bit nerdy.'

'How is that nerdy?'

'I dunno, I just have this visual of a guy with woolly brown socks tucked into his hiking boots and binoculars hanging around his neck.' Annemarie dusts her hands off one another. 'Completing the look with a sensible anorak.'

'Trust me.' I throw her a suggestive wink. 'He's not that guy.' I can't stop grinning, but Annemarie curls her lip again.

I don't care who says what. I've been waiting to feel like this forever. Always wondered if this *feeling* existed in real life, or if it was all just made up for the movies. But not anymore. Not after last night.

'Nerdy or not . . . the guy's from England, right?' Annemarie interrupts my reverie. 'Sure, what's the point in him then? Waste of time and, as Jackie would say, clean knickers.'

'What are you talking about?'

'Well.' She leans over, rests her elbows on the red-and-white-chequered tablecloth, and in a slow, deliberate voice says, 'Lexie, pet, you live here, in Ireland; the Englishman, he does not. *Comprende*?'

'Annemarie, pet, I don't care if he lives in a high rise in Moscow, drinks vodka for breakfast and wears a leather trench coat and an eye patch! You don't get it. He's out of this world!' I air-kiss the skies. 'I'm on a ridiculous high here!'

Annemarie does this thing she does when she's uneasy. She hunches her shoulders as high as they can go, so her long neck all but disappears.

'Woah.'

'*Woah*?' I go up an octave.

'Woah,' she repeats in the same tone.

'Oh, come on, you know how unlike me this is! You know I'm content on my own. You know I've given up on finding *The One* because of my apparently unattainable romantic expectations . . .'

'I don't think *fidelity* was too much to *expect* from Dermot but go on.'

'Well this guy, Adam, ticks every box,' I enthuse. 'It's the first time, God, I don't know . . . ever, that I've truly head-over-heels fancied someone like this. God, it's so exciting!'

She raises eyebrows at me.

I shoot her a look.

'Well I suppose you've never felt like this with anyone apart from Dermot . . . before you found out about his cheating that is,' she reminds me.

I half nod; it's unconvincing because it's a lie. I don't remember Dermot ever making me feel like *this*. Dermot wouldn't be worthy to lace Adam's, I'm guessing, size-twelve boots. Shifting on my seat, I catch my flushed reflection in the floor to ceiling windows. Marco's café sits directly opposite Silverside Shopping Centre, our shared workplace that overlooks the Dublin Quays.

'Sorry,' Annemarie says, misunderstanding my silence. 'I didn't mean to bring Dermot up.'

'It's grand, Annemarie – I'm long over Dermot honestly.'

She tilts her head, strokes her chin, and only just stops short of pulling on a diamante skull cap and saying 'Cross my palm with silver, my girl' or 'Gimme a pound' as she studies me. I wrap my hands tighter around my coffee cup.

'What? You think Adam is a rebound? Please! And take that fortune-teller look off your face. It's been ten months, for God's sake! Yes, Dermot publicly humiliated me. Yes, I was mortified that the whole of Silverside knew about his shagging everything with a pulse. And yes, he trampled all over me and crushed my confidence into the ground, but I'm fine now. He's an asshole and I'm over him! I don't pine for Dermot, believe you me!' I swap the coffee for my baguette, so I don't have to talk for a minute.

'Okay, chillax!' Annemarie reaches her hand across the table apologetically. 'I'm only looking out for you! I believe you, but no harm in checking in now and then. Isn't that what best friends do?'

I smile through my mouthful of baguette, letting her know it's all okay. But, actually, I wish she hadn't brought up Dermot. I feel nauseous when I think how I might well have ended up with him. Before I found out what he'd been up to, I'd assumed he was my future because we'd been together for five years. Eyeroll emoji indeed. There had never been any lengthy relationships before him, just casual ones. I'd never even come close to finding my Johnny Castle – so I convinced myself that *The One*, *The Guy from the Movies*, *The Leading Man* – was make-believe. He didn't exist. *The One* for me has always been Patrick Swayze's Johnny Castle. Perfection. Baby got it all. But I'd assumed that level of love and lust was unattainable – just scripted for the movies, not for Lexie Byrne in her ordinary life.

Until last night.

I digress.

Five years I gave Dermot – the last two living together in my apartment. *Gave* being the operative word. During that time, my parents had retired to Spain and they'd offered me – their only child – the chance to go with them, to start a new life in the sunshine, but I was happy in Dublin with Dermot. Although, after the initial honeymoon period, his true colours had slowly unveiled themselves before me. The thrill of the chase had involved him sending me bunches of exotic flowers at work, taking me to cool comedy clubs, wining and dining me in trendy open-air wine bars midweek, going on long drives into the countryside at the weekends and sending me hundreds of romantic messages . . . but once we were officially an item, all of the above disappeared.

Puff.

The smoke still lingered, but the magic show was over.

I'd hoped when he moved in with me that we'd continue to have stimulating date nights and plan exhilarating trips to Europe on cheap weekend breaks.

Rome.

Budapest.

But nothing changed because it seemed Dermot wasn't really the *flowers-flirty-messaging-having-fun-midweek* kinda guy he'd sold me. More like:

Home.

In his vest.

We are all but that next step away from toppling headfirst off the 'okay, you'll do' settling cliff. Smashing onto the rocks with the seagulls pecking at our remains.

I'm brought back to the present by a ding-a-ling on Anne-marie's phone. I watch her as I chew in the companionable quiet. Despite a night spent rolling around in that dimly lit hotel room, I feel utterly awake. More alive than I've ever felt in my thirty-nine and a half years.

'Marco's baguettes are highly calorific,' Annemarie declares as

I wipe my saucy hands. 'But, my God, just look at that dessert!' She points to a woman passing with a whipped cream and melted chocolate concoction. The woman, blushing slightly, edges her tray to her other side as she takes a seat in against the window.

'I mean, your arteries could get clogged with cholesterol just looking. But I'm such a hypocrite, I *want* it!' she murmurs as she slides her phone back into her rucksack. Unlike me she is currently obsessed with what she puts into her body. She never used to be. But unlike me, she is no longer single and, at forty-two, is thirty-one weeks pregnant for the first time. She's been through an almighty struggle to conceive.

'Oookay,' I reply slowly. 'So get one? You deserve all the whipped cream the world has to offer.'

'Uh-huh, you know I'm on my pregnancy health diet. That was Tom,' she adds with a gesture to the phone in her bag, 'just about food for later. I might do an organic roast chicken with spinach and roasties – it's a roast chicken kinda day . . . comfort food, you know?' She nods to herself before glancing back at me. 'Anyway, I'm sorry – back to you! Tell me more!'

I open my mouth to continue my – in my opinion – thrilling story of the night before, but she stops me. Again.

'Hang on a sec!' She wags a finger at me from across the table. 'Forget this Adam, for a moment. You were with that fella from Galway you said was mighty craic a few months ago. Whatever happened to him? You never told me!'

'He *was* mighty craic. We ended up in Coppers after you left. I hadn't been ready to go home just because you were – it wasn't even bloody midnight! We danced all night to the cheesiest pop songs. He was hilarious. But I didn't *like him* like him. He just, well . . . he just did.' I lower my eyes as I battle to pull apart a plastic milk sachet from the bowl on our table.

'Just did? What does that even mean?'

'Why does Marco make his Americanos so strong and what's wrong with an old-fashioned jug of milk for the table?'

'Stop avoiding my question!'

'Oh, it means he was grand for the night, but I felt nothing after . . . *it*. I just wanted to go home, hungry again, and mush a packet of Tayto crisps between two slices of batch bread in my own bed . . . then vacuum my mattress with my hand-held, so sue me!' I throw my hands up in the air, drama-queen like.

'Nothing wrong with that. But what do you want exactly, Lexie? I keep telling you, life isn't the movies. What are you looking for?'

'Oh, I'm looking for so much more.' I lower my voice to almost a whisper and lean across into her. 'I know exactly what I want now and the soundtrack beats in my head – "Cry to Me" by Solomon Burke . . .' I hum the beat.

She throws her eyes to the heavens, sucks her cheeks in, tries not to smile. She's heard this all before after all.

'. . . and I won't settle for anything less, Annemarie. Recall, if you will, the sexual magnetism between Baby and Johnny when they danced to "Cry to Me", when their bodies moved as one, when Baby says, "*But most of all I'm scared of walking out of this room and never feeling the rest of my whole life the way I feel when I'm with you . . .*"' I trail off into a dramatic whisper, a quiver of my bottom lip.

'It's called a film, Lexie.'

I ignore her.

'Johnny Castle is a fictional character.'

I ignore her again.

'Sometimes Baby is happy to just sit in the corner, drink her wine and chill the fuck out.'

'Language, Annemarie,' I say, pretending to be shocked.

'But seriously, picture that look of pure desire in Rhett Butler's eyes when he swooped Scarlett O'Hara up in his arms, at the bottom of that magnificent spiralling staircase?'

She grimaces. 'Always felt that was bit dodge actually.'

'Passion! It was passion!' I gently bring my clenched fist down on the table. 'And no, I didn't have any of that with the Galway nightclubber, whose name I can't remember. I swore if I taste a relationship ever again it will be the greatest dish I've ever eaten. It will be three Michelin stars. It will be sublime. And you know what? I think I found it last night!'

Annemarie makes a sarcastic grunt.

'You don't believe me?'

She plasters a smile on her face. 'I have no idea, Lexie. I just know you'd be better off looking for an Irish guy. Maybe give the Galway guy another date, when you're both sober. Sometimes love needs room to grow.'

'Room to grow, me hole! I want fireworks, Annemarie. Boom!' I bang the table again, harder this time. The mustard topples over.

'Shush!' She sucks her cheeks in again, pulls her chair in as close to the table as her bump will allow.

'There was no shaking after-lust with the Galway guy,' I hiss, but she butts in.

'What does that even mean? Live in the real world pur-lease!'

'It means when I left his musty, single pull-out, I'd zero fantasies about the next time we'd meet. Not one daydream about how alluring I'd be in a skin-tight dress, boho blow-dry, immaculate make-up, looking my very Lexie Byrne best . . . not once did I daydream about how I'd step down off the Galway train into Eyre Square and there he'd be, in a dark dress suit, lounging against an illuminated lamp post, one foot crossed over the other, just waiting for me . . . a busker playing "Falling Slowly", dusk falling. He'd walk over, look seductively at me then lift me up; I'd wrap my legs around his waist and . . .'

'Lexie, your leg-wrapping days at train stations are well and truly over, pet.' She snorts. 'You are seriously watching too many old Audrey Hepburn movies. Forty-year-old women don't get lifted, unless it's airlifted to hospital after a nasty fall.' She laughs heartily at her own joke, her red hair bobbling in the loose bun on top of her head.

'Thirty-nine! Stop adding on an extra year to my age!' I wave my wobbly milk sachet in her face.

'Thirty-nine and a half! That's almost forty!' She retreats and smirks at me from over her straw.

'But it's not! It's thirty-nine. I'm still thirty-nine, Annemarie!' I have no choice but to use my back teeth to open the milk. 'I don't want a life-map anymore; I don't want to have to do what's expected of me. I – I want this guy.' I study my fingernails, and just as Annemarie is about to answer me, a younger woman, star tattoos creeping down onto her hands, leans in between us, shoves me out of the way and grabs the mustard from our milk-puddled table.

'Uh, oh,' I whisper to myself.

7
Working Girl

'ALL RIGHT,' THE GIRL WITH THE STAR TATTOOS doesn't ask so much as informs as she turns to move away in her cropped top, frayed shorts, white fluffy three-quarter-length socks and black sliders.

'Eh, sorry, no, it's not all right,' Annemarie snaps. 'I'm still using it.'

Have I mentioned that Annemarie is a boiling cauldron of hormones?

The girl reluctantly removes one ear pod. She seems to move in slow-mo.

'Huh?'

'I. Am. Still. Using. The. Mustard,' Annemarie informs her again.

'Well squirt what ya want and give it back,' she drawls, dangling the mustard bottle in front of Annemarie's face.

'No thanks.' Annemarie grabs it back. 'It stays here.'

'Squirt and hand it over.' She clicks her tongue off the roof of her mouth, her eyes rolling to the whites.

'Marco!' I turn my head over my shoulder to shout at the man himself behind the triangular counter. 'Mustard row brewing.' Marco has one jar of mayonnaise, one bottle of tomato ketchup, one bottle of brown sauce and one bottle of mustard. It's a constant source of confrontations in the café.

'*Condividere*! Share!' He waves a steak knife, more than a little threatening, at Annemarie and our new enemy.

Annemarie squirts an inordinate amount of mustard onto her plate and begrudgingly thrusts the bottle at Miss Star Tattoo.

'Weirdo,' Annemarie spits.

'You're the weirdo. It's a shared mustard.' She throws me a filthy look too as she leaves. 'Ya pair of grannies!'

'So . . . go on! What the hell happened next?'

'W-What?' Annemarie's ability to switch her head space amazes me. I'm watching my back literally. I don't want to be stabbed over a bottle of mustard.

'With the Englishman?'

'Um . . . Adam,' I correct her. 'Listen, Annemarie, I know you're pregnant, but you can't just pick fights with randomers in cafés!'

'I don't give a shit. You don't just walk over to someone's table, call them a granny and then take their mustard!' she almost growls.

'Ah, c'mon.' I try a smile. 'There's a cut-the-mustard joke here somewhere.'

'No there's not.'

'I mean, it's begging to be told.'

'No, it's not!'

'Whatever.' I stir my coffee anticlockwise.

'Forget the mustard.' She raises her shoulders at me. 'What makes this guy so remarkable? Tell me that? You bounced into work this morning like you were trying out a pair of Scholl sandals on your feet. I barely recognised you. I can't remember the last time either of us turned up to work after a late night beaming.'

'I really do have a goofy smile on me, don't I?' I turn my eyes in together and she laughs. I push the bobby pins tighter into my bun, pull my chair in as close as I can.

'What's his name?'

'I told you his name! It's *Adam*!'

'His full name, Lexie! Adam whhhaaaaat?'

'Oh. I dunno, do I?'

'Lexie Grace Maggie Byrne, listen to me. Don't you dare go falling for an Englishman on holiday whose surname you didn't even get! Holiday romances always fail – you of all people should know that. Might I refer you to one Shirley Valentine! D'ah! After Dermot's bullshit, you just need a nice, honest, reliable guy to share your life with. A partner. Now stop overcomplicating life with impossible fairy tales. You'll get hurt.'

I eyeball Annemarie across the tablecloth. I'm a bit embarrassed to admit this to her but it's too late. I've already fallen for Adam.

Fallen headfirst off a cliff for him.

It was love at first sight; lust at first sight.

After one night Adam has bowled me over completely. Knocked me off my feet and onto that hotel room's king-size divan. I do a shivery shoulder roll and my eyes close momentarily as the memory tape of last night rewinds.

8

Moonstruck

I HADN'T EXPECTED HIS KISS TO BE SO SOFT. His touch so light. In the back of the taxi, he held my hand and wouldn't let me chip in for the fare. When we reached the hotel a short five minutes later, he got out first and opened the passenger door for me. *Gentlemanly*, the cynical voice in my head whispered, but are you sure it's not just because he's getting laid?

As we walked through reception, I was well aware of the look the receptionist gave us – there was a definite grin on her face. I sensed that she knew darn well Adam hadn't checked in with anyone. We took the elevator to the fourth floor, our bodies on high alert, our senses overloaded. The door opened.

I'm right back there. How could I not want to be lost again in those spectacular moments?

*

'Left,' he tells me as he takes my hand. Even in that simple syllable, I can hear the desire in his voice.

Holy crap, I think, am I glad I shaved my legs before swimming last week, and made free with my special-occasions perfume. Decent bra, check. But, still, what the hell knickers have I got on?

We stop outside a door at the end of the glowering hallway. He pulls his key card out of his wallet. Room 141. My new lucky number. His key card doesn't work the first time. We get a red light. I start to giggle.

'What is it with doors and me not getting along this evening?' Click.

Green light flashes. We're good to go.

'Again, after you?'

Inside his room, bags with roped handles are scattered across his bed; they look like gifts and stuff, but he just swipes them all to the floor and turns to me. The metallic tube light on a modest bedside table throws a soft orange light over the crisp white linen bedspread. I notice a well-thumbed detective novel, a packet of paracetamol and a *Dublin By Day* guidebook. Slowly he removes his leather jacket and drops it onto the armchair under the window. I follow his lead and take off my own jacket, drop it on top. He takes my face, oh so gently in his hands, and without further ado, leans in and kisses me. My leg bends up from the knee in a corny old film move – I can't help it.

We kiss for what seems like an eternity. I'm lost in his mouth – it's cool, slow, sensual. I run my hands through his messy hair. He moans. I'm pretty sure I moan too. I'm physically dizzy, in a sort of outer body experience, when he pulls away.

'Jesus, Lexie, I can't tell you how good this feels.' Adam bends his head to rest his forehead against mine.

'You don't have to. I know.' His skin smells so damn good. Cream. Stella McCartney. A bargain at 70% off. Suddenly I remember. I can relax. My knickers are fit for public consumption.

'This isn't a norm for me by the way,' he whispers, pulls back, studies my face.

'Me either,' I whisper back.

Then he lifts his head and with his eyes never leaving mine, he begins to unbutton his blue shirt and still I stand rooted to the spot in a hazy daze of delish, delectable desire.

'Do you have . . .'

'I have protection.' He pops the buttons on the shirt, peels it off, revealing the sexiest chest, speckles of dark hair and buff, toned arms. I stare at the trail of hair running down to his navel, to his well-worn jeans, just waiting to be reefed open.

'I don't want this to be a one-night stand. I'm not —'

I put my finger over his lip.

Then he starts to undress me.

I'm trying not to shake, to take it easy.

He puts his hands on the bottom of my sweater and I obligingly raise my arms up. He deftly pulls it off over my head – to reveal my strapless bra and we kiss again. This time his is more passionate, a little more forceful. His mouth is heavy on mine, his tongue probing.

'I want you so badly,' he murmurs, and I nod.

He reaches round and unhooks my bra, then I tease his mouth to mine as we fall back together onto the bed.

What follows is the most earth-shattering session of – forgive me – lovemaking that Lexie Byrne, aged thirty-nine and a half, has ever been blessed to experience.

9
Waiting to Exhale

'HELLLLOOO? EARTH TO LEXIE?' Annemarie knocks the hand that my chin is resting on and I jerk.

'Ow.'

'I'm assuming you're fantasising about *him*?'

'Guilty as charged.'

'Don't go all gaga over this lad now. He doesn't even live in the same country.'

'So?'

'So . . . what did you talk about?'

'Stuff.'

'What kind of stuff?'

'Everything. Films, food, life. We laughed . . . a lot! I felt this instant connection with him, you know? It's his eyes . . . they're unforgettable. It was all so easy. We were so comfortable together. The fact we were complete strangers just a few hours before felt unbelievable! But the point of the matter was that *afterwards*, neither of us got up to leave.'

'Well he could hardly leave – it was *his* hotel room.'

Always honest.

'And then what?' She's only dying for the gory deets.

'What?' I wind her up.

'What the hell happened with him is what?' Annemarie breaks into a massive grin.

'I thought you said he was a waste of time, so what do you care?'

'Seriously, Lexie, just tell me! I want to know everything.'

'Well, we put *Fifty Shades* to shame. Now, tell me how you like this for serendipity? Like I told you, I dragged myself into the Brazen Head last night for Jackie's do, which you didn't bother your arse to show up to, even for five minutes, by the way. I told Jackie you were at the cinema already to stop her calling you.' I flick my eyes at her.

'You knew I was never going into a crowded bar in the middle of town on St Patrick's night! I couldn't go even if I had wanted to – Tom had the lads round for a poker night.'

'And you had to be there why?' It's a rhetorical question. Tom's sound and all that but a tad too lazy on the domestic front for my liking. Annemarie's always cooking for the lads. She likes keeping house, but still.

'They wanted my pulled pork.'

'I bet they did.'

'Don't start.' She holds a palm up at me for the second time over lunch.

It was on the night of her fortieth birthday that she met Tom Webster. It was a whirlwind romance and marriage. We were, as fate would have it, in the Brazen Head. Tom was sharing the leather window seat with a few of us from Silverside. I'd asked him to push up so Leontia, the girl from the Tan-Tas-Tic pop-up shop, could squeeze in. His leading line was so cringe. He'd turned to Annemarie and said: 'Feel my shirt.'

Annemarie had looked at him, more than a little confused.

'Know what it's made of?'

Annemarie shook her head as he'd got down on one knee, reached up for her hand.

'Boyfriend material.' He'd lifted her hand and kissed it.

I was about to let out a long groan when out of Annemarie's mouth came this bizarrely weird high-pitched laugh.

It was kind of hysterical. Majorly manic. I hate to admit it, but after last night I maybe finally get it.

'Are you okay?' I'd stared at her quizzically.

She was still fake laughing at Tom, twisting her long red hair around her finger, she was only short of pulling a Good Ship Lollipop out of her arse and sucking playfully on it.

'Either way, you're hurting my ears!' I'd picked up my pint and she'd stood on my toe, hard, to warn me to shut the hell up, then moved up right beside Tom. I'd observed her and this goateed chap in his plaid shirt and waistcoat combo over white skinnies, shoes so pointed that airport security would have them off him as a dangerous weapon, as they'd struck up a conversation.

That was it. Annemarie was taken. They both really wanted kids and had started trying straight away. Oh, Tom had apologised profusely for his woeful pick-up line that night, blamed it on the Captain Morgan, but it had left a kinda icky impression on me, one that I haven't been able to shake. He knows it, I know it, Annemarie knows it. He's said he'd thought it was funny until he heard it out loud, but by then it was too late to take it back. To this day Annemarie still protests that she thought it 'Hilarballs!'

I drip feed more milk into my coffee cup. The Girl with the Star Tattoos takes her walnut tray and leaves her waste on top of the bin. Carrying the mustard in the palm of her hand like the Holy Grail itself, she approaches our table.

'D'ya want it back, hun?'

'No.'

'Where will I put it so?'

'Put it back on the counter.' Annemarie shrugs, rests her hands across her pregnant belly.

49

'But I got it from your table.'

'Well I'm finished now.'

'Well I'm nearer the door now, amen't I.'

'D'ya really wanna know where to put it, hun?' Annemarie's tone drops a million octaves.

'Oh. Steady on. Shouldn't you be in Bewley's dunking custard creams in yer afternoon Earl Grey?'

'Seriously, are you all right?' Annemarie stands, her plastic chair scraping the tiled floor. Protectively pregnant and all as she is, she's still a feisty one. They go at one another verbally. A mother and her young son exit the café and the door stays swinging open. The busy Dublin afternoon roars in.

'Marco!' I shout. 'Fight over the mustard again.'

'Stop wiz the facking musturd, guys, or get you out of my café. Leave the musturd on the table. Now close the facking door, man – trucker fumes are getting in!'

The mother outside flings her hands over her son's small ears and shakes her head in disapproval. Another lost customer, I think, as both women shut up instantly. I close the door. When Tattoo Girl slides out past me, Annemarie hisses.

'Seriously, Lexie, whose side are you on? I need to pee. My back is still aching. Must be from standing all day in those new flats I bought – sometimes flats can be just too flat. Now I want to hear all the juicy details when I'm back!' She rubs her lower back as she walks heavily towards the toilet.

It's her hormones.

I never gave hormones enough credit.

Vicious bitches.

They are possessing Annemarie like you wouldn't believe. Annemarie is normally a calm individual – kind to a fault, she sees the good in everyone, but not these days. These days she's a match waiting to be lit. One of the old-style, red-topped ones.

She showed me the ropes when I started in Silverside. How to deal with customer queries, pointing people in the right direction to various shops, answering phones and administering gift certificates. I got a summer job there one year stacking the new opening-hours flyers at information and never left. We've been the faces behind that marble counter ever since. It's a good honest job – lovely people, salt of the earth for the most part – but it's hard being on your feet all day, and the only real downside is we are dictated to by our David Brent impresario boss June, who Annemarie does not get along with, at all, and sometimes, I have to be honest, it's like Groundhog Day.

But hey, aren't most jobs?

'Go on will you – lunch is nearly over!' Annemarie sits back down, still drying her hands on a paper towel.

'Why are you still drying your hands?'

'Because I want to hear the full story before we go back!' She rolls the wet paper towel in a ball. That's another aspect of her lately – she's kind of forgetful, does odd things, like not binning her wet paper towel. She really isn't herself at all.

'Are you ready for this? We literally collided! He hit me with the door and knocked me flat on my back! It's like I'm making this up, but I swear to you I'm not! I'm not joking you, Annemarie, this guy literally took my breath away. He helped me up, apologised profusely and we left it at that. Inside I saw him again, well I did an *orchestrated bar-bump* like we used to. I just had to talk to him again. Had to. The compulsion was scary. So when I saw him at the bar, I hopped into the queue behind him. As he turned to make his way back, his hands full with three pints, I stood my ground, then said in my best flirty voice, "Here, let me help you?"'

'Did you really?' Annemarie is impressed I can tell.

'I bloody did.'

'Ya mad thing!'

'Yup. This guy was not slipping through Lexie Byrne's shaking fingers. I took a pint off him and followed him over to his table where we both landed them without spilling a drop. Shameful I know.'

'What if his wife had been sitting there?'

'Then I'd have Blarney Stoned her, Annemarie! I'd have stroked her hair lovingly, hoping her good luck and amazing fortune would rub off on me and gone back to a rather drunk Jackie.' I tilt my head at her. She smiles.

'He asked if I would like a drink. I said, *"No, but thanks. I just got a full glass of wine. I'm sitting over there with friends by the door."* I didn't want him to think I was alone or just after a free drink but wanted him to know where I was should he want to find me!'

'But you were in the queue at the bar!'

'Oh yeah, I forgot that. A minor detail! Anyway.' I eyeball her. 'He didn't seem to notice, but another crew of his friends had arrived and some guy called Dominic had draped himself over Adam, so I wandered on away to my seat, shoulders back, boobs out, in case he was watching me go . . .'

'And did he?'

I shake my head but immediately hold my index finger up, the universal sign of *wait there is more to come*.

'He walked past me but never came over, just smiled at me and went straight out the door. I presumed he was going to another bar, so, with a heavy heart, I decided to call it a night. I'd promised Garfield a takeaway tikka masala and Netflix in bed. So I pulled on my jacket –'

'Hang on, what were you wearing again?' she wonders.

'My pleated skater skirt – the one Dermot used to say I was too old for! The one that evoked another of his has-been references. My red off-the-shoulder angora sweater, my black boots.'

'Nice.' She joins her index finger and thumb together. 'Okay. Go on . . .'

'I said goodbye to Jackie, who was too engrossed in a very serious drinking game to pay me any heed, and I left. Outside, my hand was outstretched for a taxi, but suddenly there he was . . . again.'

'And?' She's exasperated, but I have to tell the story as it happened. I need to relive every minute – no, every second – of last night.

'Can I just tell you . . . one more time, he has these unbelievable eyes, totally melt-worthy; honestly, Annemarie, I've never fancied a man like this before ever, not in my entire life.'

'So you shagged him and?' she demands.

'Don't be so crass. I'm a lady.'

'A lady who appears not to have slept all night!' she snorts, laughing.

'Do you want to hear the rest of my story or not?'

'Yes, but we have to be back in' – she checks her Fitbit again – 'three minutes!' She stands and starts to tidy off the table. 'June is around the centre all today – I know she'll be watching who's covering our breaks since Jackie's gone.'

'Lisa is there – she can cover an hour!' I say.

'June just has it in for me – she's up to something, I can tell. She wants rid of me because I'll be going on maternity leave soon and she's still reeling from the time I took off after the . . .' She pales. I jump in before she has to say that dreaded word. *Miscarriage.*

'Right, let's go. But why don't you come over to mine after work tonight, so I can fill you in? I need to vent about him. I need to say his name over and over. Adam. Adam. A-d-a-m.' I clasp my hands together, prayer like, under my chin.

'Tom has cricket practice tonight and the lads tend to come

back after – he likes me to be there. I was going to roast that chicken, but maybe . . .'

I stare hard at her.

'Lexie, I know you think I do too much for Tom, but I like it. Please get to know him better – you two have a lot in common. A bit of support for him please.'

'I support you in everything you do, my dear,' I tell her.

She strokes her belly and twists the elasticated band on her polyester maternity work skirt.

'I know you love him, and I know Tom's going to be a brilliant father.' I smile warmly at her.

I've never *craved* children in the same way that Annemarie does. I *wanted* them sure, but I just *presumed* I'd have them. I don't admit to many people that I'm more or less okay with the probability that I won't have kids now; I found that people can be funny about women who are thirty-nine and a half who don't long for children. They all assume I must be panicking and desperate to procreate. I mean, I still might want kids, but I don't dwell on it because – well, what's the point?

I follow Annemarie across the floor to the bin. She shakes our messy lunch remains off the tray, separates the recycling.

She wants this baby so badly. Which means I do too, for her. I've held her hand through two failed rounds of IVF and a devastating miscarriage at sixteen weeks last year. Heart-breaking. I wouldn't have wished her grief on my worst enemy. Truly, the joy I feel at her pregnancy now is second to none.

'Okay, I'm sorry, what you do or don't do for Tom is none of my business –'

'It is so your business – we're best friends.'

'Well, all I meant was can he not order a Chinese, just for tonight? Is there none of that pulled pork left over he can make do with?'

Annemarie sighs heavily, slides the tray into the grooved slot provided.

'I enjoy cooking, Lexie! It's what relaxes me at home! But all right! I'll tell him. To be honest, he'll be glad I'm getting out of the house. I'd enjoy a glass of non-alcoholic wine and a thin and crispy Hawaiian maybe, but without the ham?'

'Yay!' I punch the air. 'You got it! Deal! Date! . . . I'm telling you, stress is worse for . . . well ya know . . . a little of what you fancy goes a long way.'

'Stress.' She gasps. 'You think I'm stressed?'

'A little, yeah.' Oh, talk about putting my foot in it.

'About the baby?' Both her hands wrap around the bump now.

'Aaaah, no. You just need to relax, enjoy the pregnancy a bit more, that's all.'

'Like I don't have enough to stress about without worrying if I'm stressed!'

'Everyone's stressed now and then,' I try to reassure her.

'You'll pick off the frozen ham before you put it in the oven?' she makes me promise.

I hold my pinkie out to her. 'Of course I'll pick off the frozen ham before I put it in the oven,' I repeat. 'But come round, put your feet up, have a meal handed to you. It'll relax you. You need a bit of an escape.'

'I know – you're right. I'm a constant bag of nerves, Lexie. I feel so sick sometimes, but then I think that if the baby's what's making me feel sick then that's a good sign. So I'm enjoying the sick feeling! How messed up is that? I know I talk about nothing else apart from babies, being pregnant. I'm surprised you actually want to spend time with me outside Silverside. I am really grateful – you know that, don't you?' She takes a big gulp of air. 'Honest, I bore myself sometimes. You're a good friend to listen to my self-obsessed ramblings.'

'Don't be silly – I'm always here for you,' I enthuse. 'I'm nearly as excited as you to meet this baby!'

We squeeze each other's hands and Annemarie winks at me. 'It's a date. I'll bring my ID so I can hear all about your X-rated bedroom activities!'

She holds open the glass doors to let a mother navigate through with her double buggy, staring in wonder at the chubby bare-legged, soother-sucking babies within. I wait at the pedestrian crossing in front of Silverside Shopping Centre, clutching my phone in my pocket. Silently, intensely, I'm praying for the finest man I've ever encountered in my entire thirty-nine and a half years to get in touch.

10
Cruel Intentions

'BESIDE ME HE WAS, ONE MINUTE!' a panicked young mother in a camouflage jumpsuit and velvet headband screams at me. 'The next thing I looked down and he was gone. I was weighing the bananas – the label kept getting stuck! I took my eye off him! Eoin's been kidnapped! Ring the police!' She does a 360-degree turn in her oxblood Doc Martens.

It's a hellish Friday afternoon for expired vouchers, unreadable magnetic gift cards and temporarily missing children.

'Try not to worry,' I attempt to comfort her. 'I've worked here for years and I have recovered every missing child ever reported. I've got a one hundred per cent record. I'm Cagney and Lacey rolled into one.'

She's shaking uncontrollably as she stares at me through fluttery lashes.

Lexie, I admonish myself, *you're showing your age! She's never heard of Chris Cagney or Mary Beth Lacey.*

'We'll find Eoin, I promise.' She can't be more than twenty years old, iPhone an extension of her arm. A lot of the young mammies spend a lot of time in the centre, filling their day, sharing stories for hours over cups of coffee in the Geraghty Food Hall. They help give the centre its sense of community.

'Let's get you a seat and I'll take some details . . . make a sweet tea, can you?' I ask Annemarie who is already hovering over our machine, cup in hand, as it whirrs to life.

'Just tell me Eoin's surname and what he's wearing. I promise we'll find him, all right?' I use my soothing voice as she talks to me and I take the bunch of bananas from her hand. I bet she didn't pay for them. Happens all the time. People wander up to us with trolleys full of shopping, clothes on hangers, make-up in hands, full head of highlights still wrapped in tinfoil. Returning to the desk, I clear my throat and press down on the announcer.

Normally it takes less than ten minutes for lost children to be returned. We make the announcement not only for the public but also so security can be extra vigilant. Annemarie pulls up a stool beside the mum and makes light chit-chat while we wait.

Dermot swaggers towards me, Silverside jacket on, earpiece in, radio in hand. As always, he has his lackies on either side of him, making him look far more important than he actually is.

'Story?' Dermot asks me, twisting a button on his radio.

'No sign yet,' I politely answer him because I have to.

'How're ya keepin'?' he asks, equally polite.

'Absolutely fantastic, Dermot, thanks for asking!' I smile ridiculously wide as he presses down on a button.

'Missing kid still not found, Jocko.' He talks into his radio, which hisses static as he walks back to the bench beside the escalator, turning full circle to check out a young woman taut in white fitness wear. It used to make me flinch, but now I see how tragic it is really. Just the sight of him makes me glad to be alone rather than feel so goddamn alone when I was with him.

I jerk back to reality. My frightened young mother has swooped her bawling three-year-old up in her arms, the poor mite's face roaring red, drowning in huge stinging tears. 'Eoin! My baby! Oh, thanks a million!'

'Thank you,' I say more firmly to the kind teenager who brought him over. I check to see that Dermot's clocked the kid is safe and see him muttering self-importantly into his radio.

Relief floods Eoin's mum's face, and she starts to scold him now, just like they always do. I pat her shoulder gently, reminding her that everything's fine again.

'Now, steady, would Eoin like a lollipop? Sugar-free,' I assure as I reach over the counter and pull up our clear container of colourful lollies. The grubby little hand reaches in and pulls out two.

'Uh oh, here comes June,' Annemarie informs me in a quiet voice as our boss totters over on her towering high heels. June is small and birdlike, dressed in black, with silver jewellery that jangles and clanks as she moves.

'Hello, ladies, how's it all going?' she asks, running a manicured finger along the desk to check for dust. 'Missing Jackie? Busy?'

The young mother rises, her little boy safely wrapped up in her arms. I wink at her and hand her back the bananas.

'Oh, I never paid –'

I interrupt her. 'Consider them a present from Silverside.'

'Thanks a million.' She grins, her face pretty with relief and gratitude as she steps away into the crowd.

'Good, June,' I say, my tone clipped. 'Thanks.' And I nod at her to move so I can lift the hatch, footstool in hand.

'Why aren't you in behind the desk?' she accuses, stepping smartly out of the way.

'We were dealing with a lost child there and we aren't allowed to take mothers, fathers, grannies, grandads or great-uncles twice removed behind the desk anymore,' I intone. 'Remember you made that rule?'

She gives me the side eye but isn't beaten yet. 'Did you two take your break together again? I thought we spoke about that?

I'm still recruiting Jackie's replacement. I need reliable staff.'

'Is that a dig at me, June?'

I groan as Annemarie wades in.

'You know it's illegal to discriminate against women in the workplace for needing time off after . . . well, you know exactly what I'm talking about – that and my upcoming maternity leave.'

June pouts and folds her arms, but she's so short that she can barely lean on the counter. 'I find that comment very unfair and untrue.' She stares at me while addressing Annemarie.

'June, Lisa has been here on late nights for a year – I think she knows the ropes by now. We're managing fine without Jackie, honestly. We don't need anyone else.' I replace the hatch with a purposeful bang.

'I make the decisions around here, Lexie Byrne.' She slides her tortoiseshells up her nose and sweeps her flicky hair out her eyes. I grit my teeth. I can't afford to lose my job. I've got rent to meet, bills to pay, food to buy, pet insurance. I've no family here since my parents left so I must rely on myself. Although it pleases me no end that my parents pursued their goal of retirement to Spain. For as long as I can remember, it was always there, the Mediterranean dream.

She's asserted her authority and so June clacks off on her heels. I glance up at Kilroy Travel on the third floor. It always reminds me of my mam and dad.

'Oh, wait, just you wait until we're sitting on our veranda, under the heat of the Spanish evening, eating Manchego cheese and sipping red wine, watching the sun go down over the Med,' David, my dad, would say. So, according to their life plan, and with Granny settled and happy in Sir Patrick Dun's, and on my insistence that they go, they sold the house and relocated to the Spanish resort of Nerja, with its warm winters, white cobbled streets and bougainvillea-scented air.

They'd never warmed to Dermot. Mam worried he was a bit of a narcissist. Dad worried he'd eat himself if he could. In fact, the pair of them sometimes seemed to do nothing but worry about me. I was after all, their one and only, their 'pride and joy'.

When I turned eighteen, they worried when I drank a dolly-mixture of gin, vodka and brandy from our drinks cabinet at my end-of-school ball and had my head down the toilet bowl before the beef curry was served, and they were called to collect me.

Then they worried when I had no boyfriend all through my twenties.

Then they worried even more when I introduced them to Dermot in my thirties.

And so I think it brings us both peace of mind that, with them abroad, I'm not as much of a worry to my parents anymore.

11
Blue Valentine

A DAM DIDN'T GET IN TOUCH.
No text, no call, no WhatsApp.

Nada.

Fuck it anyway.

Fuck it.

Fuck it.

Fuck it.

I am beyond disappointed. If only I knew his surname, I'd do something I never do and stalk him on Facebook or Instagram, but I don't. Damnit. Damnit to hell. I'd such a strong inkling that he'd really liked me too! More than just the physical attraction, I'd felt this sense of proper connection. Convinced it was a two-way thing.

How was I so stupid? I chastise myself as the bus drives past me full. Again. Friday nights are a nightmare, even this late. Waiting passengers moan but I don't get involved in conversations with the strangers standing with me. We're all crammed under the glass shelter as the March rain sleets down. I start to walk. I push up my umbrella, swap my shopping bag to the other hand with my pizzas and wine and start the half-hour walk home. The disappointment is actually palpable. Grey clouds hang low and ominous like my mood. I trudge, head down, along the wet pavement then pause and check the phone once more.

Nada.

Blankety Blank.

Adam's ridiculously handsome face floods my mind. I shiver remembering his touch, his voice telling me he didn't want it to be just a one-night stand, as a cloud bursts with more rain and a clap of thunder brings me back to earth. With the downpour beating on my already drowned hair, I shuffle on, my toes squelching in my open cork wedges. I check left and right then cross the busy road, but I simply can't get him out of my head. Facing into the rain once more I see a bus coming towards me. I do that half-run thing people carrying heavy bags do for the amusement of drivers safely ensconced in their cars to the next stop, which is thankfully not too far ahead. The bus pulls in, doors flip open and I step on, breathless. The windows are all fogged up. No seats, but I lean against the yellow bar, bags safely trapped between my sopping-wedged feet, and there I stand daydreaming of Adam, swaying easily with the motion of the bus.

'Thank you,' I say to the weary driver when I finally disembark. She musters up a weak smile behind her protective glass. The stop is right outside my apartment block. Inputting the code into the keypad on the electric gate, I walk the short distance across the car park to my apartment, to get supper ready for Annemarie and me. Maybe pizza and a glass or two of wine will help me forget the inimitable Englishman.

12

Eat, Pray, Love

'Tom is really happy you asked me over.' Annemarie shakes out her umbrella before she steps into my narrow, tiled hallway.

'Oh, good.' The door slams behind her, with a rattle of glass.

'He said that I really need to just believe now at seven months all is fine.' She hands me a box of Lindt chocolates.

'He's right! Good for Tom. Go on through. Oh, thanks – my faves.' We go into my kitchen, with its teal walls, the colour I chose when it became my refuge after I threw Dermot out.

Annemarie looks so cute in her denim maternity dungarees, face free of make-up and her red hair piled in a messy top knot. She looks a lot younger than her forty-two years. I silently pray that everything will be fine with the baby. At least I can spoil her tonight. No doubt she'd be making her incredible starter of home-made chilli nachos for those cricket lads, followed by the organic roast chicken, with all the trimmings if she was at home. I might gripe about Tom's lack of domesticity sometimes, but I will give him this: he most certainly only has eyes for his Annemarie. He adores her, works hard for her and can't wait to become a dad. Plus, I've never seen him with a wandering eye any time we've been out socially.

'Mmmm, what's that delicious smell?'

'Two Hawaiians, frozen ham removed before cooking as requested, and a sneaky lil ole garlic bread with cheese.' I hand her a glass. 'It's non-alcoholic, it's organic, it's at room temperature. Now sit down. I'm looking after both of you tonight.'

'Your kitchen is so modern! I haven't seen it since you got the new Bosch fridge and washing machine in,' she enthuses. 'Looks so stylish!'

'Thanks.' I sit down, cross my legs and together we admire my little kitchen. It's small but looks cool in all its shiny chrome. Since my weekends, when I'm not on shift, are mainly taken up with volunteering at the old folks' home, I saved up enough to buy myself some fancy apartment appliances.

Annemarie takes the glass from me and I pat the couch. My brushed hair is still wet, my face is freshly cleansed and moisturised. My tracksuit is comfy and my slippers well worn. Cosy attire. Annemarie sits ever so gently into my grey velvet two-seater that faces the wall-mounted TV. She drapes her legs across my lap, rests her head on my shoulder.

'Now isn't this nice?' I say.

'Mmmmmm.'

'Someone needs to take care of you too.'

'Tom does take care of me, Lexie.'

'I know he does. I didn't mean that.'

We sit in comfortable silence for a few minutes.

'You're so good to me, Lexie,' she says when I get up to fetch the little footstool and point to her feet.

'To put the aul' feet up on while I get our supper ready.' I lift her feet and place them down carefully as I pad into the kitchen. She's like fine china at the moment.

'Oh, there you are, Garfield,' she coos as he strolls across the thick cream carpet and hops up on the couch on his second attempt. She gently rubs his neck.

'How old is he now, Lexie?' she asks in a tone I don't like, as if he's literally on his last legs.

'I don't like to add it up. He's a grandad, that's how I like to think of him, and that's how I treat him,' I tell her over my shoulder as I hit play on my Spotify.

'Well, Garfield, I was called a granny today, so I know how you feel. I do feel a bit like a granny to be honest . . . and especially granny-sensitive after that stupid wagon in Marco's at lunchtime.'

'You aren't a granny, Annemarie! Neither of us are.'

'Although I do sometimes feel ancient lately. Especially when I have the cricket lads in my kitchen, drinking craft beer and eating my leftovers, as you suggested. They're all sound in fairness, they always leave the place spotless, but they are loud and this quiet is total bliss I must admit.' She sighs, contentedly rubbing Garfield's belly, his four paws in the air. Pouring myself a much-needed hair of the dog, a vulgar glass of very alcoholic red, I return and flop beside her again.

'You're welcome to visit me and Garfield any time – you know that.'

'You have the place fabulous.' She twists her head to cast a look around.

'It is nice, if I do say so myself. Literally repainted these walls again last month; the paint was left over from the dining room in Sir Patrick Dun's and they said I could take the excess home. I won't let you look in my wardrobe mind you – that's a total mess and needs a complete clear out. It's in my diary as my next home improvement. I want it minimal; apparently that'll be good for my head, for it to feel clean and uncrowded.'

'Sounds very "new" you,' Annemarie says. 'You are all Beyoncé-Independent-Womanly these days, aren't you? Like you take no prisoners.' She clicks her fingers.

'I suffer no fools,' I correct her.

'I pity the fool!' she rejoins with a bad Mr T impression.

'No, I don't hate Balboa, but I pity the fool!' I challenge her. We giggle.

'You certainly don't; if there was a positive from the Dermot disaster, it's that you really know who you are now.' She smiles at me, squeezes my knee with her free hand. 'And I do admire that.'

'Thank you.' I am a woman who now accepts compliments. 'Although I have no idea who I was in that hotel bedroom last night, Annemarie!'

'Yes! Here we go. Spill those beans! I desperately need to hear the rest of the you-and-the-Englishman-in-Dublin story, else I probably would be in bed with my eye mask and Calm app.'

'Well . . .' I start reluctantly.

'But – hold your horses!' Annemarie pushes her hand out like a traffic cop. 'Before I hear this, can I just say one thing? It's not just me? Wasn't June being such a cow to me this afternoon? I really can't deal with her anymore, Lexie. Did you see the way she stood breathing down my neck when I had to do the return on the dodgy hundred-euro gift card? When she hears I want early maternity on my doctor's orders, she'll freak. She'll try to think of a way to get rid of me, if she isn't already. I don't know what she's up to, but she wants me out. She hates that I was afforded the time off after the miscarriage, I know she does.'

'Ignore her.' I gently rub her leg. 'She's a pain in the hole.'

'She always says, "I couldn't afford to take maternity leave on my August – I had to keep on working."'

We've never set eyes on June's daughter, August, and sometimes I wonder, I really do, if she even exists. June says she has a job in Manchester but keeps quiet most of the time about her private life.

'So, enough about that misery guts. Go on, I'm all yours . . . spill. This Englishman!'

67

'Adam.'

'Adam.' She does a shoulder roll. Garfield snores under her touch.

'Ah well, I guess it was what it was . . . but he's not got back to me. Not a measly little WhatsApp.'

'Don't want to say I told you so, but . . .' She trails off, managing to look simultaneously sympathetic and apologetic.

'I'm devastated.' I shrug, hugely embarrassed that I cooed so much over him in Marco's at lunchtime. How had I got that so wrong? My instincts were obviously shite.

'Devastated! No . . . that's a bit extreme, Lexie. Really?'

'Yeah really.'

'Did you text *him*?' She kicks off her boots with her heels, revealing mismatched men's socks.

'He took my number. I didn't ask for his.'

'Rooky mistake.'

'Why would I want to text him?'

'All hail the Feminist!' She laughs and snaps out a salute.

'It's got nothing to do with feminism. If he doesn't want to see me, he doesn't want to see me. What difference does it make if I have his number? So he can ghost me? No thank you.' I twirl the glass stem in my hand, the liquid swimming from side to side.

'Okay. But all I mean is why should *he* hold that power?' she insists, and I get the feeling she's reminding me that she's the one who chased Tom after their first encounter.

'Ah, that's not how I see it. For me it's about someone really wanting to see *me* again.' I hold her gaze.

'But what if you want to see *them* again!'

'It's pointless, Annemarie, if they don't want to see me!'

'So it's okay for men to do the chasing but not for women, is that it?'

'No . . . that's not it. Of course it's totally fine for women to do the chasing; all I'm saying is it isn't what I want to do. Especially after Dermot the Deceiver. I want to be sure a man wants me, specifically. I think it's to do with being cheated on. And you've not had that experience. Tom adores you.' I take a deep breath, pushing down that scorch of shame. How could he have treated me like that for so long? 'Every time Dermot's head turned to assess yet another woman who wasn't me . . . well it ground me down. Every vaguely attractive woman who walked past us in a bar or restaurant, every waitress or bartender, or just while we were in the car stopped at traffic lights. Every time he looked, appraised, appreciated . . . I died inside. My self-esteem shrunk, curled up in on itself.'

'Why didn't ya whack him! I didn't know he did that!'

'Really? You must have clocked it?'

'Did I?' She pulls a face.

'I mean it ruined so many nights out for me. I would honestly dread going anywhere. I tried to tell him how I felt, but he'd just laugh and spew some bullshit about why would he go out for a hamburger when he had steak at home. That he was only human, or some other lame excuse. Or, best of all, that I was controlling, paranoid, jealous. It shot my confidence to hell, messed with my mind. Whatever I tried, I just felt *lesser*. And, to be honest, finding out about the actual cheating was a relief after all that. So, no, I didn't ask Adam for his number.'

We let that hang.

'Right. I get that. Makes sense. And, yeah, Dermot was one disrespectful arse.' She wiggles her toes in their odd socks. 'Do you have any raisins in by any chance?'

'Raisins?'

'Yeah, I just fancy a few raisins on the pizza.'

'Oh. No – no, I don't.'

'Currants?'

'Who has currants?'

'Rachel Allen, Nigella Lawson, Betty Crocker?'

'Not Lexie Byrne.'

'No sweat. Never mind.'

The timer sounds on the oven and I'm thankful to get away for a moment. I'm cringing with embarrassment at how I went on like an idiot about this great *leading man* I'd met. Padding over in my bare feet, I remove my burned oven glove from the hook above the rose-gold toaster that matches my kettle and pull open the door. Steam engulfs me. The pizzas are golden brown, and I flick off the switch.

'Table, my lady.' I pull out one of the wooden stools at my kitchen counter table for two.

'What do I do with him?' She nods to a snoring Garfield on her lap.

'Shift him – he won't wake.' She gently tips him onto the sofa, then comes over, washes her hands and carefully sits up at the table.

'*Bon appétit*,' I say.

'Pizza, how I have missed you!' she declares melodramatically. 'It's been non-stop healthy pregnancy foods: salmon, kale, spinach, lentils, blueberries, quinoa, cabbage, manuka honey.' Annemarie counts on two hands.

'Tuck in. You look like you need it – certainly won't do you any harm.' The words slip out and I bite my stupid tongue.

13
La La Land

HARM!' ANNEMARIE SITS UP STRAIGHT, a look of horror on her face. 'What do you mean I look like I need it? Do I not look well? You made me eat bad-baby-growing food in Marco's today, and I was riddled with guilt all afternoon!'

'Annemarie, you ate a bowl of sweet potato fries not a deep-fried Mars bar. You know how mad it sounds to feel guilty after eating that?'

In fairness to her, she nods.

'I know, I know, but my mother keeps trying to shove red meat that's practically still mooing down my neck, and she knows I'm going on what the experts say –'

'Experts? What experts?' I interrupt, use finger quotations.

'Pregnancy ones!'

'You mean your doctor?' I ask, because I know it's not true. She's never offline, always reading up on what's necessary for a *healthy pregnancy*.

'Well, no, the pregnancy onliners. Those experts.'

'Ah everyone's an expert at something online these days, Annemarie. And we're just clickbait to the experts. *Click, click, click.*' I sit forward on the stool, do a bit of a performance. Eyes wide, hand clutching chest, all theatrical like.

'Oh, that's me!'

Click.

'Oh, I do that.'

Click.

'Oh, I eat meat.'

Click.

'Oh, I drink wine.'

Click.

'Oh, I look like that.'

Click.

'Oh, I have a *problem* belly.'

Click.

'Seriously though, every model who's ever had a baby is a *mummy expert*, every overweight reality star who's starved themselves into malnutrition to flog a DVD is a *fitness guru*, every influencer is being paid to promote, every expert isn't an expert, Annemarie. Stick to your doctor's advice and stay off the internet – that's the best solution,' I say gently.

'That's not what we're talking about here, Lexie. You know I wouldn't even have conceived without my IVF experts, and now I need to pay attention to the actual pregnancy experts!'

'I know. But these internet experts aren't experts.' I raise my brows.

'Why not?'

'They're just blogger sorts who happen to be pregnant.'

'So?'

'So they aren't educated *experts*.'

'They are! They are living it. They are pregnant! Most have babies already.'

'Look, if I was famous and I told people if they melted bird shit and spread it on pitta bread, they'd live to be a hundred, people would do it. Don't you get it? We seek out the experts in the field we're most worried about. Research that's proven is nearly *always* proven by the companies who have *paid* for the research in the first place! It's all about the money. They're predators. They feed on our insecurities. I know how precious this baby is to you and Tom, but do not believe the internet, Annemarie. The internet is a bald eagle!'

'The internet is a bald eagle?' She tilts her head at me as I take a long drink of my red wine.

'Yes. And I hate how it rules our lives. Give me any other generation and I'd happily live in it, whatever else they've been through. My old folks in Sir Patrick Dun's were the lucky ones.' I swallow, replace my glass on the table.

'Right.'

I get the sense Annemarie might have tired already of my rant, but I'm on a roll now.

'Right,' I confirm. 'It's why I took myself off social media, shut them all down. And it's been so liberating.'

'Okay, Little Miss Revolutionary. In what way?'

'No longer am I jealous of the fake life that Aveen FitzWhatserface who's married to the obsessed weight-lifting guy posts, in her filtered-to-the-max world of breastfeeding, baking and bullshit. Do I need to see her breastfeeding eleven times a day? No is the answer – I don't. I get it. Do I need to see her home-made vegan choc-chip cookies perfectly positioned by her box-fresh, never opened cookery books, leaning against her NutriBullet and green matcha tea? No, no I don't. I get it. You don't eat meat, have a prize. You're not brainwashing me into wanting to be like all the other sheep. Baaahhhhaaaaaaaaaaaaaaa!'

'Aveen FitzWhatserface is in the Bahamas on a Bikram yoga and avocado retreat,' my brainwashed pal tells me. 'And she looks sensational.'

I'm incredulous.

73

'Aveen isn't sensational, Annemarie! What the hell is sensational about starving yourself? Then contorting your body into absurd positions in ninety-degree heat?'

'Aveen looks great is all I'm saying.'

'She looks great on *Instagram*, Annemarie, cop on! Because I bet she looks like a dead woman from the Famine when she wakes up every day . . .'

'Oh, here we go . . . wake me up when you're done.' She shuts her eyes playfully.

'. . . and the Bahamas is for lounging on a sunbed poolside, skimming the latest airport bonkbuster while sipping an ice-cold Diet Coke and simultaneously dipping your Ray Bans and peering out across the aquamarine ocean and not moving yer fat ass off that sunbed until it's time to saunter back to your bedroom and slather on a bitta eyeliner then go back down to the bar and sit up on the wicker high stool while you watch the open-shirted waiter shake his tight ass as he makes you a Sex on the Beach while you throw caution to the E. coli wind and eat all the salty bar nuts before ordering a chilled bottle of Pinot and a huge pil-pil prawns . . . only then can you wobble up to bed to finish your book, the windows open, listening to the sounds of the night ocean as the snow-white curtains billow in the cool coconut-scented breeze. *That's* what a trip to the Bahamas is to me, Annemarie! That's the definition of relaxing!'

'Actually, that sounds way better, I have to be honest.' Annemarie nods at me and smiles. 'No Bikram required.'

'And the final thing –'

'God, please let it be so!' Annemarie clasps her hands together and looks up to the ceiling, pursing her lips, trying hard not to laugh now.

'I will *never* reactivate my Facebook account. When I do have a "real" status update, I'll share it in "real" life with my "real" friends.' I take another slug of wine. 'Right, as promised, rant over. But tell me, did your doctor tell you to stick to this pregnancy diet?'

'Oh, we're back to that, are we? I can't keep up with you. Well . . . it's not like she told me to *only* eat them, but they are the recommended foods.'

'Grand, all right. So everything in moderation, yeah? That's the key to a happy, well-lived life, Annemarie. No depriving yourself. No regrets on your last day on this great earth that you spent your whole gift of life jogging on hard tarmac against the wind, going to bed at nine o'clock with earplugs so you can't hear the kids on the road playing, shutting out life, pouring two litres of water down your neck every day, only eating plants, rattling with supplements, trying to live forever. Because, me old pal, no one lives forever.'

'Yeah, but my reasons are different. I don't want to live forever, Lexie, I just . . .' Her bottom lip quivers.

'Oh, love –'

'I just want to carry and deliver a healthy baby, that's all.' She puts her hand protectively on her rounded tummy, leans into the back of the stool.

'I know you do.' I put my hand on top of hers.

'And I'll do whatever it takes.'

'I know.' I squeeze then she slides her hand out from beneath mine to rub her tummy in circular movements. 'Everything will be fine. I promise.'

'I'll have some pizza tonight but otherwise I'm not jinxing anything; I can't change a thing, Lexie. It's got me here, hasn't it?'

I nod. Smile at her.

'Do you know what I'm trying to say?' She holds my gaze and I keep nodding. 'Do you think I wanted to drink beetroot and carrot juice every morning? Do you think I wanted to get into bed and lie down from the minute I came home from work to the minute I woke up? Or eat all that fertility-boosting shit? Do you think I wanted to text Tom, at work, every time I was ovulating to demand he leg it home so we could have the most bizarre, unsexy sex to order? To have him inject me? To rob our relationship of all its spontaneity? I can't remember the last time I enjoyed sex simply for itself.' She gives me a weak smile, bashful. I say nothing. 'Do you think I wanted to lie with my two legs up in the air, as if that would help his sperm find their way to my eggs like a deranged baby-making Google map? Guess what? I didn't! All I want to do is carry our baby to term, deliver our baby safely. I honestly don't care how much it hurts, how many stitches I get, if I shit all over the place! I just want to meet my baby – smell, hold, touch my baby . . . our baby.' Her hand shakes as she lifts her glass. 'All I want is to keep this baby safe in here, to carry her – or him – to term . . .'

'And that's what you'll do,' I promise her again. 'But excuse me, dear lady, the pizza is ready to demolish!' I brandish the pizza cutter and carve three large cheese and pineapple slices.

'No ham, right?' She inspects the pizza as I slide it onto her plate.

'No ham, Annemarie. Jesus Christ, are you the ham police?'

But I smile at her.

She smiles back.

She lifts a slice, blows a few times and takes a bite.

'Heaven! Now come on – gossip.'

'I told you he never called.'

'But you'd a great night, right?'

'Oh that I did.'

'So allow me to make the sexy hot love vicariously?' She grins. Drops the straps on her dungarees and opens the button on the side. Exhales.

76

'Right, where was I?' Why not? I want to relive every moment regardless of the fact I'll never set eyes on him again.

'The nightcap.'

'So . . . we had a nightcap at the bar and then went back to his hotel, Jury's Christchurch.'

She makes a face not overly impressed. 'Ah well, go on, doesn't matter.'

'Miraculously we got a taxi right outside; he held the door open for me.'

'Nice.'

'Then we held hands in the back of the taxi, and he paid – wouldn't let me chip in.'

'Nice. So far, so gentlemanly.'

'Right? I was a bit morto walking past the receptionist, who defo had a grin on her face. We got into the lift; he kept staring at me, like his eyes were devouring me. I can't tell you, Annemarie, what a ride this man is. Gorgeous, leather jacket, blue shirt, faded jeans.'

'I'm no more interested in hearing about his clothes.' She flings her hands out wide. 'Tell me about his lack of clothes!'

I push my plate away, the memory of him momentarily supressing my appetite, which is unheard of. I take a slug from my wine and refill my glass.

'Go on!' she urges as I wrap both hands around the glass.

'He took my breath away. He . . . well, to be brutal, he . . . well . . . ya know . . . heard me roar!'

Annemarie bursts into a fit of coughing. I jump up and twist the tap to let water gush forth, then offer her a glass.

'Jesus wept, Lexie Byrne! That's gross!'

'Sorry, but it's true.'

I sit back down and cross my legs, rotate my bare feet.

'I was expecting more along the lines of *we made exquisite, sensitive love*.'

'Sorry. Well, what can I say?'

'Well not *that*!'

'But it's the truth . . . it was just mind-blowing, Annemarie. I can't remember the last time I wanted so much of a man in bed.' I put both hands on the side of my head and do that double-handed action of an exploding brain.

'Wow. Ah here, cut me another slice there. So how did it end up? How did you leave it? And how, after all that hot action, did he not call you?' She nods to the remaining pizza.

'That's what I cannot understand. After . . . we just lay naked, totally at ease, side by side, chatting, laughing until the sun came up . . . like we were still talking when his bus arrived at seven in the morning to bring him to the Cliffs of Moher, which is when I got dressed and left.'

'What on earth did you talk about for all that time?'

'Stuff.'

'What kind of stuff?'

'Everything . . . I told you – just life in general. Him. Me. He asked so many questions, listened to my answers. We laughed so much. And like I said, neither of us got up to leave.'

'Well, like I said, it was *his* hotel room. Maybe he was praying you'd stop chatting and get the hell outta there.'

'Believe me, I know when a man wants me to leave his bed – as do you!' I tilt my head at her.

'Yeah, I'll give you that one . . . but thank God my single days are behind me.' She shrugs happily. 'So you lay there in this hotel bed talking to this complete stranger for how many hours?'

'Three, four maybe.'

'Three or four hours' talking! I'm impressed!' She takes up the crusts she'd discarded. 'Do you have any mustard?'

'What's with this mustard craving? It's out of control.' I shake

78

my head and watch her chew them anyway. I sense that Anne-marie isn't sure what to say next.

'He asked for your number or you offered?' Hope is in her eyes; I can read her like a book.

'He asked.'

'Good! So maybe he will ring?' She wolfs down the crusts. 'How? How did he ask?'

'He said, *"Can I take your number, Lexie?"* I called it out to him. He tapped it into his phone. Then the room phone buzzed – that's when I got dressed and slipped out, while he was on the phone. He was giving some code for his booking.'

I inhale deeply.

In through the nose.

Exhale slowly.

Out through the mouth.

'But he never texted me.'

'Player?' she suggests.

'I didn't get that vibe. But it's only been a day, mind you.'

'Still.'

'Still.' I wink at her. 'I had the best night of my life.'

'Oh, come on, drama queen! It was only sex, Lexie!'

'No. That's just it, Annemarie, it wasn't only sex,' I insist. 'Are you listening to me? It was a real connection, I told you. This felt different. Like what I've been secretly hoping for. I saw stars!'

Annemarie takes this in. 'Well he did hit you with a door,' she reminds me, trying to make me smile. I don't. She nods, as only one who knows all too well what it is to secretly hope for something with all your heart can.

'What else did you find out about him?'

'Not much. He's got a brilliant sense of humour, seems really honest and loyal, loves Ireland . . .' I rack my brains. 'Is a painter and decorator and lives in the Cotswolds . . . oh and doesn't

79

travel anymore but he had an . . .' I search my memory for the word. 'Unexpected week off.'

'Unexpected? Un-ex-pec-ted? How so?'

I shrug.

'He could be married, Lexie.'

'No wedding ring. He's not married. I know he's not.'

'Did he use a condom?'

'Of course!'

'Aha! So he had a condom – what does that say about him?'

'That he has a brain?' I shake my head at her. Then: 'Actually, two.'

'Two brains?'

'No. Two condoms.'

Her green eyes widen. 'You did it twice?'

'Yeah. Well maybe a few minutes in between to catch our breaths.' I raise my glass.

'Ah, I miss those early days.' She leans back, wiping her mouth with the back of her hand.

14
Forget Me Not

I WAKE WITH A THROBBING HEAD and a raging thirst. I drank far too much wine after Tom collected Annemarie. Finished the bottle I'm afraid to say. I lift my head slowly, avoiding the drool that sits on my much-hyped silk pillow. My lashes feel clumpy. I uncurl my hand, my phone drops out onto the rug. Leaning over, I blindly feel around until I find it. I also find a curled-up, snoring Garfield. The wine and disappointment meant my sleep was seriously erratic, plus I'd kept one ear open all night long. My phone never beeped once. He simply didn't get in touch. I stretch and check it again just in case.

No messages.

'Ah seriously? Come on. What the hell, Adam?' I moan, my mouth dry. I'm sure I dreamed about him when I did sleep. I punch the pillow lightly.

'Come on, ring me! Or text me! God damnit, it's so frustrating!' I kick my legs, turn my face into the silk pillowcase and scream in it. Promised me smoother skin it did and fewer fine lines. I've seen zero results. My crow's feet aren't for turning, not unless I lie back and invite botulinum toxin into my life. Which seems unlikely given that, to date, my skincare routine mostly consists of a packet of industrial-strength wipes and a vat of Astral cold cream.

I might be in lust, but I'm back to my default of being starving the second I wake up, so I haul myself up slowly, swinging my bare feet onto the sheepskin rug and sit for a minute. Hold my head in my hands. Garfield snores like the old man he is, stacks of books piled up next to him, waiting for me. I've ditched the self-help ones and am back to reading Reese Witherspoon's book club choices and celebrity autobiographies. Dermot never read and, what's more, he had every allergy under the sun, so I couldn't have any soft furnishings when he lived with me. No rugs, no throws, no cushions, no curtains. He'd even tried to make me get rid of Garfield. Now, despite my minimalist fantasies, my apartment looks like I won a competition in one of those sixty-second runarounds to fill my bumper-trolley at a soft furnishings' depot.

Out my window I see a surprisingly radiant Saturday. The rain has given way to early March sunshine. It slides in through my open curtains, finding the gap in my blackout lining, throwing a shadow of slanted yellow light across my bedroom floor. Squeezing my toes into the softness of the rug, I stand. I'm going to need a kickstart of two paracetamols, as I've a busy Saturday spread out before me in Sir Patrick Dun's for book-club day. We discuss the book we've chosen and then I read the weekend papers and supplements out loud; sometimes I make up stories using all their names and the names of their children, grandchildren and great grandchildren. After lunch I put on some beautiful old movie full of the feel-goods, and I always play classic soundtracks on my Spotify. The old folks can't get enough of those tunes; clearly, you're never too old to dream of romance or dance to great music. I'm due in at eleven this morning, so I throw on a sweatshirt and jeans, stuff my feet into my runners and lace them up.

'Wakey, wakey, Garfield.' I run my fingers through his coat. He opens his left eye only.

'Come on, buddy – breakfast time.' His other eye opens, he steels himself and arches his creaking back. I give him a moment then together we head for the kitchen to make my first cuppa of the day and his breakfast.

The kitchen is bright as I fill the kettle for one cup. I used to go out with Jackie on the occasional Saturday night, but Sundays were hellish as you literally never got home before four in the morning. Then the hangover didn't shift for days, allowing the fear to creep in and become personal, loitering heavy in my head. But even Jackie's going now. Last night's dishes are soaking in the sink, ready for a rewash.

'Thirsty, Jimmy?' I ask my luxuriant peace lily plant.

He answers me. 'I am, Lexie,' I say in my deepest voice.

'Well allow me.' The kettle clicks off and I pour the boiling water into my cup and then refill it with cold water. Opening the French doors, to let Garfield out for his balcony air, I look out to the quiet car park, not a spare space this morning. The complex is small, only thirty-three apartments. But somehow I know no one.

'Here ya go, Jimmy.' I pour water onto the dry soil.

I throw back two headache tablets and go about my kitchen chores, cuppa at my side. Tea, the giver of life. Running water onto the dishes, I squeeze washing-up liquid in and swirl with my free hand to make bubbles, I rattle the glasses around, then twisting off the tap, I freeze.

'What the –?'

From the bedroom, I hear my phone ringing. I drop my cup and it splatters its contents onto the floor, as I Usain Bolt it.

Just as I slide across the floor on my sheepskin rug, the ringing stops.

'Noooooooooooooooooooooooo!' I dive across the bed to grab the phone.

'Please no!' I twist, getting tangled up in my duvet, staring at the bright screen at a long unfamiliar number before it goes black.

'Shit!' I cradle the phone in my hand.

'Beep!' I urge. It remains silent. No message.

'Oh, beep, you total bastard!' I shake the phone like a greyhound with a hare in its jaws. I dial into my message minder anyway. Press it tight against my squashed ear.

'*You have no new messages,*' the automated reply smugly informs me.

'No shit!' I shout again. The number has an English dial code. What do I do? It must be Adam – it has to be.

'Wait!' I tell myself as I sit up. I sit cross-legged in the middle of my bed. I undo my laces and retie them then exhale slowly. 'Give it a minute.' My heart is exploding inside me.

It rings again.

I jump up.

Sit back down.

It keeps ringing. I jump up again, wobbling on my mattress.

'Hello . . . hello . . . hello? Hello!' I say out loud, testing the sound and changing the tone up on my voice before I hit the green button.

'Heeelllllo?' I draw the word out in a remarkably bored tone.

'Hi, um, Lexie?' Unmistakable.

It's *him*.

It's my Adam.

15
Crazy, Stupid, Love

SPEAKING.' I GRIND MY TEETH, squeeze my eyes tight shut.

'It's Adam . . . from the . . . the –'

'Oh, hiya, Adam.' Bright *agus* breezy. *Maith an cailín*, Lexie Ó Broin.

I stick my tongue out so far down my chin it hurts.

'Hey!'

I pull it back in.

'Hey, hi. How were the cliffs?'

'High.'

'Told you.'

'And spectacular.'

'Told you.'

'Eh . . . listen, Lexie, I'm sorry I didn't call sooner. I actually had a bit of a family issue yesterday, so I flew home . . . I'm back in the Cotswolds.'

My heart literally sinks to my toes, like I've just stepped into a broken lift and plummeted. I fall onto my knees on the bed. I bounce. Once. Try to silence my inner cynic.

'Oh . . . right.'

Can I ask him what happened? Is that any of my business?

'Yeah . . . sorry, I had such a brilliant time with you. Really . . . I . . .' He trails off.

'Yeah, me too.'

'You did?'

No point playing it cool, I tell myself. 'Sure I did! But I think you know that?' My heart is racing so hard I put my hand across it. What's the point in being flirty? He's gone home. Damn.

'Look, I've not been playing the *how-many-days-should-I-leave-it-before-I-ring-you* card. I'd planned to chat to you yesterday, ask if I could take you out for dinner . . . but then I got a call from home and felt I should get back.'

'Sure, we're chatting now . . .' I'm up on my hunkers.

'We are, aren't we? Look, I think I mentioned things are a bit complicated my end . . .'

Oh, Annemarie was right. The man *is* married!

'. . . so I was wondering if you . . . well if you might be into coming over to visit me . . . here? If you –'

Oh, Annemarie was wrong. The man *isn't* married!

'Yeah!' I bite my bottom lip, shake my head madly. 'I'd love that.'

'Yeah?'

I pause for a split second to compose myself. 'Yeah.'

He notices my pause.

'Not too weird I'm asking you to come over to the Cotswolds, is it?' Immediately I hear doubt creep into his voice.

'No! No! Not at all.' I clear the frog that's doing tumble turns in my throat. 'Sorry . . . I want to see you again, Adam. I'd an amazing night with you.' I flop tummy down onto my bed, phone almost entering my ear canal.

'So would I . . . so did I. I haven't stopped thinking about you to be brutally honest, since you left my room.'

Ya WHAT now? Did he actually just say that?

86

Instead: 'Ah well, you had cliffs to see.'

'I did. So . . . how about you have a think about when you can come over? Let me know?'

I do calculations in my brain that Carol Vorderman would be proud of.

'I'm actually off next weekend. I'm off from the Friday. I could come on the Friday for the weekend?' I bite my lip harder.

Is that too soon? Do I sound mental? I do, don't I? That's way too soon! I gulp as if I might be able to swallow the words back in.

'Next weekend? Eh . . . that's the . . .' He pauses and I coax saliva back into my mouth. 'The twenty-fifth! Oh. That's actually perfect for me!' He sounds . . .

Excited.

'I aim to please!'

'Wicked!' He laughs his deep, sexy, dirty laugh.

'This is a bit mental,' I say.

'Can you still say mental?' he quizzes.

'No, apparently you cannot, so it's crazy, it's all a bit crazy, if you can still say crazy – I have no idea on crazy – but . . .' I laugh, feeling my hot cheeks with the back of my hand.

'But exciting though,' he says.

'Oh my God, very exciting.' I exhale my nerves.

We both pause for breath.

I laugh.

He laughs.

I twist over onto my back, hug my knees close to my chest.

'I can't get you out of my head,' he says, his voice lowering. The words registering like church bells in my head.

Dong!

Dong!

Dong!

'Me neither,' I admit. 'About you, I mean. I can't stop thinking about you,' I manage.

It's like an orchestra have started up in my head. Cellos, violins, flutes, the whole kit and kaboodle. Music swells, the conductor madly swings his baton.

'So we're doing this . . . right, the twenty-fifth, if you can get in any time after two thirty I'll be off work and I can come collect you from the airport?' he says.

'Yeah sure – I'll book an afternoon flight.'

'Amazing.' I hear the flutter of pages being turned. Then the closing of a book – is he writing in a diary or something?

'Where should I book to stay?' I feign sincerity.

He pauses. 'If you're okay with it, I was hoping you'd stay with me? At mine?'

In my head: *I was hoping to God you'd say that.*

Out loud: 'Only if you're sure?'

'Oh totally. It's nothing fancy, but I think you'll like it. We are fairly rural. Scenic, even.' A pause and more rustling of pages. 'But actually, just looking here, I've this engagement party I have to show my face at, just at our local hotel . . . so maybe I can book us a room there on the Friday night and we can stay at mine the Saturday night?' A buzzing sound comes down the line. A phone rings.

'Sounds great.' I can barely think straight but I'm aware there's a few details to iron out. 'So I'll book a flight to where?'

He laughs.

It's the sexiest laugh in the whole wide world.

'Handy to know that, all right. So if you book a flight into Birmingham, I can collect you – it's about a fifty-minute drive to my place from there. I'll meet you at the arrivals hall?'

'Grand.'

The buzzing sound again.

'Can you insert that line for Mr Pawley, cubicle four?' he mutters to someone.

'Huh? Where are you?' I ask at the same time he says:

'Right, I have to go, Lexie, I've to work – make sure you save my number into your phone, message me your flight details? I'll see you next weekend! Bring your drinking boots.'

'And nothing else?' I bite my bottom lip.

Silence.

'If I had my way.'

'How about I bring my drinking boots and a carry on?'

'Perfect.'

'Deal!' My voice feels like it's about to fly away with me, I'm that utterly buoyant.

'All I can visualise is you dressed only in those knee-high boots of yours pulling a wheelie behind you through Birmingham airport. It's some image.' His voice is low.

'One way to get through security checks quicker.'

He laughs hard again.

'I can hardly wait. Bye, Lexie.' He rings off, still laughing as Garfield eases around the door to stare at me.

'Holy shit, Garfield!' I throw the phone like a hot potato high into the air and jump up and down on the bed.

16
Untamed Heart

'HAVE YOU COMPLETELY LOST YOUR MIND?'

'Nope.' I click Silverside's out-of-hours answering machine message to *Off*.

'Then you're having a laugh?' Annemarie carefully hands me my Monday morning flat white, her face contorted at my news.

'Again. Same word. Nope.' I accept the steaming cup carefully. I wolfed down a bowl of microwaved porridge and soggy blueberries this morning, then scoffed an almond croissant on the bus on the way in. Lust is a hungry beast. I tighten the bun on top of my head, smooth out my eyebrow.

'And you thought you'd wait until Monday morning to tell me all this?' Annemarie's uniform blazer hugs her bump, the buttons straining above her swollen stomach.

'I was busy in the Brendan Behan Reading Room hosting Book Club for my Sir Patrick Dun's residents – we're reading *The Thursday Murder Club* novel and they're glued to its pages. We devoured far too many bowls of creamy bread and butter pudding.' I rub my own belly. 'Then I had to stay to call the bingo and fell into my bed at ten with Garfield, I'm still catching up on a full night's missed sleep remember?'

She nods.

'I spent hours trying to set up a raffle. I've organised it to try to raise funds to buy them a new pool table. We've just repainted the Roy Keane Games Room especially. The men like to play, and the women like to watch. Bless their hearts. It's quite odd and mildly sexist, but hey – that's what they like to do.'

'Lexie?' Annemarie interrupts indignantly.

'What, Annemarie? I'm telling you about my weekend!'

She glares at me, sits her bottom teeth over her top ones like a confounded Shih Tzu, leans against the marble counter.

'Okay, then . . . what else happened in the home over the weekend, Lexie, pray tell?' Her sarcasm only makes me more determined to continue.

'You see, poor old Paul Buckland was potting the black and he's been waiting eight months on his cataracts, so he dragged the cue through the green baize and it ripped to shreds. Three red balls and the yellow were already missing, not to mention the triangle to set up – it was ancient. Hence the raffle.'

'Get one sponsored.'

'By whom exactly?'

'I don't know, do I? Now stop messing and tell me what's going on with yer man?' She shrugs impatiently, rubs her lower back.

'I'm looking for a good second-hand one, but I can't find any I can afford – they're all over a thousand euro. I'll think of something; I have to. It's the calmness and quiet of the game that they like. Margaret Kilroy looks hypnotised by it. She can sit for hours watching the men play, crocheting her blankets, never having to look down at the needle. I always try to get her to have a go, but she says it wouldn't be proper.'

'Maybe someone can repair it?'

'Oh, I rang around everywhere – it's not worth the money. They need a new one. Honestly, they were all so down I stuck on

Calamity Jane – again – but my heart was breaking. They enjoy taking a few bits and bobs off one another in their little wagers too.'

'They play for money?' She's shocked by that one.

'Money, Annemarie, is no use to them; they play for fruit cake, packets of unopened tissues, Kimberley biscuits, muscle rub, things that *really* matter.'

'Stop! Enough of the baize. Just tell me why you waited until now to tell me about Adam inviting you to his house!'

'Well I might have to think of something because we only raised fifty-seven euro . . . and I bought most of the tickets! And well . . . because . . . we never talk at weekends anymore.'

'What does that mean? I've asked you over to ours a million times for Sunday lunch!'

'And I've been over a few times, and all I do is sit with Tom, making small talk, while you spend hours in the kitchen cooking up a storm and talking back to Donal Skehan on an iPad!'

'Oh, madam, I'm sorry for your troubles!' She hunches her shoulders.

'I'm sorry, you're brilliant, and thank you for having me, but please be careful you don't enjoy cooking so much that Tom becomes so used to being spoiled rotten that you never get taken out to a restaurant ever again!' I look her in the eye.

'Get off my case. This is about you . . . and the grim reality that you don't know the first thing about this guy!'

'Adam!'

'Adam.' She says his name like a bulldog sucking on a nettle.

'Who cares? What do I need to know?'

She guffaws. 'Famous last words.'

'Right, here's what I know! I'm *insanely* attracted to him! He's funny, smart and stimulating company. I know that he makes me feel acutely alive! What else matters? Why aren't you happy for me?' I pick the paper cup back up and blow on my flat white, so the surface ripples.

'Because what if he's a Dirty John type? What if his plan is to lure you to a remote cutesy ickle village in the arse end of England and murder you? Or worse, keep you tied up naked and filthy in his cellar for decades. No one even knows what this guy looks like! Did you even get his surname?'

'No.' I probably should know his last name, I have to admit. 'But, y'know, he did mention a wine cellar!'

'Don't mess about, Lexie – you can't go alone.'

'Well how come I am then?' I feel like sticking out my tongue at her, but I refrain.

Annemarie dunks her camomile teabag up and down, staring at me like I've lost my mind. I sip my coffee.

'Okay, it's a bit . . . reckless, but I trust him – I just do.'

'That's not enough.'

'Jackie saw him!' I suddenly recall and I snap my fingers at her as if that somehow seals the deal.

Annemarie snorts and literally doubles over, putting her paper cup on the ground.

'Jackie saw him!' Tears stream down her foundation, diluting it; when she comes back up she's clutching her pregnant stomach. I stare at her, because it's been so long since she laughed like this. I'm shocked.

'Are you all right?'

'I can just imagine it.'

She composes herself, picks the tea back up, wipes her nose with her fingers and stands ramrod straight.

'Your Honour, I'd like to call Jackie Brophy to the stand. Jackie, you say you saw the victim, Miss Lexie Byrne, on the night in question with Adam the Englishman at the Brazen Head in Dublin, is that correct?'

She clears her throat, and in a low-pitched voice uncannily like Jackie's thick Dublin accent: *I did an' all, Yer Honour. A ringer for that actor, Cillian Murphy, I said he was.*

'And do you think you'd recognise him here today?' Annemarie spins around, her hand outstretched.

Another voice change: *Defo wefo, Yer Hon.*

'Is he sitting here today, in this courtroom?'

A clearing of her throat now. *Totes.*

Annemarie is very good I must admit.

'You're hilarious,' is what I say, totally deadpan.

'Truth is funnier than comedy. Fact.'

'I was friendly with Jackie, so stop slagging her.'

'No . . . you went out with Jackie when you were at a loose end. There is a difference.'

'That's so not true!'

'Isn't it?'

'She was my friend,' I insist.

'No, I was a better friend to Jackie than any of the rest of you,' she tells me, her face serious now.

'How so? You didn't even show up to her leaving party!'

'No, but I was the one who told her to get out of here and go out to Dubai, that it was too good a chance to turn down, when she was wavering. I listened to her when she was stone-cold sober and needed help making a decision more important than whether to start off in the Brazen Head or end up in the Brazen Head on a Monday night. And you know full well I didn't show up because I am heavily pregnant and it was Paddy's night! Now don't give me the Jackie Brophy saw him line again because Jackie'd say, *"Yeah, that's him defo wefo!"* and then point out David Byrne, your poor grief-stricken dad. Jackie! Gimme a break. Sure, Jackie wouldn't have remembered her own name by that stage of the night, let alone the face of the potential killer she left you staggering off to a hotel room with! Jackie saw him.' Annemarie laughs again, dabbing her eyes with her free hand. 'Hilarballs!'

'Wow, I'm glad you got such a laugh out of your own joke.'

The phone rings and I dash to answer it. A lady from Wicklow informs me that she left a necklace with huge sentimental value hanging in one of the changing rooms on Saturday afternoon.

'We were in the Wilde Bride. I think it's on level one? My daughter, well she's only just noticed. She was trying on dresses and took the necklace off.' The woman sounds close to tears.

'Don't worry, in my experience people are usually very good at handing in stuff they find,' I try to reassure her with positivity.

'She removed it when the sales assistant was pulling the dress up over her head in case it caught, and she thinks she hooked it on the changing ring, but she's no idea really. She's wearing it on the big day. It's my fault – she'd enough on her mind with Livvy, her sister, being a complete Bridesmaidzilla! I should have reminded her to make sure she had it. It was her gagsy's . . . my mother's, her grandmother's.' She really does choke up now.

'Oh, I'll get straight onto it I assure you,' I comfort her, not wanting her to panic even more. She sounds almost beside herself, so I take her number and hang up. Then I scroll through my directory and dial the bridal shop. They promise me that they'll go check right away and call me straight back.

'I can just see myself on the six-one news, microphones stuffed into my face on the doorstep of mine and Tom's three-bed semi,' Annemarie jumps straight back. 'I'll be there, bursting out of my furry dressing gown with reporters telling me Jackie Brophy has just been dismissed as a credible witness, and they'll be shouting questions at me about the zillions of online comments slagging me for being such a shit friend as to let you go to stay in some Englishman's house when we didn't even know his surname and he mentioned a cellar!'

I look closely at her now that she's recovered from her laughing and, as the colour fades from her face, I notice she looks tired today. Pale and exhausted actually.

'Quit the catastrophising! Rest assured I'll have died happy. How about you ask June for a few days off?'

'Why?'

'You look worn out.'

'I'm fine; don't fuss. I slept for ten hours last night. Perhaps that's why my backache is even worse today. Could not keep my eyes open during *Gogglebox*. When I spilled my cup of warm water and lemon onto my PJs, Tom had to wake me up and carry me into bed.'

I smile despite myself, it's such a cute image. 'Still on thirty-one weeks?' I ask.

'Thirty-one,' she whispers back, her face flushing red, and then opens her mouth to say something else just as June reappears in front of us.

'May I have a record of any complaints by close of day please?'

'Sure,' I say as Máiréad, an elderly lady from the Liberties in the heart of Dublin, stops at the counter with her shabby gingham shopping trolley on wheels.

'Excuse me please, loves, dere's no toilet paper in de ladies on level two.'

'Now, Máiréad, the loo rolls were all filled this morning.' I turn away from June, give a very deliberate wink and wag a finger gently at her. Máiréad has a hard-earned rep as a bit of a kleptomaniac.

'Well, dere's none dere now, love,' she blatantly lies to my face, not for the first time. We've had problems with her robbing the loo roll for years. She'd give Houdini a run for his money. At first the toilet paper was just on a regular holder, so she had easy access to it. Then we secured it in one of those round metal holders, but she managed to pick the lock with hair grips. Then we got bigger holders with better locks and she dismantled them too. Then we got dispensers with just small individual sheets of paper, but still she takes them out.

'Máiréad. If I get maintenance to go check and the dispensers have been emptied, you are coming up to the office again, and this time I will alert security to call the Guards!' June tells her sternly.

Máiréad looks at me with watery eyes. I can't help but notice the stray hairs poking out of her pointy chin.

'But it's only a bitta bog roll.' She pulls a well-used tissue from up her sleeve and dabs her eyes.

'It is not your property!' June snaps at her.

'It's free but . . . I use it to –'

'Just put it back.' June leans on the counter. 'Or there will be consequences.'

'Are you accusing me of theft?' Máiréad shuffles a few feet back.

'I'm not accusing you, no – I'm telling you you're a bloody thief, Máiréad!' June bangs on the top of the shopping trolley and dust splatters.

'June? Jesus, come on.' I turn to her. 'Go easy on her, seriously, that's enough.'

'I'm the one who has to add up the accounts of what we spend on hygiene products and maintenance at the end of the month, not you, Lexie,' June snarls at me but backs away.

'She's just a lonely old lady,' I say under my breath, but I can see Máiréad's hands are shaking. 'I'll deal with Máiréad,' I tell June gently. I nod to the hatch and Máiréad follows me across.

'I don't like yer one June at all. She's always like a bag a' cats. Never even passes the time of day with me. Any chance I can have a cuppa tea first.' She perches her arthritic body over her trolley. Always dresses the same no matter the weather – a long grey trench coat with several missing oversized black buttons, black socks in green Crocs.

97

'First?' I half smile at her.

'Before I have to go and put all the bog roll back.' She pats the trolley lid. Dust rises again.

'Sure.' I go about making her tea as Annemarie deals with a new customer. I study June as the hot water drips into the paper cup and she shoots me a look that says, *Sorry*. I shoot her one back that's says, *Don't worry, it's fine*. Poor Máiréad. She never had much from life. She lives in a run-down council flat complex that is currently being demolished by developers, only her tower left, and she could very well soon be homeless. I had a meeting with the board at Sir Patrick Dun's about her, and I've been pushing to get her in, but it doesn't work like that. Most residents have family that contribute the extra money due after their pensions, or have sold houses to pay. Máiréad has neither. She lives on her pension and, I'm guessing, has no other savings or support.

'D'ya have any sort of them French cross'ougts? Or a bitta bread 'n' butter?' she asks now, shifting her yellowing false teeth around in her mouth.

'Afraid not. I have to get back to work, so you have to take the tea and go sit on the bench.' I point across the floor to the long soft bench under the chiming hourly clock.

She pulls her trolley behind her, the wheels squeaking. Máiréad takes all sorts of things from the centre: the plants, the ashtrays, salt and pepper sachets and holders, sugars, plastic cutlery, napkins, straws, piles of the free newspapers – all those sorts of things, nothing from the actual shops. Dermot goes easy on her; him or one of the other security guards check her shopping trolley when she leaves, as she's on CCTV, and just take it all back at the end of the day. They're sweet to her in fairness.

'That June one, bad cess to her too!' Máiréad turns her head to hiss back at me.

'Yeah.' I roll my eyes as I take the tea across to her. I let her get settled onto the bench and put the hot cup into her hands with their knobbly fingers and paper-thin skin.

'June has it in for Annemarie too; it's not just you. It's really unfair, but she hates the idea that Annemarie will be going on maternity leave. Don't say that to anyone now, d'ya hear me?'

I sit beside her. I know she likes my company.

'Sure, who would I be saying it to? No one talks to me.'

'I talk to you. And you know I'm talking to Kevin, at Sir Patrick Dun's, every time I'm there to get you that ground-floor corner room. It's just the bloody two-thousand-euro deposit he needs.'

She removes one hand from around the tea and pats my knee.

'I'll stuff the paper back into the dispensers after I sup this. Just keep the rolls – I make bird-feeders outta dem.' She fixes me with her surprisingly clear eyes. 'Don't worry about the fancy home, Lexie. I'm still waitin' on a letter from the council – they will get me some place. Half the block has been knocked down now – only me, Mr Macken and Peter his blind parrot left.'

'I know, but I'll keep trying for you. The council *will* find you somewhere, don't worry. But you do need to keep at them, you know?'

She nods, rummages her teeth around again, slurps the tea.

'But if they put me in the midlands somewhere, I won't go. I won't leave Dublin. I've been here almost eighty years, and I want to die here, be buried in Glasnevin Cemetery. I want to go in with me ma and da and baby brother Michael. I better admit I sup'se I'd love to get a place in that Sir Patrick Dun's, sounds nice and warm. And safe. Them three meals a day handed to you, people to talk to, TV, bingo.'

'And a pool table.'

'And a pool table if ya don't mind?' Máiréad grins and then suddenly gives me a cheeky, watery wink.

'I'll have you know I was a dab hand at pool in me day, beat

99

them all in the old ESB offices so I did. There used to be a table in the canteen when I worked as a cleaner; t'was only for the suits, but I'd play by meself when I got in early. Sharpen the skills. A pool table, well now . . . isn't that something!' She seems utterly taken at that news. 'I know you're doing yer best for me, Lexie, you're a good girl, but please don't be worryin'.' Her eyes water and she dabs at them with bent thumbs.

'Máiréad, with the amount of tissue you have in that trolley, can you not give yourself a clean hanky?'

She laughs, hands me her empty teacup, hoists herself up and scuffles away in her Crocs.

What I wouldn't give to get her into the home. By the sounds of it, she'd give Paul Buckland a run for his Kimberleys! And better still might convince Margaret Kilroy to actually play.

I slip back in behind the counter as Annemarie continues with her customer and take the opportunity to scroll through my emails. I find the one I want and open it with a click. A little shiver runs up my spine.

Voila!

My flight details. The second Adam hung up I went straight online and booked my flight for next Friday, leaving Dublin at two forty-five, landing in Birmingham an estimated one hour and sixteen minutes later. The butterflies circle my belly again. I haven't texted him the details yet. I'm not playing a game exactly, but I don't want him to think I'm *that* keen.

But I *am* that keen.

That keen that last night I attempted a DIY workout in my bedroom, using two tins of off-brand beans as weights while Garfield defo gave me a weird look. Then put a treatment in my hair, studied my magnifying mirror with tweezers in hand for any hairs on my face or chin then collapsed into bed with a face slathered with newly purchased overpriced wonder cream.

I'm *that* keen.

'I don't mean to be a Billy Buzzkill, but I can't believe you're going to go over to him. I have to be honest, Lexie, it's a bit . . .'

'Huh? What?' I shove my phone down into my skirt pocket and turn to Annemarie.

'*Desperate?*' Annemarie hooks her hands on her hips.

'Is it now.' I stand with my hand hovering over a ringing phone. 'Desperate how?'

'Come on – you've met him *once!*'

'So what?'

'So let him come back over here then, to see *you?*'

'Where's this coming from?' I ask as the desk phone rings.

'I'm being honest with you that's all,' she says as I turn my back on her and answer the call. It's a man, a proper American, left over from Paddy's Day no doubt, barking about parking. I give him directions to our underground car park. Americans are the only nationality who call up about car parking – everyone else just rocks up. I hang up. Annemarie busies herself with another customer and I try to stop being pissed off with her. The phone rings again.

'Hello, Silverside Shop –'

'It's Nancy from Wilde Bridal. Nothing here I'm afraid, Lex.'

'Oh no.'

'But the manager is looking at an autumn-winter collection for Marks & Spencer's in town so she might have put it somewhere for safekeeping. I can't call her as her phone's powered off during the catwalk.'

'Okay, I guess no news is good news as far as our lady is concerned so I'll leave it until you call me back again?'

'Sound.'

The counter is six deep. The word *desperate* gets shoved to the back of my mind and I concentrate on my work.

17
Only You

When lunchtime comes, Annemarie asks: 'Canteen or what? Please don't say Marco's bad-baby-growing food?'

'Actually, I need to do some shopping – I'll grab a ham roll on the go. Catch you after.' I undo my bun, slip my leather bag across my shoulder, pull my curls free. My stomach rumbles.

'Do you not want me to come with you?' I can see she's hurt, but negativity – I just can't deal with it right now.

'No, it's fine. You relax.' I pick up my tinted lip balm, smooth some on. 'You should sit down and read a magazine, take the weight off your feet, ya know.' I nod to her belly. She yawns.

'Is this about me saying you were desperate?'

'No.' I twist the lid back on and slide it into my pocket.

'Because I didn't mean it.'

'It's fine.'

'Look about Adam . . . I'm sorry if I've annoyed you? I'll just mind my own business.' She curls a loose strand of red hair behind her ears.

'You've a right to your opinion,' I say as Lisa slips in to cover lunch.

'Lisa, the bridal store is due to call me back to see if they found a valuable necklace. I wrote the woman's number in the lost and found book. Her name is Marie Woodcock and she left it there on Saturday she thinks . . .'

'You're going shopping, aren't you?' Annemarie whispers into my ear.

'Will do. No worries,' Lisa replies.

'Sure am. Sexy underwear, the works.' I unzip my bag and stuff my phone in. 'Call her will you if you get word while I'm gone; she's obviously very anxious,' I tell Lisa, who nods again. I lift the hatch, stride out as Annemarie follows me.

'Lexie, come on, don't fight with me. You'd do the same in my position.'

'Ha!' I stop myself.

'Ha what?'

'How often do I interfere in your relationship?'

'Never.' Annemarie rolls her eyes. 'If you say so.'

I feel the blood rush to my cheeks.

'I'm only being honest with you.' She yawns again, a double yawn this time. I see her neat, immaculate teeth.

'Well then, don't. I don't want your honesty, for once in my life. I want you to be my friend, Annemarie, not my mother. God knows, I get fifteen texts a week from my parents fretting about me; I don't need that from you too. Let me enjoy this please, yeah? I'm not some stupid kid. See you in a bit.' I walk away from the desk and step onto the escalator.

'So I need travelling clothes, but they'll also be the clothes he sees me in when he picks me up. Then I need an outfit for that night, the engagement party thingy he mentioned, and then Saturday day, Saturday night and back to the airport clothes.' I'm talking to myself under my breath, counting on my fingers, as my phone beeps and I pull it out of my bag.

I'm sorry, when r u going? x From Annemarie.

Friday 25th, I type back, send and miss the last step off the escalator so a girl slams into my back. It beeps again.

What time? I can take u 2 airport? x

Aer Lingus flight is @ 2.45 but u'll b in work only im off that Friday, u r in with Lisa. Send.

Where do you fly from to get there? x

Birmingham, I type back, send then slide onto airplane mode. I know Annemarie is standing on her own now in the Green Gables organic café, queuing for a smoothie, starving and bored silly so she's nothing better to do than to ask me stupid questions.

I've stuff to do.

I've a man to please.

I'm all about free the nipple, but I'm also all about the power of the see-through lacy bra.

I stroll in and out of the stores, take one look at the rails from a distance and know I will find absolutely nothing. Then I see Dermot, on his radio, at the emergency exit by the Final Cut. He waves. I pretend my phone is ringing. It's funny how I never saw him for who he really was until we broke up. I just believed he preferred me wearing comfortable shoes, but now I think he never wanted me to wear heels because it showed his height. Or rather lack of it. I'd be lying if I said I didn't still feel the rage when I imagine him writhing around with other women, sexting them, while I peeled spuds for a shepherd's pie. It demolished my self-esteem, though he'll never know that, the prick. Turning back, I yield outside Threads. Its lettering says: *'What, this old thing?'*

And lo and behold the faceless mannequin, the one that's built bigger than other mannequins, is wearing a long white shirt, black leggings and wedge ankle boots.

'Oh, you look nice,' I whisper to her behind the glass. My breath clouds her for a moment. If she had a face, I'd guess it would be smiling back at me.

'Good afternoon, can I help you?' an older lady I've never met before, dressed head to toe in lilac wool, asks politely as I walk in.

'Yeah, the outfit in the window, where can I find that?'

She nods in the right direction and I follow her; she shows me to two rails and mercifully leaves me to it.

I find the shirt, hold it up to me, gauge some sizes and do the same with the leggings. They looked ordinary in the window but on closer inspection are in fact faux leather leggings. Not exactly me. But feck it. Throwing several sizes over my arm I spot a short red dress and add several of the same. I extend the twelve items only policy by the time I hit the changing room, so I leave some with the young attendant.

'These are all the same PBWs and LRDs, chicken?' she tells me, confused, separating the tangled hangers impressively.

'The what?' I ask, even more confused.

'Pretty white blouse and little red dress.' She speaks fast and selects a number from a rack on the wall.

'Is it not a shirt?'

'Same thing. A no fuss number that slides easily under any jacket. Actually, these are stretch perfect shirts – they let your body move despite their body-hugging shape.'

'That's why I need to try on a few – I don't want the hugging part.'

'Just size up.' She hands me the number.

'I know, thanks.' I step behind the heavy curtain like the wonderful wizard himself, pull it across, take a long deep breath and begin the ordeal.

The trauma that is the trying on of clothes.

18
Pretty Woman

I GO FOR THE LOOSE WHITE SHIRTS to start with.

On.

Off.

On.

Off.

On.

Off.

Oh, who turned up the heat?

Is it just me or is this dressing room smaller than most? My stomach is gurgling at me and I really don't need to see my arse every time I look at my face in the oh-so-bright multiple mirrors. After four tries I find the right fit. A nice dipped open collar, long slim sleeves and it falls just over my bum by a few safe inches. Then I drag the leggings on, jumping up and down to get them up, but the first pair fit nicely and, much to my amazement, look pretty good on me.

Flattering. Very flattering. They make my legs look slim and long. It's a trying-on miracle! I'm almost afraid to breathe.

I wedge my feet into the black ankle boots. Twisting and turning in the mirror, I like what I see. A perfect travelling outfit. Not exactly comfortable, but it's the first thing he'll see me in. It must look comfortable, that's the main thing. Nothing that looks comfortable but is really nice is ever really comfortable.

Carefully, I undress and fold the miracle items together on the little stool. Next, I try on three different sizes of the long-sleeved LRDs. The dress has that stretchy material with some give, but all of them are a bit tight around my stomach. My face is starting to do that thing it does in changing rooms, turning pinker and pinker as I scramble to pull clothes off over my head. But being here suddenly reminds me of Marie Woodcock and the unsolved case of the missing necklace. I pull my phone from the crumpled heap on the changing-room floor and dial the information desk, letting my stomach muscles relax for a minute.

'Can I help you?' an unfamiliar voice asks.

'Lisa? Is that you?'

'No.'

There is a shuffling noise on the line, the receiver is dropped and then June's telephone voice screeches down the line and I have to hold the phone away from my ear.

'Helllooo, Silverside Shopping Centrrrreeeee. This is information, June speaking, how may I help you?'

'Em, it's only me, Lexie, wondering did the bridal shop call back?' I ask.

'Huh?'

'There's a missing necklace I'm trying to locate – where is Lisa?'

Again, more muffling, as a hand goes over the receiver, and I hear faraway voices.

'No news about the missing necklace as of yet,' June tells me.

'Right, 'kay, thanks.' I put my phone down and stick my head around the velvet curtain.

'Do you have this in the next size up?' I ask the fast-talking assistant.

'What size is that one, chicken?' she asks eagerly.

'I don't know – I don't look at sizes.'

'How do you know what size it is then?'

'I don't.'

'Can I look, chicken?' Tenderly she prises the red dress out of my hands.

'It's a –'

'Ahhh!' I raise my hands and block my ears. 'La la la la la!'

She backs away slowly as my phone beeps from inside the changing room. I pick it up off the floor.

Please, please, pleaseeee don't say you've changed your mind?! Adam.

The sight of the four letters of his name is enough to send me giddy. Who could have imagined a simple A and a D and another A and an M side by side could have this effect on me? I'd planned to text him after lunch, but this is even better.

All booked! I insert the airplane emoji and press send. No details, so he has to text me back. The bubbles hop. He's reading and texting. Right now, wherever he is, whatever he's doing, he's stopped because he's thinking about me, Lexie Byrne. How the hell did this happen? I mean, I nearly didn't go to Jackie's leaving do, and then I left and had there been a free taxi I'd have been gone. It doesn't bear thinking about.

Airline? ETA?

Aer Lingus flight leaves Dublin at 2.45pm. I'll send flight number after work – Lexie x

The sales assistant returns, and she hands me in another dress.

'I think this one should fit.' She looks me up and down, chewing at speed.

'Thank you very much indeed,' I say and drag the velvet back across the rings as my phone beeps again.

This time just the thumbs-up emoji. I catch my reflection in the full-length, light-bulb-encrusted mirror. I'm physically flushed but not sure now if it's from the horror show of squeezing into tight red dresses or Adam's texts.

'Here's hoping!' I tell myself as I drag another dress over my head, fight my arms down through the snug, ribbed sleeves, and this time it slides on without too much of a wiggle. She's right. This one fits a bit better. So I do the twisting and the turning thing again. The rich colour makes my skin look very clear and brings out the green in my eyes.

'Hey, looking good, kid!' I blow myself a kiss.

It's a perfect party dress. But only if I suck in twenty-four-seven for people I've never met before in my life. The full-length sleeves are a gift from heaven, the ruffling design across the middle hides my stomach magically and the V-neck is just low enough to show off some cleavage without being too titty.

'Designer of this dress, I salute you.' I shimmy back out of it and fold it on top of my other soon-to-be purchases.

Pulling the curtain across, I'm back in uniform as I head to the till. The assistant grins and gives me a thumbs up as lilac-wool lady folds my purchases. With one swipe, I'm €216 lighter.

19
Once

COMING UP THE ESCALATOR, swinging my bags by the roped handles, daydreaming of how well I'll look in my LRD, I can hear raised voices at the information desk.

'No! I won't!' It's unmistakably Annemarie. Picking up the pace, I take the final two steps together and jump off.

'Oh shit,' I say.

I see the white socks and sliders first, before Girl with the Star Tattoos reveals the rest of herself. But more worryingly June is standing beside her, her arm trying to reach the girl's shoulder. I pause, quickly twist my hair back up in my bun.

'Everything all right?' I ask, approaching the desk now.

'Yer one was standing by the desk as I came back from break and she gave me the finger!' Annemarie is positively fuming.

'Eh, I did in me hole!' the Girl with the Star Tattoos turns to me, her neck jerking like an angry chicken with every word.

'And June wants *me* to apologise!' Annemarie snarls.

'You gave me the fingers.'

'You gave me the finger first!'

'I gave my ma the finger!' she spits.

'Who's your ma?' Annemarie looks around.

'Please just apologise for sticking your two fingers up at her,

Annemarie; you cannot behave like that behind the information desk. You are the face of Silverside Shopping Centre.' June tries to keep her voice low. 'People record everything these days. I don't want a big viral finger on my hands.'

If this were a TV show, now would be the time I looked directly down the lens.

'I'm going to have you barred.' Annemarie reaches for the phone. 'I've had enough of your harassment, you wagon!'

'Hey! Thank you! That's it! That's quite enough!' June puts her hand with its multiple dress rings on the receiver, across Annemarie's.

'Annemarie, you cannot speak to August like this. It's not the first complaint I've had about you.'

'Who's complained about me?' Annemarie really is mad. 'And why haven't I been notified in writing?'

'Máiréad?' June is lying. I can see it.

Annemarie's eyes nearly pop out of her face as she drags her hand from beneath June's. 'Máiréad?'

'Yes, Máiréad,' June says as Annemarie shakes her hand out like it may have been in contact with something infected, wipes it several times down the side of her skirt.

'August?' I've been slow on the uptake but I suddenly register the name and stare at the Girl with the Star Tattoos, who is now surrounded by a small crowd that has gathered around the information desk, some sucking on smoothies, others sipping takeaway coffees.

I catch Annemarie's eye and see the penny finally drop for her too. 'Aha! Right. So this is your daughter, June? Wow . . . just wow!'

'Let's take this away from the desk, shall we?' I'm eyeballing Annemarie now. How is this June's daughter? What are the bloody chances?

'Good idea. You stay, Lexie, and you too, August. Annemarie, please follow me.' June totters a step or two on her heels. One of the heels looks lopsided to me, making her walk like she's just got off a horse.

'So you're saying you gave your mother the finger?' Annemarie moves through the hatch and slams it down. 'Charming!'

'Yeah, so what? It's a joke. Relax the cacks, hun.'

'Hey, June, go easy on Annemarie –' I try to get June's attention, but she marches off up to head office with Annemarie keeping step behind her.

'What's her problem? She's a bleedin' loon that one!' August says.

'She presumed you gave her the finger because you had that run-in over the mustard in Marco's, remember?'

'Yeah, well, I'm not having the best day ever. I'd just landed back from Manchester that morning after discoverin' my girl-friend of two years shagging Janine, our best mate . . . my ex-best mate, in our bed!'

'Oh!' I'm a bit taken aback, to be honest. 'That sucks.'

'I know, hun. I should have copped when they got matching haircuts! I came home to see if me ma could take me back, but she was at a meeting, so I went for food. I'm one of those ones who eats her face off through heartbreak.'

Every woman has something in common, I think. Looking past August's shoulders, I clock a tall man approaching the desk.

'Starvin' I've been for two solid years!' she tells me, on a roll now. 'I'd turned vegan for her, but I was constantly hungry, cravin' meat, I dreamed 'bout real-life Percy Pigs. The only thing I liked about being a vegan was the mustard chickpeas.' She clasps her hands together and stares up to the roof. 'I saturated it all in mustard. The chickpeas, the cauliflower rice, the tofu . . . all swimmin' in the stuff. But that row with your pal was the last thing I wanted. Even though I didn't need it to mask the taste anymore, I'd grown to desire it. Mustard, y'know.' Suddenly she looks vulnerable to me.

'Annemarie is going through stuff herself; no one knows the weight of anyone's troubles so just leave it, go on.' I move in behind the desk as a small queue has formed behind the tall man.

'I once read a thing on Insta that said, if everyone put their problems out on a table, you'd gladly take yer own back,' she says and follows me in behind the desk.

'What are you doing?' I stop.

'I'm starting here, hun, aren't I, this afternoon?' she mutters.

'Starting what?' I drop my bags under the counter.

'I'm workin' full-time in information, duh! I'm home for good. Ma trained me in on the phones when yous were at lunch. She said someone's leavin'?'

'Hello? Hi. Hi. If I may? I need twenty-seven five-euro gift cards please.' The tall man taps a red biro on the counter, most annoyingly.

'Hang on, August, you're starting work here, with us? That was you when I rang down earlier from the changing room?'

'Yeah, I was practisin' answerin' the calls. Then Ma said I've just to watch yous today . . . observe . . . until she spoke to yous.' She rolls her eyes; again I see the whites.

'This is going to be a prob–'

'So I've been told to go home for the week! Full pay, fine by me! She's trying to make me out to be unstable. I know what she's doing.'

Jeez, I think – now Annemarie's standing facing the desk, waving a yellow form in her hand.

'W-What's this?' she asks, doing a double take.

'Twenty-seven five-euro gift cards please!' He tip-taps again, faster now, the red ink marking the counter.

'Erm . . .' I just know this is going to blow.

'What is *she* doing behind our desk?'

I see June cautiously stepping off the escalator now.

'I'm starting work here, hun. I was working near Old Trafford at Pizza Express bu–'

'You're starting behind the information desk?' Annemarie's tone has come down rapidly; her nostrils begin to flare.

'Apparently. Taking over from a Jackie?' August faces Annemarie.

'No bloody way!'

'Annemarie!' June says from behind her.

'That's it. I'm not working with her. Sure, she's no experience? We don't even need anyone else we keep telling you!' Annemarie crumples the yellow form tight in her hand.

'Uh oh,' August singsongs.

'Annemarie.' June stares up at her with eyes of steel. 'You really should keep that formal written warning in your files for your future here in Silverside.'

'Hello! Is this an information desk or an episode of *Coronation Street*?' A smoothie is sucked dry as the straw grasps for liquid at the bottom of the plastic, and laughter cackles around the small gaping crowd. The tall man knocks loudly on the counter this time with his knuckles. 'I've twenty-seven goody bags waiting to be filled.'

'Sorry . . . can you please just hang on for one moment.' I turn to him, my index finger raised as Máiréad pulls her shopping trolley on wheels off the escalator towards us. *Oh not now, Máiréad*, I whisper in my head.

'Annemarie, I thought we'd agreed you needed to go home right now. I think it's for the best.' June lifts the hatch and comes in behind the counter. She pulls out the middle drawer where we keep the gift cards. Counting them out on the counter, licking her thumb as she goes through them, like playing cards.

'Do you, June? Is that what you think?' Annemarie's tone is deadly.

June just smiles and bobs her head at her like she's a child, very patronising like.

I open my eyes wide at Annemarie and shake my head at her. Clench my jaw and shake my head again.

'June? I'm talking to you?' Annemarie pushes.

'We both know your past history, so I'm expecting you'll be asking for early maternity soon, am I right?'

Annemarie is at a loss for words at this. As am I.

'I must have provisions in place for you dropping in and out of work.'

'June! Stop!' I say my mouth open.

'Uh-oh, uh-oh, uh-oh, oh, no, no,' August singsongs again to the tune of 'Crazy in Love'.

'Like we just discussed, I think a few days off will do you the world of good. Maybe go chat with your GP, okay? Sorry, did you say five euro on each card, sir? Apologies for the wait.' June smiles warmly at him as Máiréad shuffles in beside him.

'I found something by the Blazing Seeds & Salads bar I think is –'

'Máiréad, not now.' I give her a look.

'You think that's what I did? Dropped in and out?' Annemarie is actually grey in the face.

'Not now.'

'Why would I need to chat with my GP?'

Everyone in the queue except the tall man is staring at Annemarie.

'June?' Annemarie won't quit.

June continues to press her thumb to her tongue and count out the cards.

'I will not be accused of theft twice in the one day so I'm telling you I found a ne–' Máiréad starts again.

'Can you just leave it, Máiréad.' I wave my hand at her. June has threated on occasion to bar her from Silverside and I couldn't bear if that happened to her.

'But it might be valuable? Or sentimental to someone?'

I hold my hand up to her.

'Don't ignore me, June. I've worked here for a long time – have some respect for me please.'

My heart sinks for her. Quickly I hiss at poor Máiréad: 'Leave it into the Wilde Bride, the bridal shop, will you? They know it's missing – tell them I said to keep it there! It's very valuable!'

'All right so . . . I once cleared the table ya know when I broke, won thirty-five pounds I did, before the euro came in.'

'W-What?' I gasp.

'Playing pool. I was that good.' She shuffles off, pulling her trolley behind her. I pray that she'll actually do what I've just asked her.

'Answer *me*!' Annemarie suddenly shrills, piercingly loud.

She's seconds away from a second formal warning and therefore being fired if she says one more thing, I just know it. June will be thrilled if she continues to kick off in public and leave her with no choice. I also know her hormones are controlling her mouth as well as her body. I have no choice.

'Owwwwww!' I fall to the floor. 'Ouuccchhhh!' I roll around, grabbing my stomach, tucking my skirt in between my knees.

'What the hell?' June drops the gift cards and they scatter all over the ground, like a fifty-two-card pickup.

'My side! My side hurts! Ow! OW!' I clutch my left side, praying it's the side my appendix is on – I can't remember. I look up straight into the beady eyes of August. They're suspicious. Then I do remember – it's the right. I move my hand.

'I better call an ambulance.'

I look up again this time to see August lift the information phone with a huge grin on her face.

'No – I – I.' I raise one hand from my stomach then drop it. 'We have our own first-aid department here, but I'm fine, honestly, I just –'

'I dial one for first aid, right?' She presses a button. 'Yes, we need you please right way, on level two, information. It's an emergency! I think she needs the *theatre* right away!'

'No!' I protest too late.

'*Baby, you're making a fool of me,*' August sings under her breath.

'Please stop making a scene, Lexie!' June hisses.

'Please keep the scene running, Lexie!' August guffaws.

'Lexie, are you 'kay?' Annemarie wraps her arms around me. I can't tell her I'm faking.

Yet.

'Oh my God, don't worry, the centre first aiders will be here any second; they're only in the basement. I've got you.' She cradles me.

And sure enough, within minutes I see the neon yellow coats of two first aiders, jump-bags across them, sprinting towards the information desk. I shut my eyes tight, as if that might make them go away.

'Balls,' I mutter.

20
Remains of the Day

'I'M COMING WITH YOU!' Annemarie announces, handing me a box of Off-Beat doughnuts.

'Huh?' I shuffle my foot back into my well-worn slipper, which has slid off, as I half open my hall door to her, holding Garfield back with my other foot.

'To the Cotswolds we shall go!' she hollers, pumping her arm in the air, her tummy greeting me first. 'I've still got that Aer Lingus credit voucher to use up that my folks got us last Christmas.'

'W-What?' I stutter, and she gently pushes past me, down my hallway, her orange slip-ons clacking off her well-moisturised heels.

'It's the least I can do after all you did for me!' she calls back over her shoulder.

I shut the door; the glass rattles. What is she talking about? She must be winding me up. All I wanted was a quiet day after spending hours in the basement wasting the first aiders' time – only to be told they could find nothing wrong obviously. I follow Annemarie into the kitchen. The Lindt chocolates she brought me are on the kitchen table, with a thank-you note, as yet unwritten. They're waiting to be dropped into the basement at Silverside, for the hard-working first aiders, and to alleviate my faker guilt.

'What are you talking about?' I drape a tea towel over the chocs, so she doesn't question my regifting, as she fills my kettle. It feels very strange, us both in our civvies of a Tuesday morning.

'You really are the best friend a girl could ask for. Tom thought it was absolutely hilarballs that you did that for me. He said you're a total headcase.' She turns and hugs me to her tightly. 'You should consider an acting career – I totally bought that performance.' She claps.

'Don't applaud – I'm mortified!'

She stops.

'August didn't – she knew I'd my hand on the wrong side for my appendix. That's why she called for first aid. She was laughing at me; she knew you were about to blow your top.' I step back from Annemarie, whose freshly washed, tumbling red curls smell like shea butter.

'She knows what her mum's like – enough to drive anyone up the wall. She was just such a patronising witch in the meeting – she asked me if I was one of them *bi-populars*, I kid you not, and said I shouldn't neglect my mental health!'

'She did not?' I try my best.

'She did, and . . .'

I can't. 'And then gave you your first formal warning for *an obscene gesture* behind the desk.'

Annemarie had told me the story of what happened in the office with June at least six times in the basement, as she held my hand yesterday.

'Can you believe it? Well, hey, it's all worked out – we both have the week off work and a trip this Friday to look forward to!'

'What trip? Seriously, what are you banging on about?'

'I'm coming with you . . . to see Mr Cotswolds himself!' She moves to my couch, yawns loudly, eases herself down gently, like a pregnant woman should. Leans back, palms flat against her lower back.

'Eh. No, you're not,' I manage, confused.

She shifts her weight, pulls something out the pocket of her maternity jeans.

'Eh. Yes, I am. Look, I'm all booked! *Voila*. I'm on the two forty-five Aer Lingus on the twenty-fifth to the charming Cotswolds, via Birmingham – glad I asked you that one. I'd have flown into London! I'll book my accommodation when you get me his exact address, don't worry.' She slides her feet out of her slip-ons.

'Have you actually lost your mind, Annemarie?' I tie my robe tighter around my waist. I hadn't bothered getting dressed yet as I was about to de-fuzz. A total leg and underarm de-fuzz today and a *down-there* tidy-up.

'Stop taking the piss,' I say.

'I'm not!' She crosses her heart. 'So here's the thing. We're both off and I need a change of scenery. I talked to my doctor again and you're right, I need to relax. He said it's perfectly safe for me to fly up to thirty-seven weeks, especially a short hop over to the UK. No problem. I took your advice. I've stopped all the online *expert* stuff – it's making me totally paranoid – and I've decided to only listen to my obstetrician.'

'You're not serious? As if you're going to fly?' I quiz her.

'Lexie, you're the one who's telling me to chill. People can fly up to thirty-seven weeks . . . thirty-two weeks if you're carrying twins!'

'I don't know that, do I? I just imagine you being you –'

'Flying honestly is the least of my worries. I'm starting to worry about the actual birth now!' She folds the booking printout back into her pocket. 'Plus I'm worried sick about you going over to some bloke we don't know from –' In fairness she resists, just hunches.

'Right so,' is all I can manage. I want to say: What. The. Flaming. Hell?

'All I know is that I have to get away. Maybe I am going a bit bonkers. I'm so anxious all the time, and beyond tired, so unlike myself, it's hard to explain.' She exhales her worries; I sit beside her and take her cold hands in mine.

'Of course you can come. I really don't need you to . . . or want you to, but if *you* want to, that's different. Then that's fine.' I rub her hands like my mam used to rub mine when I was a little girl and I was too embarrassed to wear my stringed mittens she'd sewn into my coat anymore. My mam always had me wrapped up cosy from head to toe. Funny, when I look in the mirror these days for that split second, I see her looking back at me.

'I won't cramp your style I promise . . . he need not even know I'm there. I'll just hang out in the hotel, order room service, watch regular telly, maybe get a pregnancy massage and sleep, I'm so exhausted . . . and my back aches constantly and, honestly, I'd feel like a better friend if I'm nearby and I know where you'll be. It's just not an option for you to go alone.'

'I know it sounds crazy, but you have to trust me. Like you said, I'm thirty-nine and a half, Annemarie. I'm a grown woman.'

'Would you let me go to stay in some bloke's house in the middle of nowhere who I'd only met once?'

I digest her words.

'I'd like to think I would trust –'

'Would you really? Now be honest.'

'Probably not,' I croak.

'You know it makes sense.' Relief floods her pale face.

'I guess.' But I'm still trying to compute this.

'Believe me it does.'

'Tea?' I ask as I get up to re-boil the kettle and get the doughnut box.

'No, can I have a glass of milk with my doughnut?'

'Huh?' I spin on my rubber soles.

She looks at me, her hair tumbling around her pretty face, the dark freckles contrasting dramatically with the pale skin underneath. As she crosses her legs, I can't help but notice they have barely any significant difference in definition or shape from thigh to ankle – only her bulging sweatshirt indicates that she's pregnant.

'Daaaaiiiiiiiiirrrryyyy?' I growl out the word like it's terrifying.

'I know. I just really want it. Freezing cold milk. Like the way you can't pass the bakery in M&S without buying those macadamia biscuits they bake in store.'

I salivate. I don't know if you remember the old Bisto gravy ad where the kids followed the scent? Well I'm like that with those bloody biscuits. I'm lucky to make it out of the car park without eating the four in the bag. Everything in moderation is my Achilles heel.

'But *bad-baby-growing cow's milk*?' I use the same voice.

'Or is it?' She sighs.

'Well that's what you tell me the experts say.' I refrain from doing finger quotes on experts. We've had the conversation; she knows how I feel.

'Fuck the experts.'

I've trained her well, my Jedi.

'You said it, sister.'

I yank open the fridge to get the milk, and on cue Garfield purrs. I shop day by day so there isn't much else in there keeping the milk company. Some eggs, half a block of white cheddar, a large mushroom, an open tin of tuna, three-quarters of a bottle of white wine, a jar of slightly off Old El Paso sliced jalapenos and a half-bag of mini-Dime bars.

I take one of my four crystal glasses out for her, pour, then spoon a good heap of coffee granules into my cup and fill with boiling water. Dermot despised coffee granules – we ground beans and made coffee that way. I always hated it; it all took far too long for me. By the time it was deemed ready for consumption, I'd gone off the idea. I wish I'd stuck to my granules and told him to go grind his own beans! In every way.

Stirring it, I dribble some milk in and pour a full glass of calcium for Annemarie.

'What flavour?' I proffer the Off-Beat box.

'I want the Nutella Ring first then –'

I was joking.

'What?' I look in through the clear covering. Then I snap the sticker seal and the lid pops open. These aren't the usual Annemarie sugar-free, gluten-free, joyless doughnuts – these are a Willie Wonka jamboree.

'. . . then the Honeycomb Crunchy. No, actually, the S'mores!' She even claps her hands in excitement, like Julian, Dick or Anne might.

Not George – she was much too cool.

'Well holy God. Let the doughnut orgy commence!' I cheer, returning to the couch with the drinks and box.

Garfield does his series of circles before curling up on the floor at my feet.

Leisurely we gorge and sup and I do not ask her about her reignited relationship with sugar.

'Wouldn't this be bliss, doing nothing all day every day?' she says through a mouthful, her front tooth covered in chocolate so it looks like she's missing a tooth.

'Not really.' I take a bite from my Boston Crème and chew, unfolding my legs out in front of me, crossing one slippered foot over the other.

When I swallow: 'Life is not for doing nothing.'

'I'd be more than happy doing sweet feck all . . . weekdays, weekends, I'd take it all,' she says, rolling her tongue around her white-frosted lips.

'You think that.'

'Having nowhere to be every day must be the be all and end all, come on? Imagine not having to drag yourself out of the groove in your warm bed in the depths of winter? In the pitch dark and icy cold! Not having to listen to the same Christmas music with non-original singers on loop from the start of November until the end of January?'

I lay my head on her shoulder. She's right. I will admit they are the worst months in our job. We see first-hand the consequences that hideously over-commercialised Christmas brings. I've had grandmothers well into their eighties, rosary beads entwined in their fingers, shoplift toys because there was no other way for the kid's mother to get their Santa list. But I also see the goodness in people. We organise a drop-off at the desk that we bring to St Vincent de Paul the night before Christmas Eve. People leave all sorts of stuff from rolled and boned turkeys, to honey-glazed hams, to selection boxes and brand-new toys. For the last eight years Annemarie and I have donated €100 each, to be spent on toys for the collection. We wish we'd the income to be able to give more. One year, Annemarie had poked me in the ribs so hard I'd yelped.

'Look! Lexie! Look!' she'd hissed as a very young dad pushed his son on a shiny blue tricycle by the red handle. The boy's little face was lit up. 'We bought that; I know because I got us a ten per cent discount because it had a long scratch on it!' she'd whispered in my ear.

It had felt so damn good.

'Our job isn't so bad,' I remind her.

124

'Says who?'

'Says me. We have each other . . . and a pension!'

'When the baby comes' – she sucks her thumb, runs her tongue across her teeth – 'well, ya know yerself after the maternity leave, June is right. I'm not going back to work. I want to be a stay-at-home mammy.' She looks sheepish, as if I'd be cross with her.

'You're joking, right?' I drop the half-eaten doughnut back into the box on my lap, wipe my fingers off each other.

'I'll miss you obviously, but it's not like I won't still be seeing ya, you know.' She hunches, as if worried how I'll respond.

'But, sorry to be crass, can you afford to do that?' I'm more than a little surprised. Tom's job as a salesman in Sailor's Supplies, a sailing shop near the East Link Bridge, doesn't exactly pay a lot – as far as I was aware, Tom relies heavily on Annemarie's contribution to pay her half of his mortgage. *Their* mortgage as it is now.

'Tom's going to start teaching sailing at the weekends. Don't look at me like that, Lexie. He can charge up to a hundred and fifty euros an hour for a private lesson.'

'And there's a big market for sailing lessons in Dublin?'

'Apparently.'

'What about his matches at weekends? His pints with the lads down the cricket club? That all adds up.'

'He'd stop all that. We talked about it.'

I don't allow my eyebrows to rise and choose my follow-up words carefully.

'Hmmm . . . sounds great, Annemarie, but I wonder, shouldn't Tom be qualified to teach sailing? Maybe tell him to check that out. He may need a teaching certificate. Insurance, all that stuff? Just before you guys make any big financial decisions.'

'No, I mean he's a great sailor.' She pauses, digests my words on top of her doughnut.

125

'I'd just think about it, carefully you know. Pensionable jobs are hard to come by, not to mention the massive Silverside perk you're entitled to of using the Huckleberries crèche for free! That's a pretty brilliant perk. Like, it's unheard of really.'

'I know, but I'm going through all this to be with my baby. I want to be the one who's there for the first crawl, who sees the first steps, hears the first word.' She takes a breath and it's one of those jumpy ones that gets caught in the back of her throat.

'But you'd literally be twenty steps away if the baby was in Huckleberries.'

I'm not convinced Annemarie should throw in the towel on her job. At least take the maternity leave and then see? Okay, so maybe Tom can provide a whole extra income with this teaching idea, but I'm still not convinced. The last thing she would need is to quit, only finding out later they couldn't manage. June wouldn't take her back, I know that for a fact, plus she'd lose the free crèche.

'Why don't you just have the baby, take your couple of extra early weeks maternity leave and see how you go? Don't make that decision now . . . not when you really don't have to.'

She digests my words.

'I'm excited to meet this Adam chap now.'

'So am I . . . No, hang on, I thought you said you were staying out of the way? Come on. He'll think I'm very strange – like actually perverted – if I bring my heavily pregnant best friend along on a dirty weekend, ya know?'

'I'm joking. I'll stay far, far away.'

'Annemarie, he's collecting me from the airport! It's a good drive to his house.' I pull my Boston from her S'more, pink icing fluttering onto my dressing-gown lap.

'Hold onto yer wig, will you! Tell him you travelled with a friend but she's doing her own thing. I'll straggle behind and grab a taxi to the hotel. Tom's given me some extra spending money, bless him. Don't worry, Annemarie Rafter will be fine. You won't even know she's there.'

'Why are you talking about yourself in the third person?'

'She feels like an adventurer. She can't remember the last time she had a bitta craic!'

'That's just odd,' I tell her.

'From Annemarie,' she says as she blows me a kiss.

This is very far from ideal, I think as I stuff the last bite into my mouth and Annemarie rests her hand across her rounded tummy.

'Cheers.' I pretend to catch her kiss in my hand. 'Fancy going halves on this one?' I add as I pull a sprinkled vanilla frosted from the rapidly emptying box.

21

Up in the Air

'IS THERE ANYTHING YOU FANCY?' I turn my head to Annemarie, who's also flicking through the on-board menu.

My adrenaline is off the charts.

My wedges can't stop a-tip-tappin'.

My mouth is like sandpaper.

I've been dreaming about Adam every night, several times a night. In all the dreams I'd been chasing him upstairs, but the steps turned into marshmallows and I sank into them. I've been pruned and pampered to perfection down to my every last overgrown hair.

Taking slow deep breaths, I try to contain myself as we bounce through the thick grey clouds. I've never known a week to drag by so slowly. But I'd made good use of Wednesday and Thursday evening by cleaning out the bookshelf in Sir Patrick Dun's and taking a collection of books in from a local college that were donating. I've had no luck with sourcing a pool table or my raffle. I saw one for sale in an old community centre off South Great George's Street, but I need to raise €950 to pay for it. So far, I have €69, so I need to think of a plan B.

I went to Máiréad's run-down flat twice, but she wasn't in either time. The whole place is now more or less a building site and I was really worried for her well-being. I'd popped in to see everyone at Sir Patrick Dun's last night, but especially to see Kevin again. I'd appealed to his better nature to give Máiréad the one spare room, and while he is the gentlest of giants, he has a board of directors to answer to, and without the €2,000 deposit she simply doesn't have a chance. I have no savings to contribute. Kevin promised to talk to the board for me, and I played Go Fish in the Pond with the residents while we drank hot chocolate made using warm milk with Cadbury's Flakes.

'Huh?' Annemarie says now, dipping the magazine and gazing out past the passenger by the oval window, into the vast blueness at thirty thousand feet.

'Do you want a toasted cheesy thingy?' I skim through the glossy pages.

She pulls her oversized cream hoody up over her neck, ties the strings under her chin.

'Why are planes so bloody cold?' she asks, like a little girl lost under the heavy cotton material.

'And how come so many women get travelling style so right and I always look like I've been trapped in that teeny loo for a week?' I reply.

I can't believe I'm going to see him in an hour or so. I'm going to touch him again. Feel his hands on me . . .

Be still my beating heart.

'Dunno. Are you on or off dairy?' I flick back to the menu with its slightly ambitious pictures.

'Off again. No thanks, I feel stuffed for some reason. Like really bloated.' She rubs her belly under the hoody. 'And my back is still in bits.' She arches.

'Jeez, you're great craic altogether.'

'I'm sorry. But you go ahead and get a toastie. It's your holiday! Don't mind me.'

'No, I'm going to have a wine. Settle the aul' nerves like!' I point pointlessly to the picture of the quarter bottle of wine.

'I just can't get comfortable.' Annemarie yanks at the seat belt with the extended piece. She's been a little on edge since the incident in the taxi this morning.

*

'Wow! Chrissie Hynde eat your heart out, babe.' She'd hung her head out the open taxi window like an excited puppy. I'd played up to her. Strutted through the electric gates of my apartment car park. Feeling good in my sharp white shirt, faux leather leggings and high wedge ankle boots, bumping my wheelie case along noisily behind me. You know that feeling when you really know you're looking your personal best. When any Beyoncé video plays in your head as you do final checks of yourself in the mirror. In fairness, I had pulled out all the stops. I'd been seated at the blow-out bar at a quarter to nine this morning, large Americano in hand, then straight into Silverside, avoiding level two, to get my make-up done by Zoë in Flawless. The fluttering fake eyelashes had better last the weekend as she promised.

'Semi-permanent, Lexie – trust me, they won't budge,' she'd told me matter-of-factly, with a mascara wand perched in between her multicoloured train-track braces. As she was carefully laying the individual lashes out on her workspace and twisting the cap off the mini tube of glue, I'd seen Máiréad trudge by the window, but I couldn't get off my seat. She didn't see me as she stopped to pull a tissue from her sleeve, but I'd smiled when I saw it was a fresh roll of toilet paper. I'd watched her dab her wet eyes. She'd leaned against the glass, nodding to people and muttering 'Good mornings' and 'Hellos' only to be sidestepped every time. As she passed a youth handing out flyers, she'd put out her hand to take one and he'd just ignored her too. Didn't even seem to see her. I'd had to fight the lump in my throat as Zoë told me to lie back and close my eyes as she set her magic lashes in place.

Annemarie had started singing 'I'm Too Sexy', head hanging all the way out now, huge smile on her make-up-free face.

'Hilarious aren't you . . . but too much?' I'd asked worriedly as I bent down and leaned in her window.

'No, you look amazing, smoking hot, Lexie.'

'Sure?'

'Totally – digging the lashes! They make your eyes look huge. Your hair looks incredible, you really are leaving no stone unturned! That outfit is on fire.' She does our John Travolta move, all jazz hands like.

Wella, wella, wella, huh.

'What this old thing?' In return I'd performed my best Southern belle impersonation as I twirled for her.

'Oh!' She'd sat back in the seat, bolt upright.

'You okay?' I'd turned back to face her through the window, and she'd groaned when she shifted.

'Yeah . . . I –' She'd held her stomach, stared at me.

'What? What is it?' I'd reefed the taxi door open.

'Can I put yer bag in the boot, Mrs? The meter's running here,' the taxi man had asked me, not making any effort to move, talk radio on far too loudly.

'No, it's fine – it can go at my feet.' I'd got in, never taking my eyes off her.

'I'm a bit crampy, Lexie.' Her eyes had suddenly filled with wet tears.

'What, like your-period-is-coming crampy?' I'd gasped, trying to be matter of fact.

22
The Bodyguard

I— I DUNNO.' SHE'D TAKEN A DEEP BREATH, held it, released it ever so slowly.

'Let's get you home?' I'd leaned in closer to her, my hand ready to unclick her seat belt.

'No, wait.' She'd shifted her position. 'It's gone now. Started in my back like a jab and moved round . . . just leave it, okay? Like you said, stress is so dangerous – change the subject. I mustn't dwell. I'm grand. It was just a cramp. I get them. A Braxton Hicks.'

'Are you sure?'

She'd nodded as I'd settled my wheelie at my feet, clicked my seat belt and observed her.

'I probably ate my Weetabix too fast.'

'If you're sure?'

'Totally sure. It's gone. The midwife said they're perfectly normal at this stage of pregnancy – believe me, I've checked.' She'd allowed a long breath to escape. 'I've been so looking forward to this weekend!'

So I'd told the driver Terminal One while I'd rattled on about my last night's prep, about the hour-long phone call between me and Adam, but she'd been quietish all the way along the

M50 to Dublin Airport. As we pulled into Terminal One, I got
a text.

Is it really today?!!

From Adam, with a smiling emoji and a GIF of Will Ferrell as
Elf jumping up and down.

'He's keen, I'll give him that.' Annemarie had laughed and I'd
put my arm around her and hugged her close to me. 'I'm fine.
Stop fussing.'

*

She looks absolutely fine now.

Her usual pale self, but she's never been one you would
describe as 'blooming' during this pregnancy. I'm still a little
concerned about her flying, old wives' tale or not. But she's a
grown up and this is her decision.

'You sure you're feeling all right?' I lean in.

'Yeah, I've just no appetite, although you know I detest plane
food. It smells weird and tastes like it was made seventy-two
hours ago which it was . . . because by the way, it's totally legal to
have plane food chilled for up to five days before serving. Fact.'

'I don't care about plane food. What are you talking about?
I'm talking about earlier . . . in the taxi?'

'That was just a Braxton Hicks, perfectly normal. I'm fine now
honestly. It was just that one cramp . . . and I have started eating
sugar again!' She clicks her fingers. 'That's probably it! I'm just
so tired, all the time. Sugar definitely doesn't agree with me – it
zaps all my energy.'

'Well just sit back and relax.' I nod to her tummy, hidden under
the hoody. 'Maybe lay off the sugar again, Augustus, okay?'

'Foah suhr, Mr Wonka,' she agrees with an attempt at an Austrian accent.

I reach up and press the call bell. A steward approaches, holding on to each seat top as she moves through the bumpy cabin.

'Yes?' She smiles at me – her cerise pink lips so bright they're almost blinding.

'Oh hi, can I get a white wine please?' I squint.

'You have to wait for the trolley I'm afraid.'

'Oh, do I? I didn't realise.'

'Yes.' Bigger smile. 'We'll be coming through the cabin shortly with light refreshments and duty-free.'

'Right. Thanks, but now that you're here, any chance I could jump the trolley queue?'

'Sorry, that's not possible I'm afraid.' She throws me a funny look, then leans up and flicks off my call bell.

'Hold on a minute . . .' Annemarie pipes up.

Her mouth opens to say something but thankfully she thinks twice and Miss Cerise Lip moves away.

'Let's look at the jewellery?' I suggest, pulling out the string compartment in front of me and removing the other in-flight magazine.

'In a second – I need the loo.' She releases herself and, with a bit of a struggle, squeezes out past me.

I breathe out a sigh of relief. I love Annemarie to bits, but really all I want to do is to focus on Adam right now. To bathe in this glorious excitement. That might be selfish, but it's the truth.

Adam.

Those eyes.

That dirty laugh.

That *body*.

Oh Lord, what am I letting myself in for? How will it be with us in the cold, sober daylight of another country? Will we feel the same? I know I will. Will he? I'd let Annemarie in on the fact that we'd done it twice. She was definitely impressed even if she hadn't pressed me for more details.

But if she had . . .

Seriously, wow.

If my brain was a movie, trains would be zooming in and out of tunnels.

Windows would be steamed up.

People in beds would be half covered in crisp white sheets, lighting up post-coital cigarettes.

Resting the glossy magazine open across my faux leathers, I lean my head back, close my eyes and slowly recall him.

23
Some Kind of Wonderful

HE'D RUN HIS HANDS DOWN THE CURVES of my slightly sweaty
body.

'God, you're gorgeous . . . your skin is so smooth. I could just
stare at you. For hours.'

I didn't say: 'Oh, I'm not.' Or, 'Oh, go way outta that, I need
to lose a stone!'

Because for whatever reason I believed him. Felt protected in
his arms but also felt that he felt protected in mine. A brand-
new feeling for me. I was still panting, my fringe stuck to my
forehead. I'd shifted position to lean on one elbow, just looking
at him. I hadn't felt self-conscious as loose skin rolled around
and my breasts played peek-a-boob among themselves.

'I give up! I can't find you!' the left boob was probably calling
out to the right.

'I'm under here!' Triumphant, the right boob, smug.

'I didn't know you could get under her back!'

'Me neither!'

The revelation of making love to him was shocking, just as I'd
thought it would be.

Tantalising.

The connection of our skin went deep – it went flesh to bone, seemed to move with our blood, our veins pumping passion. He'd lain naked, on his back, beside me.

'Jesus Christ,' he'd panted, pushing his damp hair off his face. His strong arms taut, his armpits filled with tufts of soft, dark hair.

'Almighty,' I'd added with my heart still beating like an erratic woodpecker.

He'd laughed.

'Yeah, you got that right – almighty is about the perfect word.' He'd rolled out of bed and gone to the mini fridge. I'd admired the masculine contours of his body as he leaned to open it and removed a bottle of water. He'd twisted the lid free and drank from the bottle.

'Eh, ever hear of a glass?' I'd only half joked; he wasn't perfect after all.

'Shit, sorry.' He'd gone into the bathroom, returned with a small glass and poured some water out for me. I gulped it down in one go as he slid back under the hot sheet beside me.

Skin meeting skin again.

'I think it's safe to say we've swapped enough germs already?'

We'd lain nose to nose. I was so aware of him, his strength, his nakedness, his whole being. I'd wanted to touch his perfect face, run my finger along the lightly tanned skin on his cheekbones, but I'd stopped myself. *Too intimate, Lexie*, I'd told myself. He probably just wants you to get the hell out of his bed, but I hadn't cared. Until he threw me out, I wasn't for moving. If the fire alarm had sounded, and panic ensued on the corridor, I'd have taken my chances.

'You're amazing.'

'Not so bad yerself.'

He'd leaned in and kissed me again. Not the actions of a man who'd had enough and just wanted some shut-eye now. Or had to text his girlfriend to say his battery died, or that he'd dropped his chips and someone had cycled over them, then a car splashed him and that he'd just got back to the room to charge his phone up now. It had been less than fifteen minutes since we'd finished making the most incredible love I've ever experienced. It was straightforward passionate sex, no circus tricks, no slurping, no mad stuff, neither of us trying to go all tantric like Sting and his missus. Adam's body just responded to mine. The soft and the hard of his kiss was unique. Dermot sure as hell never kissed me like that.

The hum of the air conditioning in the hotel room was drowned out by his soft moans as I marvelled at his perfect pressure on my swollen lips. It was slow, then fast, then he'd stop, pull away, look into my eyes, run his hand through my hair, stroke my cheek ever so lightly, then kiss me all over again. I'd pulled away eventually, breathless. Caught my breath. Wriggled away, down a little, between the soft white sheets and the thick goose-feathered quilt. He'd moved after me. I'd looked for his dark eyes under the duvet with the dim orange light from the lamp on the bedside locker still flooding in from overhead. I'd wriggled further down. Again, he'd followed me. It had been almost completely dark, and I didn't know if he could see me anymore. Then I'd shifted my body and lay myself, as gently as I could, on top of him.

Slung like a gun holster ready to make a move.

It was the most erotic contact I've ever experienced. Horizonal, we were almost the same length in limbs. I'd inhaled the manly skin of his neck. I'd been trembling as he'd wrapped his arms around me from underneath. Held me even tighter, our bodies becoming one. His breath in my ear, heavy and hot . . .

24
My Fair Lady

ANNEMARIE ELBOWED ME IN THE SIDE as she clambered over me to her seat. 'The trolley's coming!'

'Ow!' My eyes sprang open to the bright artificial lighting of the aircraft.

'You were miles away. I was standing there trying to get into the seat . . . I was like, *Lexie? Lexie? Lexie, the trolley's coming.*'

'Sorry, I was thinking about Adam.'

'Course you were.' She shakes her head.

'What?' I study her expression.

'Nothing.'

'I can't help it, I'm like a teenager, after the first Frenchie in the local community hall disco, with the glitter ball above my head. Every song I hear I can relate to. Adele has never meant as much to me.' I rub my side where her elbow just jabbed me.

'That's pretty sad.'

'That's not pretty sad. That's pretty wildly exciting actually, Annemarie!'

'Each to their own. I've got the weirdest metallic taste in my mouth – it's rotten.' Annemarie smacks her lips, rolls her tongue around and pulls up her rucksack from under the seat in front. She removes a large bottle of water she'd bought post security

139

checks. Normally, she carries one of those bottles, with fresh fruit chopped up and wedged down the middle. You know the ones? They scream: *Look At Me Right Now I Will Live Longer Than You!*

Eventually the trolley jingle jangles to a stop beside 22A, our row.

'Can I get a white wine please?' I ask giddily as I watch the steward jerk open a drawer, take out a small green plastic bottle and a plastic glass and hand down my nerve settler. I need it. The wine, however, is definitely not chilled – in fact it's positively warm.

'Eh, do you have any cold ones by any chance?' I ask, handing it back up to her.

A shake of the head. 'No, I'm afraid not.'

'Extra ice?' I plead.

'I'm afraid it's only two cubes per passenger – we don't have a lot on board.' She leans her weight onto the crowded trolley.

'Oh, look it's fine, I'll swap it for a red instead,' I say as she puts the white wine back into the warm drawer, hands me a red, and I pay her. She rummages for my change in her bumbag.

'Anything for you?' She smiles at Annemarie.

'Can I get a glass of milk?'

'I'm afraid –'

'I'm afraid you've none. Not your fault. Grand, I get it. No thanks, I don't want anything else. I only want a glass of cold milk.'

Annemarie rubs her tummy and tries to smile back at her, I'm glad to see. I flip down my tabletop and pour the red wine into my plastic glass, settle it into the little round groove on the doily.

'I've a value pack of Minstrels in my bag,' I tell her.

'No, I'll just have my water. It's this milk craving I have, it's weird, and I thought we just discussed the fact I'm off sugar again?'

'Oh, right, we did.' I sip the wine. I'd say it's bitter enough to kill a colony of ants.

'And here, while you were away in fifty-shades-of-fantasyland, I logged on, paid for ten minutes for the Wi-Fi.'

She holds her phone up to me.

'So?' I'm confused. 'I thought we were looking at the jewellery?'

'Nah, I never see the point in buying my own jewellery – it gives me no options for Tom to get me Christmas or birthday pressies. So shall we Google image where we're off to, my teenager-like friend?'

'Yes please!' I rub my hands together.

'I mean, I want to cyberstalk Adam obviously, but until you know the surname of the man whose remote house you're going to sleep in for two nights, my stalking hands are tied.' She grins sarcastically at me.

'One night. We're in the Moritz hotel tonight, remember?'

'Whatevs. It's such a stunning place the Cotswolds – here, look.' She kicks her bag back under the seat in front and scrolls through the imagery of the most beautiful villages I've ever seen.

Picturesque.

'I mean, it's just fitting that he's from such a bootylicious place.' I sigh.

'How ridey can he be, Lexie? I mean, you're fangirling at this stage!' She smiles, tilts the phone down so I can't see it now.

'Like the ridey-iest lad you've ever seen in your life. Shall I put it into context for you?'

'Again?' Her brows meet.

'If you wouldn't mind?'

'Go ahead.' She purses her lips.

'Right, you saw Baby's face when Johnny walked into the breakfast room. He's that! He provides *that* chemistry! He's Johnny –'

141

'More likely *Heeeeerrrrrre's Johnny!*' She does her best Jack Nicholson impression and laughs at her bad taste attempt at a joke.

'Shut up. I've been waiting so long for this. You will die when you see him. No, you won't see him this weekend, but I'll take pictures of us, or is that a bit . . . creepy?' I grimace.

'You better take pictures! And get his bloody surname! Now look at all those gently rolling hills. It says they rise from the meadows of the upper Thames to an escarpment, known as the Cotswold edge,' she informs me, lifting the phone screen to me once more. I can read the same stuff she's reading but her voice is soothing, so I leave her off as I sip my sulphuric, piss-of-the-devil wine.

'Lovely.' I nod.

'Oh look! The Cotswolds are a popular place for filming movies and television programmes.'

'See – fate!' I tell her.

'Some of Harry bloody Potter was shot there . . . I didn't know that! Tom would be all over that. He's such a Potter head. *Bridget Jones's Diary*! *Downton*? This is going to be a deadly trip. Kate Moss lived there! Lexie, did you hear me *Kate-nothing-tastes-as-good-as-skinny-feels-Moss!*' We like to slag Kate for that ridiculous interview whenever we get the chance. For example, just before we tuck into Marco's home-made, melt-in-your-mouth hot chocolate mess.

'The Moss. She lies,' we chant together, in perfect timing, spoons aloft, then bang them off each other and cackle. I'm thrilled to see Annemarie so unexpectedly bubbly all of a sudden. It's infectious but suddenly I feel sick. My stomach lurches.

'What am I doing?' I grip the phone from her in my fist as she looks at me, my upper lip starting to sweat.

'And at last . . .' Annemarie says.

'And at last what?' I wipe the sweat and swallow a belch.

'At last you're copping on that this is nuts.'

'What if he sees me now without his beer goggles and is like, *What the hell is that? That's her?*' I gasp. In fairness we'd had a decent amount to drink, not to mention the dreaded shots.

'Eh, what if you see him and are like, *Eh, what the hell, that's him?* I thought Tom looked completely different when we had our second date.'

'Date?! You mean when you dragged me to that aul' fellas bar because you saw on his Insta stories he was there. Hardly a second date!' I snort out a laugh. Then stop when I see her face. She's lost her smile and her mouth is pursed like a deflating balloon.

'I hate when you say that.' Steely.

'Sorry, I –' She does look extremely pissed off.

'No, you always say it. You know it winds me up.'

'I don't mean to –'

'Stop saying it then. Sometimes in life you have to take the bull by the horns and that's exactly what I did. Tom was never going to chase me. It's just not in his nature. There, I've said it, are you happy now?' Her expression is dark.

I feel terrible.

'Calm down. Jeez, that's not what I meant.'

'You're always skirting around that fact, so what?'

'No. I –'

'Trying to make out like I'm some desperado who turned up everywhere he –'

'Hey, hang on. That's not true!' I try to dig myself out of this hole.

'Maybe I don't want all this.' She looks around her.

'All what? A Boeing 737?' I try a joke.

'All this drama you seem to crave.'

'Drama? Because I –'

'Maybe I love what I have, Lexie; maybe it's more than enough for me. Stop trying to put yourself in my shoes; we wear completely different sizes.'

'No, we don't – we're both a size six.'

'Shut up. You're so not funny. You know what I mean. I don't want a row right now; I'm telling you I don't feel up for it.' She shifts uncomfortably in the seat. 'So let's just google famous Cotswold people, okay? Didn't Amanda Holden have her affair with Neil Morrissey there? In some hedgerow? Let's check that,' she suggests by way of ending the conversation, and I sit back relieved as she types into the search engine, and we look at Amanda's never-changing face. It's a peaceful moment but is over far too soon.

'What the?! Ahhh!' I yelp as the seat in front reclines back rapidly.

'Ahhh!' I bang the seat. 'I don't believe this!' I freak out as a head peers from around the seat.

'Oh, I'm so sorry.' She flips the seat up and now the bottle topples and spills the remaining wine all over me.

'Stop moving the bloody seat!' I yell. My crisp white shirt is now drenched in stinking red wine.

'Oh no way!' Annemarie drops the phone into her lap.

'S-S-Sorry. I – I . . .' an English accent stutters at me.

'What have I done to deserve this?' I unfasten my belt and step out into the aisle. Annemarie, for once, says nothing but pulls wet wipes from her bag and hands them to me.

The girl in front stands out from her seat now too.

'Oh I . . .' She has her hand over her mouth; she's proper mortified.

'Oh listen, it's not your fault. I just don't get why people put their seats back? There is no space.'

'It's so bloody rude.'

Ah, Annemarie's back.

'Rude?' she says, making a face at Annemarie now. 'It's not like I did it on purpose see.' She's dressed head to toe in denim. Denim shirt, three-quarter-length ripped jeans and red slip-on shoes. I can't help but notice that she's rather beautiful.

'No, I'm sorry, it is rude and reckless. What if she'd had a boiling cup of coffee, huh?' Annemarie questions. 'What if someone had a baby on their lap?'

'I – I . . .'

'I mean, you know the space is confined as it is? Like, what do you think that extra inch is going to give you? The seat in front of you isn't pushed back I bet?' Annemarie's knees buckle as she pulls herself up to see the seat in front of the one in front; mercifully the confines of her seat belt pull her back down.

'See? It's basic manners to know that. Like what extra comfort were you expecting?'

'Um.' She doesn't quite know how to respond. Not many people do when faced with the Annemarie Inquisition.

'Like this?' Annemarie brings her index finger and thumb together with about three inches of space in between, right up to her squinted left eye.

'It's fine, Annemarie – it was an accident.' I eyeball her as she plonks back down, and I stare at the state of my shirt. It cannot be salvaged. To make matters worse, I'd checked in my wheelie case as there wasn't enough overhead space as usual, and although I'd booked priority boarding, Annemarie hadn't, so I'd had to wait with her. And now I must wait at the baggage carousel to change and it's messed up my entire, meticulously matched, what-goes-with-what weekend capsule wardrobe.

'I'm sorry. I can pay for half the dry cleaning?' She reaches down under her seat for her bag.

'H-Half?' Annemarie splutters loudly.

'Is everything all right here?' It's Miss Cerise Lip come to see if we're about to kick off.

'Yeah.'

'Oh, dear me.' She spots my shirt. 'Let me get you a hot towel right away.' And she sways away again.

'Please. I'll happily pay half?' Ms Denim opens her leather purse now.

'It doesn't matter,' I say.

'Wha' are ya doin', woman? Ignore her! Sit back down. T'was an accident like,' a male voice pipes up with a strong country Irish accent.

'Forget it,' I say.

'Sorry again.' She sheepishly slides back into her seat.

'I'm sorry but you'll pay *half.*' Hormonal Annemarie just can't help herself, clicking her seat belt loose and squeezing her face in between the two seats in front.

'Yes,' I hear.

'Unbelievable!'

I pull her gently by the hood.

'Oh, relax will yiz. T'was an accident.' The man twists his head over the seat as Annemarie pulls her head back out and looks up at him.

'Who's talking to you?' Annemarie demands.

'Take a chill pill, darlin'.' He laughs. Definitely West of Ireland. His face moon-like and friendly, his tweed cap lopsided.

'Annemarie, please, leave it!' I hiss at her.

'All I'm saying is she ruined her shirt and yer one only offers to pay half the dry-cleaning bill? That's ludicrous!' She isn't listening to me.

'Come on now, in fairness yiz shouldn't be drinking yer heads off at three o'clock in de afternoon like. Although . . . I would if

I could, but I can't!' he snorts, laughing, his eyes all but disappearing into his beefy face.

'Frank, stop,' the wrecker of my outfit says.

'I'm not drinking actually; I'm expecting, and for your information, my best friend here, well it happens she's a nervous flyer, so it's to keep her calm – medicinal if you will.' Annemarie sniffs.

'Did ya hear the one about the priest and the red wine?' He swivels round some more.

'No,' I say before Annemarie can.

'D'ya wanna hear it?'

'No.' Annemarie beats me to it this time.

'Frank, please. Everyone is listening. It might not be appropriate. You might offend someone – you know what you're like?' his wife or whoever tells him in worried voice.

'Yeah, Frank.' Annemarie sticks her tongue out at him. 'This modern world isn't your friend!'

'Seriously, stop it now. You're just being weird.' I pinch her arm lightly.

'Ouch!' She rubs it like I'd thumped her as hard as Katie Taylor herself.

I'm afraid if she insults him anymore, we'll be arrested at the airport and I won't get to see Adam.

You can't say boo on a plane nowadays. But that's not going to stop our new friend Frank.

'An Irish priest is driving along a country road when a policeman pulls him over,' he begins. 'He immediately smells alcohol on the priest's breath and notices an empty wine bottle in the car. He says, *Have you been drinking?* The priest says, *Just water*, and the cop replies, *Then why do I smell wine?* The priest looks at the bottle and says: *Good Lord! He's done it again!*'

Frank bursts into shaking laughter, slapping his thigh hard, and the whole row in front seems to shake, then turns back around.

'The old ones are the best,' I say over the seat, then hiss at Annemarie: 'Leave it now please.'

She grits her teeth. 'Don't give up the day job,' she adds far from quietly.

'Jesus, what is it with you and starting fights?' I whisper into her ear.

'Me? Huh? I was only backing you up. Where's the credit for having your back, huh?' Annemarie slaps her chest, looks appalled at my accusation and shifts again, arching her back in the seat.

'Leave it please.'

'A bit of thanks wouldn't go astray.'

Why will she not leave it?

I ignore her. I just want to stay out of trouble for the rest of the flight.

'Ladies and gentlemen . . .'

Speaking of.

'. . . we will be beginning our descent into Birmingham Airport in approximately fifteen minutes. Please ensure your tray tops are up, that your seat belts are securely fastened and that your seats are in the upright position. Cabin crew prepare for landing please.'

I clip up the table.

'Do you want a mint?' Annemarie offers. 'Good for the ears to suck on something.'

I take one, pop it on my tongue.

'Just . . . just be chilled, okay? I didn't mean to offend you earlier. You're supposed to be here for a rest, to chill out, remember? Pamper yourself.' I swallow the minty goodness. 'I'll change in the toilet when I get my wheelie and fix my face. I'm sweating after all that.' I suck again, lower my hand and point into the fabric of the seat in front.

'As you wish. No problemo.' She drinks from her water bottle as the plane descends through the grey clouds and we bump around before they part. I lean across Annemarie to get a closer look.

'Are you ready?'

Annemarie, who hates landing, takes my hand in hers. Together we squeeze our entwined fingers and suck hard, as the Boeing sets down smoothly on the runway. Some people applaud at the back as the aircraft comes to a slow stop, like they never really expected to make it.

'I'm thirty-nine and a half, Annemarie, I'm ready for anything,' I answer eventually. But what's really going through my head is, *Please let the electricity of Adam be real; please don't let this be some big Lexie Byrne illusion.*

25

From Here to Eternity

W E'VE NOW BEEN STANDING HERE for twenty-seven long
minutes.

'That's the same case that's been around three times now.'
Annemarie states the bleeding obvious, leaning on her wheelie's
extended handle, sucking hard on a mint. I check my phone.

'I know!' My wheelie is nowhere to be seen. My entire weekend-
on-wheels has vanished. My clothes, make-up, the subtly sexy
undies I bought online.

'Adam's outside waiting for me!'

'You go. I'll wait for your case and meet you at the Moritz
hotel, simple.' Her cheeks are indented from the intense sucking.

'You booked the Moritz?' I'm incredulous.

'Yeah, where did you think I was staying? That's where you
said the party was tonight, right? I got a really great deal on a
single.'

'Y-You're not coming to the p-party, Annemarie!' I stutter.

'Eh, I know that! I have zero desire to go to any bloody party.
I just thought it was the best place to be if you need a get-out
later, ya know?' She holds her stomach, rubs around it in swift
movements.

'You okay?'

'Yeah. Thought that cramp I had in the taxi earlier was coming back but I . . .' She shuffles around her case, arches her back. 'It's gone again.' She laughs, crunches on her mint.

'How can I go out to him looking like this?' I say near tears.

'It's not that bad. I mean he could think it's tie-dye. Oh shit, look who's coming.'

I turn and see the couple from the seats in front walking down past the conveyor belts the opposite way to one of the exits.

Mercifully, they don't see us and pass by – he's on his phone and so is she. She so small and delicate, he so large and robust.

'I have to go.' I'm so on edge as Annemarie pulls her hoody off up over her head.

'Here!' She stands in a khaki vest top, her freckles the only tinge of colour on her arms. I take in the bulge of her pregnant stomach.

'Seriously, a hoody and faux leather leggings! Who am I – Cher?'

'Chrissie Hynde . . . on her day off?' she offers.

'I don't need to hear another shit joke right now.'

'Up to you?' She dangles it in front of me, more like the proverbial carrot than I'm comfortable with.

It's getting so late. I'm terrified Adam will leave. I have no choice. Nothing else of Annemarie's stuff would go near me. I unbutton the wine-splattered shirt and nip into the ladies across the way to change.

'Lexie!' Annemarie calls minutes later as I slip into the hoody.

'I'm in the middle loo,' I call back, crumpling the shirt into a ball.

'Got it!' she sing-songs.

'No!' I fling open the door and there she stands with our two cases, at the end of a queue.

'Oh, thank you God!'

'And don't call me God.' She laughs. A woman rounds past me and takes the toilet I've just vacated.

'Right, I seriously have to go as I am. I've left him standing there for long enough. Come on.' We move back out to the arrivals hall.

'Please, go on ahead. This is your weekend; I'm just here for safekeeping. I'll see you later at the hotel. Are you going to his house first or straight to the Moritz?'

'To his house I think.'

'Text me his address when you get to his house.'

'How am I going to know that?'

'I dunno – ask him?'

'I'm not doing that.'

'Look at his post!' She clicks her fingers again, delighted with this idea. She does that thing she does with her hair – she swoops over and when she returns to my eyeline, her curly red hair is constrained on top of her head in a knot.

'Here goes. My nerves are fried right now. Wish me the best of luck!'

'I wish you the best of fuck.' She holds her back and breaks her heart laughing.

We hug.

'Are you sure you're okay? I feel bad. Just come with me?' I plead.

'Go! I'm going to call Tom, tell him I've landed. I'm just fine. I'm actually looking forward to the solitude. Thinking time. I've nowhere to be; it's all good. I'm happy.'

'Okay, I'll see you later at the hotel.' I kiss her cheek and take my leave as she continues to chuckle at her own lame joke. When I get near the exit, I sneak a look back over my shoulder; she makes for a slightly sorry sight standing there in her maternity vest, but she's chatting animatedly to Tom, mobile phone to her ear. I came here to see Adam – she knows that. I believe she's happy.

Turning back, I'm under the sign for the arrivals gate and I head for it. My legs suddenly feel like jelly on a plate.

'Please be the man I think you are . . . oh please, please, please let this not all be some mad decision on my part, some fantasy illusion I've conjured up with the help of Senor Pinot and Senorita Grigio,' I rant in my head – then stop. Take another baby step. Smooth my hair back. Stop again. Lick my index finger and run it under my grey-kohl-lined eyes as another straggler of a passenger walks past me and alerts the sensors which open the electronic sliding glass doors.

And there he is.

Boom!

Adam.

Dressed in his leather jacket and the same faded jeans, he's leaning his long body on the railing that separates arrivals from the pick-up point. He's eating an apple, chomping on it, his jawline delicious.

He sees me almost the same time I see him.

Eyes meet.

I swallow.

We both smile.

He turns and throws the apple core, aiming it skilfully into one of the round openings in a nearby bin.

Sweet baby Jesus are the only words that jump into my dizzy head. I slide my sweating palms down my new leggings, and they stick.

My feelings are the exact same. It's like déjà vu, a movie flash-back, as though I'd just seen him outside the Brazen Head last weekend. Can it only be last week? If beauty is in the eye of the beholder, brand me Ms Lexie Byrne-Beholder with a hot iron.

With his two hands pressed down on the railing, he pushes himself off and stands upright as I walk on through. If he thinks I look crazy in a cream hoody and faux leather leggings, it isn't registering on his face – but what is registering, and breaking, is the cheekiest grin I've ever seen.

The distance between us closes. Just the way his body moves, how his arms swing when he walks is unbelievably mesmerising (by which I mean a total turn-on) for me.

We come face to face.

26
Serendipity

HIS EYES MEET MINE.
'Hi.'

'Hi.'

'How are you?' He's still smiling like he's ridiculously happy about something.

'I'm good, yeah.' I purse my lips, trying to rein in my own smile. It's so wide I feel like the Joker.

He pushes his hands deep into the pockets of his leather jacket.

I fix the shoulder strap on my bag.

'This is a bit mad,' I admit.

'A bit . . . but good mad.'

Oh, that voice.

'Oh, very good mad.' I manage a little flirt, pull at the strings on the hoody.

'Is it a bit too Hollywood to confess that I really wanted to pick you up and swing you around?' he asks.

'Not at all. I'd have run and jumped only I thought, ya know, I'm no Jennifer Grey – I might poleaxe you.'

'I should have opened my arms, given you a signal really. I'd take my chances.' He laughs, his chiselled jaw my focus of attention. I don't think I've ever quite seen anyone who looks like Adam. The symmetry of his face is hypnotising. The way his eyes dip, edged by lush dark eyelashes, those deep dark brown eyes – I could lose hours just staring into them. He's the stuff of my dreams, but however handsome he is, he's humble. That's the word I've been looking for.

'Watch it!' is what I say as, playful, I step lightly on his toe.

The equivalent to the pigtail pulling playground palaver. People scuttle past us, and I'm acutely aware of the second glances and double takes he receives from both men and women. Announcers intone names for final calls and unattended baggage warnings, but still we stand transfixed by one another.

'Thanks for coming.' He takes his hands back out of his pockets.

'My pleasure.'

'I didn't think you actually would . . . like I know you said and all, but I was standing here waiting and thinking, *Adam, she ain't coming, mate.*'

'Sure, you knew I was on the flight, ya mad thing. Sorry I took so long, bags took ages.' I flick my blow-dry. 'I – I . . .'

He just leans in and his lips lock with mine. Both his hands rise up the back of my neck and hold my head tightly. It's hard and passionate, my eyes flicker from open to closed and then, from the corner of my eye, behind his back, I see a red head, her mouth open, wide. It takes me a minute because she's in a long black cardigan but it's most definitely my Annemarie and, God forgive her, she's winking madly at me.

I pull away a little, but still we kiss numerous times – pecks, maybe four of them, soft and sensual. He puts both his hands on my cheeks.

'Sorry, I couldn't help myself.'

'I'm glad.' I tug at the strings on the hoody this time to level them, trying to pretend she isn't there. I kinda want to tell him that it's not my hoody, that this isn't my signature style.

'Sorry. Here, let me take your –' He looks down now. 'That's all the luggage you have?'

'It is.' I tilt my head at him, lick my lips.

'Nice one.' He nods as Annemarie disappears through the doors.

'I'm all about a woman who doesn't pack seven cases for two nights away.' He moves his hands down his cheeks onto his neck where his silver feather chain swings.

'Ah, I'm very low maintenance, Adam. I was just thinking . . . eh . . . are we still going to that party you mentioned? The engagement party?'

'Oh yeah, God, we have to! Be more than my life's worth if I bailed on that,' he drawls, sounding less than excited about it. 'If you're still okay with that? Not having second thoughts?'

'No! Absolutely not. Sorry I'm a bit . . . my friend actually travelled over with me, but she's on a pamper weekend of solitude so she's just gone past us.'

'Oh!' He looks relieved. 'I would have liked to say hello. Not Jackie? She's in Dubai, right?' He can't help but raise an eyebrow.

'No, it's Annemarie. She's expecting a baby in a couple of months. She just wanted to. . . . Oh, never mind, oh man, my heart is beating so fast!' I make a pin hole with my mouth, exhale heavily.

'I know . . . mine too. I got here an hour and a half early just in case I hit any traffic. And then necked three espressos.' He holds his hand out straight – it shakes slightly.

'Shall we?'

'Shall we what?'

'Shall we get outta here?'

'Oh yeah, sure, let's go.'

He reaches for my hand and every hair on my body stands to

157

attention. I find it intoxicating the amount of people who look at us and I don't know why. Because he's with *me* I suppose.

'Let me just pop to the loo and change out of my travelling clothes.' I let go of his hand, reach down for the handle of my wheelie. Just as well I threw in jeans and a grey top for flying home in.

'Don't worry, you're fine as you are. You can change for the party at mine. My hope is that we get in and out of there as fast as humanly possible. Come on. Shall we, Lexie?' He says my name again, takes my case in one hand and my hand in his other and we drift away, this time walking through arrivals and out the main door. Outside, the late afternoon March sun is shining.

'I'm just over here.' He points straight ahead, pulling his car keys from his jacket pocket.

We cross at the pedestrian crossing and I spot Annemarie strolling amongst the long queue at the taxi rank, chatting to people. She turns her head. Now guilt engulfs me. What was I thinking agreeing to this? This is stupid – we have to give her a lift.

'Adam, I see my frie–' I stop as I see Annemarie get into a taxi with an old couple at the top of the queue.

'I thought we'd go back to mine now?' he speaks at the exact same time as me.

'Sorry go on –'

'Okay. I think we both need an early drink I was just going to say. Then head to the party for sevenish?'

A drink. Praise be. I'm the thirstiest girl in the world.

I know what she's done – she's shared a taxi with someone going her way. She used to always do that, pre-Tom – find someone going her direction on long taxi-rank queues. Split the fare, shorter queue time plus she felt safer. Knowing she'll be in her hotel room soon, I relax.

'Prinks!' I smile.

'Prinks?'

'Pre-drinks – it's what the kids call it.'

'Right. I haven't heard that one yet. All ahead of me I guess.'

We walk to the short-term car park and he points his bunch of keys at a black car. It beeps; the lights flash. He opens the passenger side for me, and I sit in, admiring the cleanliness of the car and the fresh lemon smell. He slides in beside me. There's something about how he turns the key in the ignition, glances in the rear-view mirror, that seems so normal. Like we're supposed to be sitting here in his car, not taking into account we didn't know the other existed a few weeks ago. I have one of those moments so flooring that my heart actually skips a beat.

27
Roman Holiday

I TURN TO FACE HIM AS HE STARTS THE ENGINE. 'So stranger,' I flirt, 'I don't even know your last name.'

'I know. I couldn't stalk you on social media either. Isn't it great?' He laughs, turns to face me long enough to wink at me.

'I suppose.' I think about it. 'But I'm not on social media.'

'You're not?' He slides his parking ticket into the machine and the barrier rises, then indicates, keeping his eyes on the road as he waits to slip into a break in the busy airport traffic.

'Nope. I'm an old-fashioned gal.' I do a yee-hah cowgirl impression and knee slap myself as he laughs.

'That's so rare nowadays.' He twists his shoulder now to get a better view of the passing traffic. The Brummies are all in a hurry it seems.

'Well no, I did have it for years but there's just no spontaneity with social media . . . it's all premeditated. No one can surprise you anymore.'

'And you like surprises?'

'Who doesn't? Well, good surprises.' I take a breath; it needs to be said. 'In the absence of online stalking, I know almost nothing about you. And, I'll be honest, Annemarie – that's my friend who flew over here too – she's really here because she freaked out a bit about me coming here on my own, because . . .' I let the sentence hang.

'Right. She sounds like a good friend. So she need not worry. Had you started investigating me last week here's what you would have found out. Are you ready?'

Jesus, am I?

'Drum roll.' He takes his eyes off the traffic and turns back to me, then beats his long fingers against the steering wheel, in an excellent drum roll impression.

'I'm divorced.'

'Oh.' Light tone.

Shit.

He hadn't mentioned that up at the bar, just that he'd never met the right woman, right?

'Yeah, a while ago now. We were childhood sweethearts, very innocent. Probably never should have got married to be honest, but she got pregnant, and well . . .' He's back looking out the window.

Oh, he's got kids.

'Thank you kindly!' he says and raises his hand as he pulls out into the traffic.

'So you'd have been able to see all that, and see my daughter, who's eleven . . . and . . . I wanted to tell you in the hotel room, but I guess I was desperate not to put you off before you got to know me.'

'Eleven? Oh lovely,' I can't help but interrupt. A flashback to the photograph I saw springs to mind. 'What's her name?'

'Freya. Well, the iPad addiction's kicked in, she doesn't want to hold my hand outside our four walls, definitely can't be seen to kiss me in public so any of that mushy daddy-daughter stuff now takes place in the hallway before she leaves to walk to school.'

'Okay,' I say. In the hallway? Before she leaves for school? What now? My head races. I cross my legs.

'And you'd see that I'm actually a nurse and not a painter and dec–'

'Shut up!' I'm immediately suspicious and turn my head to look at him.

'I will not.' He laughs as we immediately hit a set of red lights. He pulls up the handbrake.

'Come on, are you really *a nurse*?'

'You don't believe me?'

'It's all a bit *Dirty John*.' I'm instantly reminded of Annemarie's words.

'I don't lie.' His eyes meet mine. He rubs at the light stubble on his chin.

'You told me you were a painter and decorator? Was that not a lie?'

'No, not really, you asked me what I did. I'd been finishing a painting job on the outhouse just before I met you, though I'm not very good . . .'

He leans across me and pulls up a laminated badge on a red string from the dashboard, hands it to me.

'Why didn't you tell any of this?' I say as I study his smiling face in green scrubs and NURSE ADAM COOPER printed in bold with a long serial number underneath.

'You left in a bit of a hurry and . . .'

'But we've been on the phone?'

'It doesn't matter, does it?' His dark eyes suddenly implore me.

I shrug. 'No, I guess not.'

'I mean I'd understand if I told you I was out on parole from Strangeways and you were a bit freaked, but I have my reasons for not shouting about my profession when I'm socialising, trust me. As soon as I say I'm a nurse, it dominates conversations like you wouldn't believe. People still find it somewhat amusing that

I'm a nurse. I've heard all the lame jokes. It bugs the shit out of me if I'm perfectly honest.' He drops the laminate in the side pocket, releases the handbrake and drives on.

I think for a moment about my own reaction and I get why he didn't tell me. And, for crying out loud, Annemarie's going to have a field day with this information.

'I didn't want anything to stop you from staying with me . . . rightly or wrongly. I just wanted to be in the moment.' He glances at me.

'I get it. I wish I could tell you I'm really a Victoria Secret's model but unfortunately I still work in a shopping centre.'

'You like what you do?'

'You know, weirdly, no one's ever asked me that, but I do like my job. I mean as much as anyone can. If I won the lottery tomorrow, I'd be out of there faster than you can say *what job satisfaction*? At least you have that in abundance.'

He glances at me again, nods, turns his head back to the road, smiling.

'So you're a nurse. Tell me more.'

'I'm an A&E nurse at our local hospital with shared custody of Freya. We're practically next-door neighbours; well, they're across-the-road neighbours. Freya lives with me week on and week off but stays at her mother's every weekend, mainly because her school friends come for sleepovers now and well . . . as is the world we currently live in, some parents feel more comfortable with them staying at her mother's.' He rolls his eyes.

'Oh, I see. Is that tough? On her I mean? The moving all the time?'

'Nah, it's all good. She's pretty great – actually she's the only reason I'm on social media, so I can follow her and watch what's going on. She was allowed a TikTok account when she turned ten last year, just following kids in her class and the village. It's a world to them now, isn't it? But like you, if I had my way, I'd be well hidden.'

This is a lot to process.

He lives across the road from his ex-wife, and they share custody of their young daughter. The sweat starts to pump out of me, and I thank God silently for Annemarie's thick cream hoody cos the white shirt would have two massive wet patches right now. I can't move my legs for fear of them squeaking.

'You know?' he prompts me back to the moment.

I say: 'Absolutely. What drove me insane was the people who were friends with me, the ones who never post a single thing, these old school friends, knowing all my stuff, wanting to see my private life, yet not willing to share their own. Nosy I call them. The Green Button Beaky Brigade Annemarie calls them. Always lurking online, sticking their noses in, and soaking up everyone else's dramas.'

'Couldn't agree more.' He shifts up into fifth gear as we hit a long open road.

Oh, what did you expect, Lexie? No one who's thirty-nine and a half comes without at least a bag of something on their back. I digest the reality of his new-to-me situation and calm myself down as we spin towards the English countryside in the most companionable silence. There is literally nowhere in the world I'd rather be right now. How many moments in your life can you truly say that? If I could bottle and sell how I feel right now, I'd be up there with Alice Walton, the world's richest woman, making the big bucks.

'Anyway, Lexie, they're all my skeletons. Now, your turn.'

He keeps his eyes on the road, drives at a good pace. Not too fast, not too slow. I like how safe I feel with him in his car.

'Right.' I cross my faux leather legs, slight squelch.

He puts his hand on my knee.

164

A shooting shiver runs down my spine.

'Well . . . I've no *skeletons* to speak of. I live alone, I rent an apartment, I work full-time like I told you, I'm an only child –'

'Oh, do you like being one?' He looks over at me.

'Being an only child?'

'Yeah!' He nods repeatedly.

'Not really. I'd have loved a sibling to be honest.'

'Don't be crazy – siblings are a complete nightmare. I keep telling Freya that.'

He indicates, takes a left turn. I know it's a raging cliché, but even the way he drives is sexy – how he changes gears, the way his body leans back into the seat when he works those pedals; even the way his fingers lightly hold the wheel turns me on.

'No serious relationships since that one you mentioned?' he asks.

'Uh-uh.' I shake my head.

I make a snap decision not to tell him any more about Dermot, and the trauma of his infidelity. I just don't want to. I don't want him to judge me. I don't want to be perceived as a heartbroken victim or make him to wonder why Dermot would choose to cheat on me.

'Lucky escape.'

'Any kids?'

'No.'

'Would you want kids?'

'Yes . . . well, em, no. I dunno.' What did I just say? That was a most unexpected answer. But straight away I recognise why I said it because I've never met anyone like him before in my life. He changes everything. He keeps his eyes on the road as I look at him.

'Good.' He nods.

'Which answer?' I ask, more than surprised at myself.

'Both.'

'You do or don't want more kids?'

'I dunno either.'

We both laugh.

'I thought I was over the idea of having kids, and I am – sort of. Unless something . . .'

'I'm the same, unless it was . . .'

'Yeah . . . unless –'

'Exactly,' I help him out.

'It's amazing, you know, having kids. Freya is the best thing to ever happen to me, but I . . .' I hear hurt in his voice for the first time. 'Ahh I'm probably too old now to go back there anyway!'

'You're only forty-two! Men don't have to worry about age in the same way! Lucky bastards.'

'Can I ask your age?' He's laughing.

'Thirty-nine . . . and a half.'

'And a half – that's wicked!'

'I didn't foresee us discussing kids on this car journey for some reason.'

'I've been through it all already so it's, well, sorry . . .'

'I was expecting the *So-What-Is-It-Lexie-Byrne-Is-Looking-For* question much later tonight.' I try to swerve the subject.

'Again sorry, I'm nervous . . . Lexie *Byrne*.' He swallows loudly.

'It's fine,' I say.

He nods, breathes. 'It's best to get it all out now before we get to my house?' His eyes flick over at me, hypnotise me again, and then back to the road. 'I mean Great Tew, our village, is pretty small, so we all know one another – it's a bit like one big family. The last census in 2011 recorded our population at one hundred and fifty-six souls. The village raised Freya as much as we did so far.' He shifts gear. 'And you'll see pictures on my walls and my daughter's stuff scattered about the house so . . .'

'Can we save the *so-what-are-you-looking-for-long-term* questions until I've had another glass of wine?'

'A . . . nother?'

'A . . . fraid so.' I shrug in my best *what-can-you-do?* way and admit, 'I don't normally drink during the day obviously, but this is a very special occasion.'

'Absolutely. It's like the first day of a summer holiday or something isn't it? Like being at the airport at midday and having a drink? I've a bottle chilling in the fridge. Pinot Grigio, I remembered, right?'

'Exactly right – straight to the top of the class, Adam.'

He laughs again. He really seems to think I'm funny. If I could jump him in that driver's seat I would.

'No more serious chat – that's it now. I just wanted to be honest with you from the get-go. I'd no time to play the mysterious man card or to break it to you gently.' He raises his eyebrows at me, and I can tell he's relieved to have it all out in the open. 'I've the whole weekend off, which is very rare, so I'm planning to enjoy every second of your fantastic company, Lexie. I've been counting the days.'

His phone rings, he presses down on a button set into the steering wheel and a voice rings out around the car.

'Hey, didn't you say you'd be at the airport this afternoon?' a female voice echoes from above my head.

'Yeah, I was – I've left though,' he says.

'Ah darn, but never mind. Some agricultural machine broke down on the farm and we had to talk the staff through the problem on the phone, so we're only leaving the airport now. I've an ice sculpture being delivered to the hotel in fifteen minutes. I just want tonight to be perfect – you know me. We'll grab a cab for the drive. See you later, do not be late and please wear your good suit!'

'I'm not wearing a suit.'

'Please, Ads, for me . . . for my album? Pleeaaaaassseeeee. I've booked a cool photographer,' she begs.

He takes one hand off the wheel and rubs his chin. 'All right, if I really have to. I have to go. See you later.' He knocks her off.

'Who's that?' I ask.

'My sister. See how lucky you are?'

'Oh, she sounds stressed?'

'She's always stressed. She's a perfectionist, control-freak type. She went to Doolin on a yoga retreat three years ago to try and find herself, but she found a farmer instead and never came home. I'm not sure she's cut out to be a farmer's wife though – she hates mice and was a vegan before she met Frank!'

'No way?' I chuckle. 'Oh right! That's who you went to see in Clare?'

'Yeah, that's Deb.'

'Oh! It's your *sister's* engagement party tonight?' The penny drops. Spins.

'Yeah, sorry, I thought I said?'

'No. Won't she mind me gatecrashing?'

'No. Not at all. I told her all about you when I was in Clare.'

'Are you sure?' I'm a little taken aback.

'Totally. My plan is to say hi, have a bite and get out of there as fast as we can. Don't worry, Deb won't even notice – it's a big do,' he reassures me.

'Okay.' I take in the scenery as we whizz by green fields, slow-paced grazing Gloucestershire cows, wandering sheep and riots of drystone walls, and in what seems like no time at all, we start to pass quaint little shops. It's becoming all twisty roads and picture-postcard English countryside.

'You don't like suits?'

'I don't like being told what to wear, especially by my sister.'

'And your parents – what about them?'

'Sure, they're around. Yours?' he asks me.

'Um, yeah, they live in Spain. Any other siblings?'

'One is more than enough.'

Us sitting side by side is so easy. So relaxed. We drive on, listening to the low hum of the radio, and before long he slows down and turns the car into a narrow, overgrown laneway with brambly hedges high on either side.

'Is this a road?' I ask.

'Yeah, we're all well used to it. Let's hope we don't meet any tourists coming the other way.' He grins at me, then holds the wheel steady as I look out at the stone walls inches from the sides of the car. The road gets bumpier beneath us. Then my eyes widen as we emerge and the most delightful row of cottages appear, trailing leafy plants growing in zigzags among them.

'Oh wow,' I say, my eyes wide, as we drive past them via a tree-lined drive.

'It's a pretty place all right. Not too far to go now. This is Chipping North. You interested in history?'

'Absolutely.'

'Well, they call our Great Tew the loveliest corner of the Cotswolds.'

'*Soooooo* pretty,' I say in awe. 'Don't get me wrong, I adore Dublin, but this is like an escape from modern life.'

'Wait till you see Great Tew. Tell me to shut up any time you want me to close my boring tour mouth?'

'No! I'm loving your tour-guide vibe.'

'You are? Okay, well.' He sits up straighter and rolls the window down halfway. A breeze floats in and I welcome it. 'So, Miss . . . Byrne, Great Tew was constructed in the nineteenth century by a landscape gardener, John Loudon, as part of an extensive park overlooking the Worton Valley – just wait until you see his trees still standing to this day. People often call it a picture-book village because it's all charming thatched cottages, gabled roofs, mullioned windows and –'

'*What* windows?'

'Mullioned. You know, more than just glass – heavy stone beams that block your view if you try to look out.'

'Fairy-tale-like things?'

'Pretty much. It's still very old England here, miss. *Shrek* or *Toy Story*?' he suddenly asks.

'*Shrek*.' I don't miss a beat.

'Me too!'

'There is a whole lot of Princess Fiona in me.'

'And Shrek in me. Actually, speaking of fairy tales, near my village are the famous Rollright Stones – you've heard of them, right?'

'I'm afraid geography is possibly one of my weakest links. Goodbye.' I do my best Anne Robinson.

'Well never mind – what you lack in one area, you make up for two-fold in another is my motto. They say they're earlier than Stonehenge. The story goes that a lord of the province aspired to become King of England, but that wasn't okay by the local witch, so she turned him and his knights into lumps of stone.'

'Well . . . lumps of stone may better serve the people.'

He laughs again and points out the landmarks of his home-town – his old school, the local church, the football pitch he'd spent so many hours practising free kicks on, until: 'Here we are. Home sweet home.'

The sound of wheels crunching over gravel makes me turn and look out the window as he manoeuvres the car through an open gate, then kills the engine.

'Oh.' I swallow.

28
Great Expectations

I'T'S DEFINITELY NOT ONE OF THOSE PERFECT thatched-roof cottages that we cooed over on Annemarie's phone. But it certainly has a unique charm. It seems to stand slightly unevenly, almost crooked. Detached, with a wild rose-covered façade, slightly run-down, the large garden pleasingly overgrown. Wheelbarrows, buckets, a scorched old sun lounger, a pink scooter, bikes and tins of paint sit scattered among the thorny brambles. The square building itself is pale stone brick, and the many windows are small with black shutters on each side, but I notice a long crack in one as he opens the car door for me and I step out.

'I need to do something with the garden, you're right . . . and get around to fixing that window.' He reads my mind. 'And paint the gate!' He laughs.

'No. It's lovely – really authentic and homely, ya know?'

'I like its imperfections. It was unloved for many years because, as you can see, it's slightly lopsided in the earth, but it's a listed building. It's completely original.'

The touch of his hand as he takes mine, and the thought of what's to come, has me all a-fluster again.

'It's gorgeous; I'm mad about it.' I really am. I feel the authenticity of it that he must have fallen for.

'You're a bad liar.'

'I'm not lying. It looks like a real home!' I step closer. 'I can just visualise cosy Sunday afternoon roasts, watching *It's A Wonderful Life* by the crackling fire, twinkling Christmas lights outside.'

We stand side by side looking at his home and he squeezes my hand. Then he lets go as he turns to the boot to get my case, stops again, leans his weight on the back of the car.

'We barely know each other, I know that, but . . .' He drags both his hands down his stubble. 'But I – I just think . . . I mean I just have to say . . . is this too good to be true? How did this happen? How has no one snapped you up before now?'

My heart makes its way up into my mouth and I literally can't speak. It's jam-packed with emotion in there.

'It's mad, all right. I don't want anything to spoil it.' My smile says it all as he pops the boot, gets my case and takes my hand again. I'm overcome with this feeling of being protected. Together we crunch down the driveway, the smell of wild lavender engulfing my nostrils.

'The wildflowers are fabulous. I've a potted peace lily plant I christened Jimmy – that's about it.' I find my voice as we reach the hall door.

'Soooo many keys.' He rummages. 'We all have keys to each other's houses around here; it's very communal!' he mumbles, searching through the bunch. It's a canary yellow with *Rosehill Cottage* painted in peeling-off red lettering. I take a moment to look around at my surroundings more closely. A row of four other thatched cottages sits directly across the narrow road. I wonder which one is his ex-wife's. Low thick green shrubs surround them, bicycles lean, unlocked, against them. There's a yellow water pump, a red post box, and a winding road that leaves my eyeline where rustic fences swing beneath huge evergreens that bow over the sides of the white roads. He selects the right key and pushes the door open.

'After you,' he says, picking up my case, and I step inside Adam Cooper's home.

29
The Holiday

OH, BUT INSIDE TAKES MY BREATH AWAY.

'This is beautiful!' I say out loud this time, doing a 360-degree turn and barely avoiding standing in a dog bowl on the ground. This house is like an oyster – odd and uneven, even sharp, from the outside, but when you dive in, its honesty and originality embraces you. I feel like I should be walking around tapping walls, opening presses and oohing and ahhing like on some grand design TV show. Inside is all exposed beams and original brick, sanded floorboards and little else. Magnificently minimal.

'I've left Spangles in the utility room in case you aren't a dog lover. Probably should have mentioned her before. You're not allergic, are you?'

I shake my head, unable to stop my gawping as he shifts the dog bowl outside the door with his foot then leads the way down a couple of flagged stone steps into the farmhouse-style open kitchen.

'No, I'm completely happy with dogs,' I add as we step onto the creaking floorboards into the kitchen.

'She's Freya's – a rescue dog, really friendly, but I never expect everyone to like dogs. I'll just let her out the back for a bit, you can meet her after,' Adam explains as a warmth embraces me.

'Garfield was a rescue too. He's residing in an old folks' home until I return. To be honest I think he prefers it there. He gets far more leftovers,' I call after him.

A tall rustic table in the centre dominates the kitchen, surrounded by six well-worn leather bar stools. A colossal black Aga burns warmly in the corner with uneven chopped logs stacked up high on either side. It's an old-fashioned farmhouse layout that is irresistible.

'Welcome – please make yourself at home.' Adam returns, as if reading my mind again and I pull my bag from over my shoulder.

'That's just how I feel. It's like a home from home.' I follow him to the fridge. It has an array of colourful magnets covering it, holding up drawings, flyers for gymnastics and ballet, a hospital rota and a school timetable. A whiteboard hangs with a marker on a red string and I read, scribbled in a child's handwriting:

Don't Forget Money for School Tour Friday £15!!!!!!!!!!!!! PLEASE AND THANKS!!!!

E x

He pulls open the door and removes a bottle of white wine and two glasses. Being me, I can't help but sneak a look at what else he has in there. I'm happy to see normal stuff stacked up, like packets of ham for lunches that make you gag when you first peel them open – you know the ones. Behind them processed cheeses and yogurts. It's not a fridge full of avocados and celery. A row of pictures hangs on the back wall in a straight line in white frames. I don't look but I'm dying to see them properly. Adam puts the wine and glasses on the table and removes his jacket. A tight fitted black T-shirt is tucked in, but one side has come loose and hangs over his silver-buckled belted jeans.

He indicates the wine. 'We're on holidays, right?'

'Exactly! You've such a fab home,' I tell him honestly. 'So much heart.'

'It does have heart – that's the exact way to describe it! Well thank you! I'm so pleased you get it. I've had it for a few years now. It was a complete run-down shack when I bought it so I've been doing it up when I can. My family like to tell me it's still completely run-down, but I like to call it a work in progress.'

'It's so not run-down . . . inside. It's genuine.'

'Right?' He nods enthusiastically and it's pathetic how much it pleases me that I'm pleasing him. The ceiling is low here and he seems to take up so much space.

'I'm trying to keep it as true to its original self as I can but still have it functional, like Wi-Fi, ya know. Freya's room, mind you, is like a modern-day vomiting bug hit it, but I want to keep improving the house. It's just time-consuming. Everyone tells me to knock it down but it's a protected building! And if I wanted a new house, I'd have bought us one.'

'You've done the work yourself?' I ask, my eyes wide.

'Yeah, bit by bit.' Jokingly he flexes his muscles, but still my butterflies bash around. 'Like I said, I'd actually only finished painting the outhouse before I left for Ireland, so I wasn't really lying when I told you I was a painter and decorator. It's kind of all I do in my spare time, sadly.'

'Incredible. Well I think it's amazing.' I pull back one of the stools. The wood burning in the Aga smells divine. Like Christmas is waltzing around the kitchen with Halloween.

'I'll get there.' He laughs. 'It's my forever home so I'm not too worried.'

His forever home. I ingest that comment.

A bowl of ripening fruit cowers in the centre of the table. I can hear Spangles barking outside as I drape my bag over the back of the stool. Above me, copper pots and pans of all shapes and sizes sway melodically.

'No doubt my own fault as a parent but Freya does next to

nothing around the house, and I'm flat out most of the time at the hospital, so the household chores go amiss a lot. I'll give you the very small tour later, if you like?'

I nod.

'I tell you what, you won't be as impressed with my apartment,' I say before I think.

He's on it like a flash. 'Is than an invitation, Lexie?'

'Let's wait and see, shall we?' Lexie Byrne, ya divil ya, what a reply.

I notice a pile of opened cards on the table. All *Thank You* cards as far as I can see. He offers me the bottle and one of those spiral corkscrews.

'I can't believe you're in my kitchen.' His voice drops and he holds my eye as he places the bottle in between his knees, uncorks it with ease and pours, stopping halfway, asking my approval on the amount without words.

'The cards?'

'Patients, so kind, really no need.' He smiles.

'Fill 'er up.' I laugh. 'FYI, can we talk about my hoody? So, I was wearing a white shirt, but this woman on the pl–'

'Well you won't be wearing it for long I hope.'

I blush as he puts the smallest drop in his glass and puts the bottle back in the fridge.

'You not having one?' I ask, slightly confused.

'I have to drive later so I'll just have a small sip . . . until we get to the hotel and I'll be free to have a few,' he says, coming back and manoeuvring himself in between my legs as I perch upright on the high stool.

He hands me a full glass and I can feel him against me.

His scent lingers in the air, mixing with the woody smell of the Aga.

'It's not important now, my hoody story. Cheers, Adam!' I tip my glass against his. He tilts his head as if seeing me for the very first time, his dark eyes taking me in.

'God, you're beautiful,' he says softly.

I'm not sure anyone has ever told me that I was beautiful.

Sexy, yes.

Beautiful, no.

There is an ocean of difference in how that word makes me feel.

My phone rings out in my bag.

'It doesn't matter,' I almost snap as I make the first move, arch up and kiss him softly. Our tongues entwine and our breaths come easy. He groans softly. My phone continues to ring until thankfully it rings out. With my free hand, I feel the back of his neck, dance my fingers up into his hair, and he arches his back now. Eventually I pull away, although I could kiss him forever.

'Mmmm,' he moans and rests his forehead against mine.

'Mmmm,' I repeat.

'This is so nice,' he whispers.

'I know,' I whisper back, my mouth a little dry.

'I can't tell you how much I want you.'

I laugh. 'I think I can feel it.'

'Oh sorry.' He doesn't look sorry.

'Don't be.'

He moves against me again and we kiss, harder, more forcefully. I want to devour him, but I also want to hold a little back. When we break, he says: 'Forgive me.'

'It's fine.' I want to pull him back.

'I just don't want to ruin a thing . . . to rush a thing. Let's talk. I want to know everything about you.'

'Talk. Okay . . . here's a question I do have. Most men, I think, would boast about being in the medical profession. Why don't you?' I'm asking this so I have the answer for Annemarie more than for myself. I'm starting to overheat now in the hoody. My armpits are starting to properly perspire, and my industrial-strength deodorant is in my case.

'How can I put this?' He takes a sip of his wine and puts it down, then pushes his hands deep into the pockets of his jeans. My eye is once again drawn down to those neat hips.

'In plain English?' I offer as I force myself to concentrate and tug at the strings of the hoody, pulling it down a little from my neck.

'Right so. This ain't very PC, Lexie, but sometimes I've met women . . . out . . . and once they hear I'm a nurse, I see a shift in their romantic interest.'

'Are these blind women?' Jesus, Lexie, bad joke – he's a nurse. He laughs though.

'You'd be surprised honestly. A lot of women just lose interest, like it's still not considered a "manly" profession. Doesn't pay like a doctor and the hours are crap. I'm made to feel like my career is a second-best one – a lot.'

'You can't be serious?'

'Deadly.'

'Like your job.' I bite my lip. What *am* I saying? Oh, don't mess this up now, Lexie, by saying something really stupid and offensive. I flatten my fringe with the palm of my hand, but he throws his gorgeous head back and laughs, and I start laughing too. It's the nervous release we both need.

'Brilliant! That night in Dublin, I couldn't stop thinking how refreshing it was to have a conversation with a woman who has a wicked sense of humour!'

'I felt the same! Isn't it though?' I'm so relieved.

'I didn't feel I had to watch what I was saying, it can be difficult to have a good laugh sometimes, without offending someone.'

'I agree. Everyone is *desperate* to be offended about something.

179

I'd never intentionally be offensive or want to offend anyone.' I shrug.

I watch him move back to the fridge, the way his jeans hang perfectly on his hips. He has this ability to fill a room. I find it hard not to stare at his perfect bum as my phone shrills again.

'It's grand, I'm not getting it,' I inform him as he returns with the cold bottle and tops up my glass. I'll need sustenance soon enough if we're out for the night in a couple of hours. But right now: 'This is the life. To the weekend.'

'I'm so glad we have all of tomorrow to just chill out as well,' he says.

I raise my glass again as he resumes his position in between my legs just as my phone stops ringing, his presence once again all-consuming.

'I know it sounds crazy, but all I want to do is kiss you.' He runs his hand through my hair.

'All?' I say flirtily and move my mouth as he leans in and kisses me softly, our lips touching and parting sensually, but almost immediately my phone rings again. Oh, why didn't I put it on silent?

'Sounds like someone *really* wants to speak with you. Do you not want to answer it?' Reluctantly I move him from between my legs and rummage deep down in my bag for my phone.

It's Annemarie. Of course.

'Sorry!' I say as I hover my finger over the green button.

'No worries at all. I'll just let Spangles back in, give her a treat,' he says and walks, or swaggers as I see it, towards the fridge.

I slide my finger across as he leaves with a small bag of Good Boy Chewy Chicken Strips in his hand.

'Hello?' I say, impatient.

'Listen carefully, it's only me!' It's Annemarie.

'I can't talk now, Annemarie. I'll call you back later, yeah?'

She ignores me. 'He's all right, I'll give you that. . . I managed to share a cab with a beautiful old Scottish couple. They had eleven children! Imagine that? Eleven pregnancies! I promised them if they come to Dublin, I'll show them around. Gave them my number. Oh my God, there is the most amazing spa here, Lexie. I've booked in for an Indian head massage in an hour; the room service menu has fresh strawberry and raspberry smoothies – my favourite; I have a Jacuzzi bath that I obviously can't use because ya know . . . but this hotel is shamazing! Are you there? Hello? Hello? Lexie? Can you hear me?'

'Eh, I can't talk right now I said.' I plaster a smile on my face, but I know my voice is tense as Adam struts back in and heads over to an old-school stereo system on the countertop.

'Ohhhhhh, Jesus Christ.' She stars to pant. 'Oh no! I knew it! Most rides like that are hiding something. Look at Ted Bundy. He was a ride. And a mass murderer. Are you okay? I think I can hear panic in your voice? Just say . . . shit! We need a safe word. Okay, safe word, safe word . . . say tampon for no and . . . and . . . sanitary towel for yes! Can you do that, Lexie? Can you do that for me, pet, easy now,' she says Stanislavski-ing her way into Liam Neeson.

'T-T-Tampon,' I stammer unintentionally and go to hang up as Adam looks over at me quizzically. I turn my head.

'TAMPON!' she squeals before I can cut her off.

'Sanitary towel! I mean sanitary towel!' I hiss, clasping my fist around the phone, trying to shield my mouth, squeezing it to my ear before she calls the bloody Metropolitan police!

'Are you sure you're a sanitary towel? Promise me that you're a sanitary towel?' she implodes.

'I am! I swear to God!'

'Say it again – I'm not convinced.'

'I am a SANITARY TOWEL!' I yell at her and hang up,

throwing my phone back into my bag. Adam's leaning on the counter, his long fingers lingering on the round dial of the stereo, still staring at me.

Oh shit.

'Oh . . . I'm just. I'm . . . it's a game we play in work.' Oh, lopsided cottage ground, swallow me up.

His eyes narrow.

'Like the lotto . . . the lottery . . . except, em, we guess women's hygiene products. I – I was this week . . . a sanitary towel.' I gulp, colour rising in my cheeks as I frantically turn my phone to silent.

'Okaaaaay.' He stands up as some random golden oldie fills the air. 'Once you're sure you're okay.'

'Oh, I like this tune, ' I say inanely, still shook. He must think I'm a raving lunatic. 'Completely okay,' I add, hoping the redness in my face is diluting somewhat. When I get my hands on Annemarie . . .

'Come on then, tour time – only if you want to? We'll leave the wine cellar; you need a torch to go down there.' He reaches me now and picks up our glasses.

'Course I do.' I follow him out the kitchen door, my eyes devouring the sway of those perfect narrow hips.

We go left, down the hall of exposed beams and brick and enter the living room. Two floor-to-ceiling sliding doors open out to a large, paved patio with a rusted garden swing and see-saw set, and a weather-beaten, free-standing barbeque. The garden is massive, like half a football pitch. I see the freshly painted white outhouse, sparkling in the weak afternoon sun. Its trees hang low, their shapes spectacular. I take in the living area: an inglenook fireplace, a much-loved dog basket, a low-slung couch that's covered with a knitted throw and which, unusually, sits alone in the centre of the room with only a small old-style TV on a stand in front of it. It's basic to say the least.

'Cuuuute.' I hold my wine glass tight for fear I'll spill it.

'Living room.' He opens his hands out wide.

I laugh. 'Go way?'

'Telly.' He points to the small TV and combined DVD player.

'No way?' I exclaim.

'Badly ripped couch under throw.' He nods to the couch.

'Get the hell out of here, Adam, you goddamn genius! Underneath is a couch? Well I never!' I do the universal sign for mind blown again.

I laugh.

He laughs.

'I've plans for it, don't worry. I'm building on a conservatory for the views and thinking of knocking down that partition wall and open planning the whole cottage.'

From the corner of my eye, I spot a substantial pile of DVDs stacked up by the TV, some out of the cases, scattered across the carpet. Squinting slightly, I make out the covers of *Taylor Swift LIVE*, *The Next Step*, *Mamma Mia*, *Mamma Mia 2*. I cast a closer look round. The room has recently been tidied I'm guessing, as an overflowing box of Lego and arts and crafts are in a concertina box by the door. It's sort of shocking to me for some reason. It's the only real proof of Freya I've seen so far apart from the fridge, not that I've been looking too hard but . . .

He clocks me. 'Freya's.'

'Oh right,' I say.

'Although I have to confess, I do get a good belly laugh out of watching Pierce Brosnan trying to sing.'

'Oh, me too!' I wholeheartedly agree.

'She's not here obviously.'

'No, I remember you said she stays with her mam at weekends.'

'I like how you say *mam*.'

'Yeah?'

'It's so Irish.'

'What do you say?'

'Mum, mainly.'

'Are you a mummy's boy?'

'Well maybe just a little bit.' He sticks his finger into his cheek, twists it. Laughs again. 'But yeah, Freya spends weekends across the road at night, but she's in and out of here all the time too, if I'm not at the hospital.'

'Do you not have odd hours as an A&E nurse?'

'I used to do a lot of nights but I'm mostly days now to suit my lifestyle with my daughter. They've been really good to me at Cotswolds.'

'I'd say you're really good at your job, Adam, because you really know how to treat a woman.'

He raises an eyebrow.

Oh. My. God. Lexie, did you really just say that? The numb-skulls in my brain are doing the conga, blowing on bugles.

And just like that I feel the numbing effects of the alcohol on my nerves. It's doing exactly what it's supposed to do, loosening my lips, and I'm delirious that I'm here.

Ecstatic.

Euphoric.

Elated.

He stands in front of me. I can feel his breath on my face.

'You know, when you left my room in Jury's, I lay on the bed for a few minutes just thinking wow . . . what the heck just happened there, Adam mate?' He puts his glass on the TV stand; dust rises in the late afternoon sunlight.

'I know, me too,' I say.

'I boarded that bus to Clare, shattered but hyper . . . I couldn't sleep. My first week off work in . . . I don't know how long, and all I could talk about to my sister was this incredible Irish girl

I'd just met. This woman who I just immediately clicked with. This incredibly real person. Honestly, Lexie, I was beginning to think you didn't exist. I couldn't wait to get back to Dublin and see you again. I put your name and number into my phone and I kept looking at your name . . . the letters . . . like some kind of pathetic, lovesick teenager just waiting to ask you to dinner the next night, and then Freya called – she'd had a setback in her mum's house, so I had to come home to sort it out.'

'Oh no. What happened?' I'm not sure how I sound so normal and ask the right question, after that speech.

'Well I had to fly back so fast because Martha, my ex, she has this on-off boyfriend, Graham, who has two boys. It's off again now apparently, but they're still friends and that was the issue Freya had when I was in Clare. Clint, one of his boys, was in Martha's and took Freya's phone, went through all her private messages on TikTok then he wouldn't give it back – started texting her friends, sending pictures from her phone, the little brat! Freya was distraught.'

'Little brat is about right!'

'Right? Martha didn't seem to think it was that big of an issue – said it's what kids do. But Freya begged me to come back and sort it. Seems a bit of a melodrama but . . .' He drapes his arms around my waist, pulls me close.

'Good!' I say. 'She's a lucky girl to have a dad like you. On her side.'

I swallow, clutching my wine glass tight. I have to ask the big question.

'So how long have you been divorced?'

'Four years.'

'So. What happened?'

30
The Way We Were

H E SCRATCHES HIS FOREHEAD, drops his hands. 'Oh.'
'Oh?' I repeat at a higher decibel.

'The divorce. Are we going there now?' He runs his hand down the back of his strong neck, scratches.

'We don't have to?'

'I don't mind.'

'Must have been hard, especially with your daughter still so young?'

'Oh, it was. It was hard on everyone obviously, and to be brutally honest with you, it's a part of my life I still despair of. Martha, well . . . she's –' He stops, checks himself. Then I see him physically tense up.

Shit. What have I asked? Do I even want to know the answer?

'Let's just say that Martha's still very *present* in my life. We get on as best we can, for Freya's sake.'

'So you're still friends?' I'm trying to work out whether that's good or not.

'I wouldn't call us friends, no.' He shakes his head. 'But she is in my life every day, more or less.'

Did he just grimace?

And he's not answering the question I realise.

What happened?

'That's great that you aren't at each other's throats or anything.'

He picks up his drop of wine, swirls his glass, concentrates on the small movements.

'But . . . after . . .' His colour is turning slightly pink. 'I guess Martha thinks I'm still single and therefore she thinks I'm being unfair because I don't have anything other than Freya to talk to her about, but still she tries to wangle herself into my life as much as she can, all these years later. Deb tells me the stuff with Graham is a ploy to make me jealous.' He raises his shoulders.

'Why?' I'm finished my glass of wine.

'She's angry.'

'Because you split up?'

'You don't want to hear all this now, do you?' His dark eyes dip.

'I do.' Or do I?

'Here, let's sit down then?'

I nod. I'm aware I'm a little giddy and don't want to be prying too much, but I've got the feeling I'm about to hear the gory details of his break-up. We both sit back into the couch, not an inch of space between us. He pulls at the neck of his T-shirt as though it's choking him.

'Here's what happened. When Freya was two, I decided I wanted to become a nurse. I gave up my job in insurance when I got a place in Kings College in London, the finest school in the world, the number one faculty for nursing in the UK.' He shifts slightly. 'I was really lucky to get in.'

I nod, listening intently.

'So, to backtrack a bit, my marriage to Martha was a quick affair in Cheltenham register office when we discovered she was pregnant. Not long after, I moved to London, during the week, to get my degree so I could provide a better life for us. It was

187

tough. I came home every weekend, but I wasn't really properly around for the next three years of Freya's life.' He takes a drink, studies my expression, puts his hand on my knee.

'It was a very tense marriage from day one, Lexie, but I tried – *we* tried – and for a while it seemed like we might make it . . . but then I.' He suddenly stops.

'Must have been sad for you all?' I prompt.

'Right, but Martha did all the hard work in those early days.'

'So what happened?' He needs to spit it out.

'I've no excuses, but even now I'm riddled with guilt and I have to live with that. I feel shit about what happened every day, that's the truth, but at the time I felt I had no other way out.'

Oh no. What did he do?

'What did you do?'

'I had an affair.'

Fuck it anyway. Another Dermot. My bubble is bursting.

Pop.

Pop.

Poppidy, pop, pop. Pop!

'But please don't think the worst of me,' he implores, squeezing my knee.

I shake my head slowly. 'So she was on her own here with the baby and you were in London with another woman?'

He shakes his head too, wipes his nose with the back of his hand.

'No, worse than that. The affair happened way after . . . when I was settled back here. Freya was in school, I had my job in Cotswolds . . . but I was having an affair with Jess, a friend of Deb's, and a work colleague.'

'Oh. Wow. That *is* shit.' I wince then whistle.

'Really bad. Horrendous. Despicable. No excuses.' He holds his hands up.

'Except . . .' I allow.

'Except I was looking for a way out. Being away for those few years had kept us together. When I came back full-time, I was so miserable. I'd fallen out of love with Martha long before Freya came into our lives. Of course, I should have left her sooner, not cheated on her and humiliated her. It was appalling. I did try to tell her how I felt, but it felt like she just refused to listen. Like she didn't have time to talk about that stuff. Martha's a great mum but, for me, a stubborn partner. We'd been together, on and off, since school, just kids really, it was always are-we-aren't-we for so long . . . anyway, that's what happened. It went on, sporadically, for a summer. I have to live with what I did and everyone knowing it, because everyone talks in this village. To be honest, it's why I've never had a serious girlfriend since the divorce.'

I'm quiet.

'Do you think I'm terrible?'

I think of Dermot and how humiliated I was when he cheated, but something in Adam's face softens me. I can feel the shame at how he behaved oozing from his pores in a way I never could from Dermot. His regret is palpable. It doesn't feel rehearsed or put on for me. It's there in his physicality. I'm not making excuses for him, or am I?

But, oh, Annemarie will explode at all this.

'I don't know the situation, I suppose. Who am I to judge?' I try, keeping my tone neutral.

'I'd fallen out of love with her but, again, no excuse!' He holds his hands out wide this time.

Like an open book.

I nod.

I look down into my empty glass.

'Not easy on anyone.'

'No, but the blame is all mine. I moved out and back in with my folks in Bourton-on-the-Water for a few months. People in the village were really good to Martha. She always had an array of babysitters at her disposal, and I was always around if I wasn't on a shift.'

'So,' I can't help but interrupt. 'Did you tell her, or did she just find out?'

'Oh, no, I told her.' His dark eyes are sad. They dip again and don't rise to meet mine. 'She wanted to move on from it, for us to try again, but it was never an option for me.'

Ouch. I don't know Martha and I can't help but feel terrible for her. But I can feel desperate hurt from him. No one is this good an actor.

'Martha tends to get her own way . . . a lot. People always do what she expects them to do, but I have to hand it to her, she was very fair when it came to Freya . . . fast forward, the decision was that we should have shared residency for her.'

'Okay, so how does that work?'

'Martha was really keen that it should happen. She felt it was only fair we both raise our daughter, together. It was Martha who suggested I buy this place to be near them, so I bought it, and now my daughter has two homes across the road from each other. Martha is very much still a part of my life whether I like it or not.'

'Fair enough,' I acknowledge.

'She's still gutted we broke up if I'm being completely honest. I don't think she ever thought we'd actually divorce, but I – Look, it was over for me long before I did what I did. But I'm over the moon that I can be so close to my daughter. She's the light of my life.'

I nod. He runs his hands up and down his thighs.

'Does all this change how you feel about me?'

It probably should but it doesn't. It's how he's telling me the

true story. The pain is visible in his eyes, in his body language –
it's as though he still hasn't quite forgiven *himself*.

I shake my head softly.

He smiles, more relaxed now. 'Yeah, so overall it has its
moments, this co-parenting malarkey.'

'I bet,' I say.

'I – I never wanted Freya to have to divide her time between
two sparring parents but . . .'

'Of course, you didn't,' I interrupt. All of a sudden, he looks
like he might just cry.

'Right.' He takes a long deep breath; his eyes finally meet mine.

'But you stepped up to the plate – you are here for her.'

'I do my best.' He knocks out a salute. 'I don't want you to
think I'm *that* guy.'

I stop him.

'Do you actually want to talk about this?' I ask with a lighter
tone to my voice.

Because I don't. I don't want to digest all this now, here, today.

'No . . . not especially.' He laughs, then sighs with relief. 'Not
at all.'

'Good. Because Adam . . . Adam . . . I've forgotten . . .' I tip
my head with my index finger.

'Cooper – Adam Cooper.' He extends his hand. I take it, our
hands cold from the wine glasses.

'Because, Adam Cooper, you're right: the past is in the past.
It sounds to me like you're an amazing dad. I don't want you to
feel obliged to tell me every detail that sucks about your past.
I'm sorry I asked.'

'I'm glad you know. I'm just excited to be with you, now . . .
here.' He stands up.

'Me too. I used to endlessly rewind the past and worry about
the future but –' I stop myself. Do I tell him about living with

191

Dermot? Remind him that I was cheated on, or is it going to make him feel worse, because I don't want that.

'But?' He prompts me to give the rest of my answer.

But nothing, I think. Instead: 'But I never thought I'd be here right now . . . with you . . . feeling the way I do, so yeah, I want to live in the moment forever.'

'You do?' he asks, his eyes sparking.

Bull by the horns, Lexie, I think. I put my wine on the floor and get up, and as I face him, I pull Annemarie's hoody up over my head and stand in my white camisole top with the new pink and black bra underneath, sucking in over the leggings for dear life.

'I do,' I say, possibly a little too bridal-like.

He moves into me and kisses me hard, holding me against his body with a force that shows me how he feels about me.

'I think I have to do this.'

And effortlessly he lifts me, and I wrap my legs around him. Our faces inches apart, he walks with me in his arms out the door and down the dim, tapering hallway.

I don't feel like I have to say a thing or make a joke about how heavy I must be.

I don't feel heavy.

I feel heavenly.

31

The Sound of Music

I ROLL OFF HIM. 'SWEET BABY JESUS.'

'You may actually kill me, woman!' he gasps and pulls the duvet up from the floor over his sweat-glistening body.

Me beside him, our naked bodies heaving.

'I didn't think it could be this good.' No point in lying to the man.

'You're amazing.' He rests his hand on my belly. 'This is unreal.'

'I don't know about that. I've a strong suspicion the amazing-ness might be thanks to you!' I laugh and his hand jiggles up and down gently on my body.

In other times and places, I'd have been excruciatingly aware of my slightly flabby bits. But right now, I really couldn't give a damn.

We catch our breaths, synchronised now in our gasps as I cast around his tidy bedroom, a glass cabinet, crammed with books.

'Have you had many women?' I drawl, slipping into my quotes before I realise he doesn't have a clue what I'm saying.

His eyes cloud.

'Sorry! It's a quote from *Dirty Dancing* – I was just joking!' I'm mortified, cringing so hard at my own idiocy.

'Have I what?' He moves his hand up to his head and runs it

through his hair, and then he twists onto his side, his muscular shoulders holding him up, veins visible in his biceps.

'It's what Baby asked Johnny.' I pause, unsure of how far to spill the beans. 'I'm obsessed with that film, don't mind me.'

He studies me for a moment. 'I know. I've seen it. Are you asking if I'm a bit of a slut?'

'I don't like the word slut, but it still doesn't sound as *slutty* when it's about a man.' I try to make it into a joke.

It works. He laughs.

I laugh too and turn on my side as well.

I'm happy to leave it at that but he picks up my bait.

'I'd say, oh, I dunno . . . oh, maybe a hundred women.'

'Oh, you don't have to – A hundred!' I'm very high pitched and my head slips out of my hand, resting on my elbow.

'I'm messing!' he laughs out loud.

'Phew.' I compose myself, reset my head back in my hand.

He looks amused. 'How many for you?'

'Like, including you . . . nine,' I admit even though I don't have to.

'Nine?'

'Nine!'

'Nine!' He pitches louder and suddenly, at the exact same time we both start shouting NINE! Like Germans saying 'No!' And then we fall onto one another laughing.

'Stop!' I plead. 'I have to pee!'

'But seriously' – he wipes his eyes – 'that's not a lot. Now I do feel a bit slutty that I truthfully don't know.'

'Well, if the sheet fits.' I laugh playfully.

'Ah come on, Lexie, this isn't the greatest conversation.' He rolls over onto his back and folds his arms up behind his head. I focus on the dark tufts of his armpit hair. 'I'm only getting over my admission of adultery. Help me out here.'

He is beyond intoxicating and I need to shut up. His past isn't any of my business.

Do I like the fact he's capable of cheating?

No.

Am I his girlfriend?

No.

And what do I care if he's had consensual sex with the whole Philharmonic Orchestra. I'm here with him now.

'It's been quite a while. I mean I've had opportunities after the divorce, but Freya was my priority and . . .well not since Jess have I really liked anyone enough to . . .'

Jess. Who is Jess?

'Jess?' I study a thumbnail, feigning disinterest, lying on his chest, glad he can't see my face.

'Jess was, well, the woman I had the affair with that summer.'

'Oh yes, sorry! Of course. Lovely name Jess!' Good girl, Lexie, I sound easy breezy.

'Yeah, she's a great person. We work together – she's a paediatric nurse at the hospital. We just started chatting on night shifts over machine-made coffee, and I suppose I offloaded on her and she listened. I dragged her into my mess really; she had to deal with the whole village pointing at her too – but it wasn't, ya know . . . I just didn't feel like . . . *this*. How I feel when I'm with you.'

The magnificent specimen turns to face me again, leans over and parts his lips to kiss me lightly on the mouth. We linger on the ease of the kiss.

'This feels different, Lexie, don't you think?' he says quietly when he breaks away for a moment, I nod and he kisses me again, then he stops, like he has more he has to say. 'You feel fresh, new, different. I never know what you're going to say next, there is something about you that makes me curious and intrigued.'

His lips come in harder on mine, then break away again. My heart thumps. My body aches.

'I mean when we met, how you played twenty questions with me, how your mind works, I've never met someone like you before. And when I saw you again . . . when you walked through the doors at the airport, my stomach flipped, I just knew,' he whispers.

'So did I.'

Thank God we've got away from the women-of-the-past chat. This is turning into the greatest conversation of my life.

This is what I've been waiting for.

He has it all.

Have I found *him*?

'Although I think I only like the name Jess because it was Postman Pat's cat's name.' I do an imaginary facepalm. Did I really just come out with that at this moment?

'See? It's stuff like that I just can't get enough of.' He laughs and leans out of the bed, rummages. 'Oh shhiittttttt!' Look! It's late – we have to get to the Moritz!' He jumps up, undoing the strap on his silver watch. 'I'm going to jump in the shower and feed Spangles. Do you want to get ready here or would you prefer Freya's room next door? She has an en suite too.'

'What?' I just want to stay in his bed until the day I die.

'To get dressed for Deb's party?' He tilts his head at me, puts his watch on the dresser.

'Oh. Oh right.' I nod and frown and clamber my naked body up out of his warm bed.

Shit.

Shit.

Shit.

I don't want to see any other people. I want the world to stop turning.

'Eh, yeah, you're right, I better.'

'Gimme five,' he says.

I walk across his bedroom, absolutely aware of his eyes all over me, yet almost enjoying that feeling of being completely exposed, and I strut out the door and down to his kitchen to get my case. It's toasty in the cosy kitchen and suddenly I think, Christ, what if Freya decides to come back for some reason? I jog into the living room where I see Spangles, the cutest, furriest little black dog, curled up in her basket, sleeping soundly. Gratefully I pull on Annemarie's hoody. I can also do a little snooping down here, I think, as I hear the power shower roar, and my bare feet creak on the floorboards as I creep back into the kitchen, where I look at all the mounted pictures. There are a few of a much younger Adam and his parents I'm assuming, at his graduation. Lots of nursing certificates.

'Phew,' I whisper to myself as I run my hand down the frames. So many of them all side by side, up and down the walls. My eyes dart. Lots of baby pictures of Freya, then toddler years and then childhood pictures. Her on a small green bicycle with a young shirtless Adam, beaming, holding the saddle of the bike; one of them with red noses standing proudly by a snowman in the front of Rosehill Cottage; one where she's on Santa's knee. A pretty, smiling child, with dark hair and unmistakably Adam's brown eyes.

'You all right, Lexie?' Adam calls down.

I jump.

'Fine!' I call back as I look at one more picture on the wall and my heart bungee jumps into my stomach. Adam, Freya and I'm assuming Martha, at what appears to be Freya's tenth birthday party if the I AM TEN badge she's wearing is a clue. It's the picture I clocked on his screensaver, the Fedora hat – it's Martha who's wearing it. I can't see her face that well, but I can see her svelte figure, generous mouth and boho-chic style all too clearly.

A hairdryer sounds.

I pull my phone out of my bag, typing a text to Annemarie at speed.

You ok? leaving now for hotel. Send.

The bubble bounces; Annemarie is texting me back.

Fine. How's everything? Goooooooosssssss! Spill! dyin to hear all! In room 128 btw x

The hairdryer stops.

'Lexie? Just thinking, would you prefer to get ready at the hotel? You probably would, wouldn't you?' Adam calls down the hallway.

'Yes actually,' I register, 'it would be easier. I might need a bit more time than you. My dress badly needs an iron. That's a better idea,' I yell back as I instinctively pull the hoody over my head again. Never have I wanted to be so naked in front of a man in my life. Never have I felt this confidence in my own sexuality. I take an upturned cup from the draining board with a picture of a cute dog on it and fill it with water from the tap.

Clutching my bag under my arm, I stuff my phone back into it then sling it over my naked shoulder. I make my way back down the narrow hallway when suddenly Spangles makes an excited beeline behind me, growling and barking wildly.

I start and scream.

32
The Graduate

W HAT THE –' COMES THE YELL from Adam's bedroom.

I don't know what to do, the little dog is still yapping wildly at my bare feet.

'Spangles!' He's in the doorway now, still wet, still stark naked apart from his open white dress shirt. 'Come here, girl. Stop now. Behave.'

Spangles quietens; with her tail wagging madly she trots over to Adam.

'Good girl. Sorry, Lexie, she's just over-excited. Are you okay?'

'I . . . I thought she might bite me. I just got a shock.' I stand in the hallway, slightly shaky, the cup of water in my hand.

'I'm sorry, she's normally so friendly,' Adam says, but his eyes seem to be fixed on the cup in my hand.

'It's totally fine.'

Then, as I take a drink, he almost shouts, 'Oh, no! Lexie! That's Spangles cup! We put her water in it.'

Immediately I spit – no, I spray – the water from my mouth right into Adam's face and all down his clean white shirt. I drop the cup and it shatters, as Spangles darts into Adam's bedroom.

'Oh. My. God!' I gasp, absolutely mortified as Adam wipes his face.

'Thanks, but I just had a shower! I'm fine, don't worry. It's only a cup. Here, girl. Here, Spangles, shush now,' he coaxes her back out. He picks her up. Soothes her with sucky, kissy noises that, quite grotesquely I admit, I find a turn on. Inappropriate, Lexie.

'I'm so sorry –'

'Oh no!' he cries.

'Oh what?'

'Ffffuuckkkk! Oh shit! On no, Lexie! Her eye is missing! Shrapnel from the shattered cup I'd say!' He holds her up high over his head, her four stubby legs dangling, diminutive black paw pads waving at me.

'W-What?' I shriek.

'Yeah! It's gone! Quick – look for it! Shit! Maybe Jude, our vet in Banbury, can reattach it!'

I'm on my hands and knees, scrambling on all fours, feeling around the floorboards for her little eye.

Then I hear a weird noise. I look behind me to see Adam, literally rolling around naked on the ground, clutching the little dog, crying laughing.

Positively howling.

'W-What?' I shout at him.

He's creased over laughing now. And the penny drops.

'Oh, you absolute bastard! You PIG!' I roar as reality dawns and I look at Spangles with both confused eyes where they should be.

He's literally beside himself.

I can't help it; I try to stop it. I even pinch the bridge of my nose so tight it hurts, but I explode into laugher with him.

'Oh, I'm sorry, your face ... I couldn't resist!' He points a shaking finger at me as Spangles wriggles free.

'B-Bastard, I will so get you back for this,' I repeat, giggling so much my belly hurts.

'Ahh, c'mere pet, see . . . she's fine.'

Spangles trots back over to Adam and we both sit up and carefully I stroke her unbelievably curly, soft fur.

'Sorry, Spangles,' I utter as Adam gets to his feet, collecting the debris of the cup.

'See? Isn't it great how we have the same sense of humour? That's the thing . . . if I'd done that to anyone else, they'd have been horrified. I haven't laughed that hard in ages.'

'You're the nurse, but even I know they say laughter is the best medicine?'

'It's true! It decreases stress hormones and increases infection-fighting antibodies, thus improving your resistance to disease.' He puts on a nerdy fact-knowing medical voice and slides imaginary glasses up his nose.

'Is that actually true?' I'm very sceptical.

'Lexie, laughter triggers endorphins, feel-good chemicals – that is an absolute fact!'

'Good to know, Nurse Adam,' I joke but, again totally inappropriately, calling him Nurse Adam excites me way more than it really should.

'So I'm not sure that whatever you plan to wear to the party can be much nicer than what you have on right now?' he asks, standing over me, a dangerous glint in his eye.

I'm hypnotised. It's hard to look away.

'I got a dress. Red. Known as an LRD.' But then my phone starts vibrating among the contents of my bag, still scattered on the ground bedside him.

'As soon as you answer that, we have got to hit the road.'

'Right!' I grab the phone. He walks back into his room. I hear him dump the cup-debris in the bin.

'Hello?'

'Lexie?'

'Yes.' I sigh. June does this all the time – calls you up then says your name and waits for you to confirm.

'Good. I just wanted to call to say that Máiréad has been arrested. I found that missing necklace in her possession.'

'Huh?'

'The necklace Mrs Woodcock lost in the bridal store has been found in Máiréad's possession.'

'What? No! She told me she had it! It was me who told Máiréad to leave it back to the shop.'

'Well she didn't.'

'When did you find it on her?'

'Just after you'd left – she was on the elevator and Dermot saw her looking at it in her hands.'

'She was going down to leave it into Wilde Bride, like I told her to!'

'She's in Store Street Garda station now, and she gave you as her next of kin.'

'I'm out the country, June!' Oh, poor Máiréad. This is all my fault. I should have taken the necklace off her when she told me she had it.

'Why is she giving you as her next of kin?'

'Because she has no in else in the world. Are they prosecuting her?' I brush my bare foot along the uneven floorboards, then I turn and walk back down the hallway into his bedroom. Adam's getting dressed in front of the freestanding wardrobe mirror, in a fresh white dress shirt that hangs open over his tight black boxer shorts, his hair still the tiniest bit damp.

'Okay?' he mouths at my reflection.

'Work,' I mouth back as he fastens his watch back on.

'So what can I do?'

202

'Call the station. I have the number here, but before you do, Mrs Woodcock has asked me to inform you she has left a substantial reward for you.'

'For me?'

'Yes. You took the call – she credits you for finding the necklace.'

'I don't want a reward. I'm just glad they got it back. It was her mother's – lots of sentimental value.' I root around the floor for my faux leathers then I hold my fingers to my head as if I'm suddenly remembering something. Because I am.

'Actually, did you say substantial?'

'That's what she told me.'

'How much is substantial?'

Adam moves to the next button, his eyes never leaving mine.

'I don't know. It's here, behind the counter, in a brown envelope with your name on it.'

'Open it.'

A rustle. Then: 'Two thousand euros!'

'W-What?' I raise my eyebrows so high my eyes sting. He stops buttoning.

'It's a cheque made out to cash! Turns out that necklace was worth a lot more than simply sentimental value she told me, quite the antique.'

'Well.' I clear my throat. 'I better call the station.'

Adam continues to button up his shirt, a very quizzical look on his face.

'Please call out that number to me.' I start to input the numbers June calls out into my phone and I ring off.

'Sorry, Adam, but I really have to make a very quick phone call. You get ready and I can take it in the car if I need to.' I dial the station and give them my name and why I'm calling. A lovely young policewoman tells me that the Woodcocks aren't pressing charges against Máiréad.

'She has nowhere to go,' the police officer tells me. 'It seems her place is literally about to be demolished – so she can't go back there – and the council say she's refusing to take up the residential home place in County Offaly. She is free to go, but where? I've just given her a ham sandwich and tea; to be honest, she seems terrified, the poor thing.'

This needs sorting, and now. I swoop into action.

'Okay, thank you. Do you think you could take her to Sir Patrick Dun's, off Grand Canal Street, please? They have a spare room which she can use. I'm going to call ahead to say you're on the way.'

She readily agrees, checks the address with me and I get on to the home administrator.

'Orla!' I don't give the poor woman time to catch breath. 'I'm lodging the deposit on Monday – yes, two thousand euros; you know you can trust me – and in the meantime a Máiréad Farrell will be with you shortly. Quite the celebrity, she's getting a police escort!'

'Is she a relative, Lexie?' Orla asks.

'No, well . . . kind of. She's my very good friend. I know we need to cross all the Ts, do it properly, but she has a state pension, and we can work out the rest as soon as I'm back next week. I've talked to Kevin about her – he knows the deal. We just needed the deposit for that corner room, you know the one, and now I have it.'

Orla agrees and promises to go about getting the room ready for Máiréad.

No sooner have I rung off than my phone rings again.

'This is my mad boss again, listen! She'll ask me to confirm my name,' I tell Adam as I hit loudspeaker.

'Hello?' I repeat.

'Lexie?'

I say nothing.

'Lexie?' she repeats. Adam and I chuckle. 'Lexie?'

'Yes, June!'

'I never got to ask if you're feeling better?' Her voice goes high. 'I got your note in.'

Adam pulls a face, checks his watch.

'Much,' I say quickly.

'Good. You're a big asset to the desk. August really liked you. I hope when Annemarie comes back, we can all find civil ground. Perhaps you both can come to my apartment for a bite one evening? Let bygones be bygones.' She hangs up.

I'm gobsmacked. A compliment from June is unheard of. Maybe August being around is a good thing after all.

'C'mere.' He zips up then fastens the button on his trousers, not a glimpse of overhang to be seen – just those V-shaped lines of tautness on either side of his abs. 'Everything all right?'

'Yeah, long story. I'll fill you in later. But it's all good.' I smile. I'm delighted, so relieved for Máiréad. This is a great day.

He sits on the edge of the bed. I can't stop staring at him. He pats the sheet and then I crawl onto the bed. I feel like Michelle Pfeiffer in *The Fabulous Baker Boys*, when she slinks along that grand black piano. I feel utterly sexy around this man. I've never felt this way in all my thirty-nine and a half years about myself. He wraps his arms around me.

'I know I said this at the car earlier, but I have to say it again. We barely know each other, I get that, but this is too good to be true. How did this happen?'

'I dunno . . . right place, right time. Maybe we just got lucky.' I whisper the end of my sentence.

'I don't believe in luck.'

'Everything in life is luck,' I whisper again.

'So you think there's a reason you and me found each other?' he asks.

'God knows, but what are the chances, ya know?'

'But surely fate is made up of choices – it can't be chance.'

'So you think this is fate?'

I'm in seventh heaven – he really seems to like me as much as I like him. I can't resist. My body aches and tingles as I straddle him, kiss him hard on the mouth, feel him move beneath me.

'I think we're going to be late,' he groans as we part lips, and he turns me over and lays me down gently on his bed.

33
A Room With a View

OH, ADAM! WHAT A BREATHTAKING HOTEL! These gardens! It's like driving onto the set of *Downton Abbey*!' My nose is literally pressed up against the window of his car and I do feel my Duke is by my side. We had driven deeper into the countryside to the Moritz, and it is gloriously old-fashioned, sprawling and stunning.

'What's not to adore about your enthusiasm, Lexie Byrne?' He laughs at me and I can't take it, him in his dress suit. He looks like the best James Bond in history.

Double oh whammy.

'Your sister is right – suits suit you.'

'Yeah, you like?' He raises his dark eyebrows a few times. 'Every significant occasion in my life has been celebrated in the Moritz. It feels like part of the family at this stage.'

The tall black sign for the hotel is perched high on the steeple roof. Two extending turrets reaching into the pink evening skyline. Locals sit chatting on rustic benches outside, drinking gin and tonics in those oversized, cucumber-filled tumblers, and kids run wildly, freely through the vast gardens and high mazes, everyone dressed to suit these surroundings.

'Will I get to sightsee any of these beautiful Cotswolds of yours tomorrow?' I implore. I think I'm falling in love with them nearly as much as him.

'Yeah, but it's not the kind of sightseeing I had in mind.' He rubs his hand up my leggings, which are starting to feel sprayed on. I cannot wait to get changed. They are positively stuck to me. I have two frying jumbo sausages for legs under here. But I'm so goddamn happy. My dad always says happiness is like disco music – don't analyse it, just dance to it. When I'm with Adam, I am the Dancing Queen herself.

'I'm starving, oh my God – I just realised I never offered you anything to eat?' He breaks my thoughts and parks the car directly in front of the main revolving door of the hotel. We both hold on that and both laugh like schoolkids.

'Can you park here?' I ask when we stop giggling.

'You know the way you thought I was cool because I never said I was a nurse? Watch me demolish that perception of me.' He turns over a small laminate that is sitting on the dashboard the other way round. '*Voila!*'

I read it.

MEDIC ON CALL.

'I'm *that* guy.' He slides it across into the middle of the window in full view. 'Most days I'm covered in shit, piss and blood, so I take the perks of the job wherever I find them. This has been a running joke between me and the lads for years. So I just keep it up. Tradition, ya know?'

'Oh well, Adam. This is the icing on the cake. You mean you never have to look for parking?'

'Nope.'

'That is the equivalent of getting the Key to the City.'

'I know, right?' He clicks his seat belt and leans into me and we kiss again. My lips are bee-stung swollen, and I like it.

'How is any of this possible?' He twists my hair between his fingers.

'Yeah, it's mental, isn't it?'

'You can't say mental, remember?'

'Oh, sorry, I keep forgetting.'

He clicks my belt, which I find terribly romantic, and yes, I'm well aware that I can click my own belt, but I like how he does it for me.

'Let's go – we need to get you into the room and get you changed for the party.'

'I'm a bit nervous now,' I tell him honestly.

'Why?'

'What if they think who's yer one?'

'Yerone?' He looks confused.

'Yer one – it's an Irish saying. What if they don't like me? Like, it's very soon to be meeting them all, don't you think?'

'Lexie, of course they'll all like you. But let me tell you something about the Coopers.' He takes my hands in his.

'Oh.' I sit up in the seat, less threatened all of a sudden.

'The Coopers are a little like the Simpsons, I'm afraid. We're a very close-knit bunch. Family is incredibly important to us all. I complain a lot, but between you and me, I don't know where I'd be without them. But there will be a lot of us in the one room this evening.'

'I'd have adored a big family. I only have my mam and dad.'

'My mum and dad are lovely, but they'll only stay for a couple of hours, then they'll retreat to their house in Bourton-on-the-Water, where they'll sit in their two well-worn armchairs that flank the fireplace, their expensive red decanting and the *Radio Times* marked out with their night's TV ahead. Goggleboxers, the pair of them. They dote on Freya though – we're very close to them.'

'They sound so sweet!' I mean it. I like the sounds of Adam's parents already. My kind of people.

'The best. Although it's Deb who's the eternal family get-together organiser. Mum and Dad prefer the quiet life but don't want to let Deb down, so they trudge along to all these events she organises.'

'Does she organise everyone?' Simple question.

He looks at me as though I've just explained the theory of evolution to him.

'She does. She's the Controlling Cooper. Though I've no idea why we all let her.' He lets go of my hands and opens his door, gets out, comes around and opens my door for me, which I'm getting scarily used to already. 'Though I don't think it's a good idea for me to come up to the bedroom while you get changed.'

Accepting his extended hand, I step out of the car laughing. We lean back against the closed car door and, like two magnets, we kiss again before we step into the glass-and-wood revolving doors of the magnificent Moritz hotel.

34
Frances Ha

ANNEMARIE STANDS BY THE WINDOW in her single room, despairing of me. Her hands squeezing her hips, her red curls knotted on top of her head, dressed in the fluffy hotel robe and flat white slippers.

'My hole he's an A&E nurse! Are you insane, Lexie?'

I zip open my case sitting on the floor.

'He *is*. I knew you'd say this!' I throw my hands up in the air. 'I swear my mother wouldn't be as suspicious as you are, and you know how much she worries about me!'

'So when did he *decide* he was a nurse?'

I don't like her tone.

'As soon as I got into the car at the airport. He showed me his staff pass, for God's sake . . . and don't be so smart.'

'Come on, Lexie, I'm just looking out for you. You don't think that's weird?'

'I have to iron my party dress!' I moan up at her as I pull the crumpled red dress out, trying in vain to smooth the wrinkles from it.

'That's red flag warning number one right there, spoofer alert. Well what was his house like?' She can't help herself. If there's another thing Annemarie is obsessed about, it's property. Intrigued is she with *Grand Designs*, *A Place in the Sun*, *Location, Location, Location* and any home-improvement shows she can find on TV. Not to mention her frightening obsession with Kevin McCloud. He was in Silverside one day and she almost lost her shit.

'Oh, Kevin! Jesus, it is you! I love *Grand Designs* so much. Mr McCloud! HELLO! KEVIN!' she'd roared in his face as he'd passed by the desk with a small, nervous wave of his hand. She'd had to sit down for ten minutes to recover.

'Stunning,' I kinda lie, closing my eyes as I say the word. I mean it's really quaint and I'm all over it, but it's no Home of the Year winner.

'Go way?'

'Out of this world?'

'Like how?'

'Innovative.'

'Really?'

'An architectural miracle,' I sing, looking to the skies.

'Go way?' Her cheeks puff up.

'But what do you care? He's a pathological, lying mass-murderer in your mind, yet you still want to know what tiles he uses in his en suite?'

She moves her head, an uneasy circle of her neck.

'Were there any signs that it was actually his house?'

'What does that even mean?'

She defends herself as I stand up and shake out my dress.

'Is there an iron in here or will I just get into my own room?'

'Like was there any photos of him in the house, or did you see any bills lying around with his name on them?' She pulls out a drawer in the desk to reveal a small travel iron attached to a lead, then rests her hands on her lower back.

'It's his house, Annemarie. I saw his staff pass, graduation certs. Now stop.'

'Of course you did.' She curls her lip at me. 'Sure, anyone can print anything these days! Don't be a dummy. Thank God I came with you.' She pads across the carpet and flips down the ironing board, then sits carefully into the wicker swing chair by the window. Outside, the Cotswolds sun slides down, throwing a shadowy orange over Annemarie's pale face.

Take this, Annemarie, I think as I spread the dress out along the board.

'Oh, and forgot to tell you, he's divorced and has an eleven-year-old daughter called Freya.'

I omit the affair.

'And the hits just keep on comin'!' She throws her head back and laughs.

Something inside me twists. A rush of blood to my head and anger boils. Very unlike me.

'Sorry but what's so funny?' I stare at her.

'Sorry but it's just, well ... he's full of shit, so this deep *connection* ...'

I watch as her fingers do bunny-ear quotation marks on *connection* then tip my finger off the iron to see if it's hot enough.

'. . . you think you have with him. Come on, Lexie, like last week he told you he was single because he just never met the right woman, that he was a painter and decorator. Now he's a divorced dad who's a male nurse. I'm no Miss Marple, but I smell a very large rat! His history has all changed dramatically, wouldn't you agree?'

I focus on ironing the top part of the red dress, careful not to burn it, but I do think about what she's just said.

'I still haven't told him the gory details about Dermot. He knows I was cheated on in the past – but I didn't tell him it was my last live-in boyfriend or all the mortifying details. Does that make me some cat-fish-type person?'

She looks at me, her skinny legs swinging, and makes a face.

'I'm not getting into this now.' I finish my ironing job. 'Anyway, for your information, please stop slagging him because I'm pretty sure I'm falling head over heels in love with him.' I flick off the iron at the mains, sit on the double bed and try to peel down the leggings that are totally stuck onto me.

'Course you are.' She swings slowly like a child, the wicker chair turning and swaying from side to side.

'Oh, come on.' I grind my teeth as I inch them down, my legs red raw underneath. I finally pull them off and fling them into the case.

'So what's the plan now?'

'He's downstairs. I have to get changed and go down; we're an hour late already. We were . . .' I look at her and blow out my cheeks slowly.

She knows that means sex.

'Urgh.' She curls her lip.

'What?' I'm more than a little hurt.

'I'll give you this, I only saw the side of him at the airport, but he looked like a fine thing. Not quite my type but . . .' Pulling her robe across her large bump, she ties the belt tighter.

'There's only one Tom, Annemarie, that's for sure.' I laugh now, harder than I meant it to come out, but her finger quotations comment has really bugged me. Pulling her cream hoody off, I drape it over the trouser press, slip on the spare robe she's offered me and go into her bathroom. I've been bursting to go for about an hour. Adam's toilet was in the bedroom and, stupidly, I didn't want him to hear my wee.

'What does that mean exactly?' she calls in to me from the bedroom.

'Oh man I was bursting!' I relax on the loo, my legs stinging.

'I said, what does that mean about Tom?' I can hear the

sharp tone in her voice now from the other side of the door.

'I'm doing a wee – do you mind?'

'Answer me.' Her voice suddenly goes up a couple of octaves.

'I'm joking, Annemarie!' I tear some sheets from the toilet roll and am immediately reminded of Máiréad. Bloody thrilled I am about that windfall, and her place in Sir Patrick Dun's. That's a real reward. Wait until I get a new pool table. It's my mission when I get home. Perhaps Máiréad can get the women all playing too now. The thought of the faces on all the residents thrills me as I flush, wash my hands with the luxurious pomegranate-scented soap. I pump some hand cream out and rub it in, but as I open the bathroom door, Annemarie is standing right there.

'Woah! Are you okay?' I back up a step as I ask. She does that thing again that she does when she's uneasy – hunches, a disappearing neck. It's a very high hunch, so she's more than uneasy – she's angry. I feel a hormonal outburst arising.

'Grand.' But she walks away.

'Oookaayyyy,' I say as she perches on the edge of the bed, her head down, studying her nails.

'Right, I better go into my own room and get changed.' I zip up the wheelie case and stand it up. Suddenly you could cut the tension with a knife. Carefully I fold the red dress over my free arm. 'If you're sure you're okay?' I turn to her.

'Yup,' she says, but her lips do that parting sound thing – she clips the word and clicks her tongue off the roof of her mouth.

'Sure?' I look at her.

'Positive.' She clicks again, gives me a huge fake smile.

'Oh, Annemarie, what? I have to go.'

'Go.' She pushes herself up off the bed and pads to the door, opens it and stands aside.

So I do. I go.

I walk out and down the hall to find our room, 126, but when I hold the key card to the door to open it, it flashes red.

'Oh, for feck's sake, these bloody things!' I say as I hold it up again. This time, I get a green flash and I slip in.

'Oh yes,' I gasp as I rest my case and the door slams behind me.

We've a magnificent view overlooking the mazes, gardens and ponds. A stunning four-poster bed with gigantic fluffy snow-white pillows and chocolates upon them. I can't help but think all I want to do is be in it, under the immaculate cool white sheets with Adam, but I set about getting ready. Pulling on the shower cap, I drag myself in and out of the hot shower, then into the red dress. It's tighter than I remembered, but I wangle myself in. I pair the ankle boots with it and style my hair up in a sleek high ponytail, then stand back and look in the mirror.

'Not bad, Lexie Byrne . . . if you didn't have to breathe.'

Grabbing my make-up bag from the case, I ease myself onto the bed. With my compact mirror in one hand, I brush some foundation on, dab cover stick under my eyes, blend, wand on lashings of jet-black mascara over my falsies, pencil my lower lids in a smoky grey, smudge with the sponge on the end of the pencil and apply clear gloss.

'Bloody hell.' I shake my head because now all I can think about is Annemarie. 'I knew this was going to happen,' I say aloud.

Leaning across the bed, I scan the instructions on the phone, pick it up and dial 0 then 128.

'Hello?' she answers after one ring.

'Annemarie, it's me. Look, I'm sorry I've upset you.'

A beat.

'It's fine.'

'Obviously it's not fine. You know I like Tom, a lot.'

'Hmm.' She grunts.

'All I ever said was he could do a bit more around the house for you. Cook the odd meal? That's all. Now do you want me to bring you up anything? I feel terrible – you're sitting in that room all on your own. I knew I'd feel like this.'

'No, thank you. I'm happy out here on my own.' She's still clipped. Very clipped.

'Don't do this,' I plead, the phone receiver resting under my chin as I chuck all the contents back into my make-up bag and fasten it.

'Do what?'

'Let me go back down to Adam, feeling like shit.'

'I'm sure you'll forget about me the second you see him.' Still clipped.

'I won't . . . Come on, let's just forget this and I'll pop back up soon to see you. I –'

'What is it about me being married to Tom that you're so jealous about anyway?' Not clipped now – well and truly pissed.

'W-What? I am not jeal–'

'Oh but you are.'

'Can I finish?'

'Suuurrrre, go ahead,' she says in her most condescending tone. 'I've nowhere else to be, more's the pity.' Smart arse.

'I'm not remotely jealous of your marriage to Tom.' I clear my throat; my hand starts shaking. 'Why would I be?'

She doesn't answer me.

'Although you always said you wanted to marry a farmer . . . with lots of land and . . . well that wasn't Tom.'

'And you said you wanted a Michael Collins type. Ha! The irony!' She snorts loudly.

The dress is digging into me a little, so I have to stand up.

'I don't have time for this, Annemarie.'

'No, course you don't, Lexie. Go be with him, yeah? The man you love after meeting what . . . twice?'

I stop my hand shaking by clutching the receiver tightly; my nails white with tension under the maroon polish, I imagine.

'Says she who wanted to marry Tom the moment she heard he was single that night in the Brazen Head.'

The words leave my mouth before I process them.

'You *are* jealous I met Tom, Lexie. Seriously, I want to know why?'

'Is that what you honestly think? Let me assure you I'm not!' My voice is aggressive now. I know that.

'You know what, Lexie, I did this for you – I came here with you because I thought it was dangerous and a bit . . . desperate if I'm honest, flying to England to meet some bloke you met once all on your own. Come on!'

'*Desperate* – that word again?' I'm aghast. Deliberately so.

'Yeah, *desperate*.'

'Annemarie, you know better than anyone that desperate is the one thing I have *not* been! I let it go when you said it in work, but I won't let it go now. It took a lot of strength to straighten myself out, and I swore after Dermot I'd never settle for anything less than someone who's really worth it. I've said that over and over to you! How can you of all people call *me* desperate?'

'What does that even mean *settle*? You say it like it's a disease!'

'Because I *settled* for Dermot when he showed that much interest . . . because I was thrilled and slightly amazed that he fancied me over everyone else at Silverside! As if that made me special enough. I just settled.'

My phone rings out in my bag. It can only be Adam.

'I just assumed I loved him, and I did, of course I did in some way, but it wasn't this. It was never like this . . . ever.'

'Like how it is with this Englishman?'

'His name is Adam.'

'Adam *something* right?'

'Adam Cooper actually.'

'But, and I don't mean to rain on your parade, you do know that Adam is probably going to do what guys like Adam do, Lexie: love bomb you, play you along for a while, mess you about, then move on to a new model.'

'Maybe.' It all sounds horribly feasible. I've a lump in my throat now.

'It's just sex, Lexie,' she says almost kindly, like she doesn't want to disappoint me. 'Hormones.'

'No. It's far more than sex. Adam has *it*. Don't make me analyse what that is, but let me tell you –'

'So that's how you want to live your life now, is it? Copping off with sexy blokes who dazzle you with their movie-star looks? Putting yourself in dangerous situations and then trotting on back to your apartment to curl up with Garfield?'

That stings. How dare she? 'I happen to like living alone,' I protest. 'Don't make out my life is somehow *lesser* because I don't have a Tom, waiting on me to feed him and all his loser friends too. No thank you!' I'm fuming now.

'Tom's friends aren't losers!'

'If you say so!' *But I bet they think you are a walkover* flashes spitefully into my head.

'You might be happy alone, but honestly I can't fathom what you want from life. Like no family . . . nothing?'

'Ohhhhooooo . . . don't! Don't go there! My life isn't nothing just because I don't have kids! Is that what you *really* think?'

'N-N-No – I – I di–' she stutters, gathers herself and tries again. 'I just wondered if maybe you were upset with me and Tom starting a family, that's all.'

'Why *would* I be upset?' I twist my fingers together to stop my hands shaking, I'm that incensed.

'Because maybe deep down of course you want kids, but Dermot took all your good years.'

'All my good years? Where are we here – in *The Handmaid's Tale*?'

'You know what I mean. I just wish you'd be honest with me!'

Honest? I can give her honest. Here goes. 'Get this, Anne-marie! I don't see the point in being in a relationship for the sake of it. Like, what's the point? What is the fucking point in being with someone who isn't right just because you're scared of being alone and your biological clock is ticking? I'd rather be on my own than be with someone who isn't my soulmate.'

'Life isn't about *soulmates*, Lexie! Grow up!' She's telling me off like a frustrated mother with a child, but I won't be cowed.

'No! And don't ever throw my *GOOD YEARS* at me ever again! I've seen too many women get to my age and panic . . . run around like headless chickens and then just settle for the next available guy . . . like, HE'S GOT SPERM! *He'll do!* Like I just gotta have kids and I . . . I don't want to be that person. I don't want that life. I want something more.'

'Careful, Lexie.' Her tone is dark.

'Careful of what exactly?'

'Of saying something you don't mean.'

We both need to be more than careful, I think; this conversation is hurtling towards the break-up-because-it's-broken cliff. I make a huge effort to level out the stress surging through my body. 'Can I tell you something, Annemarie, that I really do mean? I'm angry at the unfairness that we have to think about this now. I mean, it's not an issue for men . . . but the moment we hit thirty-five it's like, you've got to decide *now* or it's going to be too late! And literally that change happens in those five years in our thirties. And it's like, what the hell? And now you have this tiny gap of time to find *the* guy. Find the one you're going to spend the rest of your life with? I just think that's crazy!'

The line is quiet; our breaths are loud.

Then: 'But I thought the Englishman *was* the one, Lexie?'

Smart arse. Can she not just stop it?

'Who knows, right? Situations change, ideals change. Maybe I will have a baby with Adam! Maybe we'll have fucking quadruplets!'

'God.' Her voice wobbles. 'I wish I didn't come.'

'I didn't ask you.'

'No, I know you didn't ask me, but I came anyway because you're my best friend and that's what friends do – they support one another, are honest with one another, are there for one another, but you know what . . . I'm really sorry that I did now.'

I bite my tongue. My phone rings out again.

How did this escalate so out of control? I don't want to fight with her.

But then.

'In fact. Fuck off, Lexie.'

'No, you fuck off, Annemarie.'

I'm not sure which one of us hangs up first, but if I were a betting woman, I'd say it was a photo finish.

35
Reality Bites

A SLIGHTLY SPITTY, SLIGHTLY JOLLY bald man in a tux points his green bottle of beer in my face.

'You're yer one from de row behind us!'

'W-What?' I take a step back on the luxurious carpet.

I'm standing with Adam by the boutique bar in the packed function room. Every inch and edge are covered in twinkling silver and white fairy lights. Round tables sit close together covered in starched white cloths. In the centre are see-through, glitter-holding silver balloons and ice-blue candles in tall three-tiered silver candlestick holders, burning brightly. At the far end of the room on a stage covered in red velvet, three violinists play Bartók, Violin Concerto No. 2. I only know this because a small screen sits above them, projecting them and the name of the piece they're playing. Kind of karaoke for intellectuals. A huge banner in the shape of a love heart reads DEB & FRANK™ and sways above an ice sculpture. My breathing is just about back to normal but I'm still trying hard to calm down inside. Obviously I didn't tell Adam I'd had a blazing row with Annemarie, who is in fact up-bloody-stairs. My guess is he's probably forgotten all about her.

''Tis you!' A huge guffaw.

'What?' I say again. He's vaguely familiar actually.

'Frank, are you all right? This is Lexie. What are you talking about?' Adam stares at him, pulls at his tie as if it's choking him already. The central heating in the room is blasting.

'He must think you're someone else.' Adam turns to me and moves me a few feet down the bar, away from him, miming too many drinks with his cupped hand to his mouth.

I tug at the red dress. Oh, come on. How the hell did I convince myself that this fitted in Threads? It's far too tight and I'm still on edge after that horrible row with Annemarie, jangled to pieces. How could she think I'm jealous of her and Tom or upset by the fact they're going to have a baby?

Or am I?

Jesus, am I?

Pulling at the underarm of the dress, I try to create some space between my recently shaved skin and the itchy fabric. This isn't the time to be feeling so desperately uncomfortable.

'That dress is amazing on you,' Adam whispers in my ear. 'You look unbelievable.'

Oh, Adam.

I look at him. *Forget about everything else*, the numbskulls in my head shout at me. The little people who run my brain are all on my side it seems.

Just enjoy being with Adam! they all shout at the tops of their squeaky voices through megaphones.

You can sort things out with Annemarie later on. They tip-tap into my brain.

'Thanks.' I want to kiss him but I'm not feeling his affection as openly in this room, and I get that.

'Wait until I get you upstairs . . .'

'I don't know if I can. I just want to get out of this dress and . . .' I'm distracted and I'm starting to feel more than a bit awkward because that bald guy at the bar is now craning his head to stare up at us. Why is he so familiar? Adam clocks him too.

'Listen, I told you we don't have to stay here long. Ignore Frank – I don't know what he's at. My plan is as soon as we can, we're out that door and up those stairs, some chilled bubbles and –'

'What's the story with the meal?' I ask. 'What time will that be?' I'm not looking forward to it at all, even though I'd gladly eat a scabby man's leg through a gate post. I can barely breathe as it is in the dress, so the thought of sitting and having to eat in it, making small talk, isn't one I'm cherishing. I haven't smoked a cigarette in five years, but right this very minute I'd give anything for one. To take myself out into the cool, open air of the outside, sit at one of those rustic tables, maybe order a pint of cold lager and just spark up.

'Knowing Deb, she'll milk this night for all it's worth, so don't be surprised if she doesn't serve until ten-ish.'

'Ten-ish?' All thoughts of a nicotine hit banished, I put my hand over my mouth.

'I know, I'm famished too.' He pulls at his tie again. 'You really do look sensational, Lexie.'

I suck in so hard I'm sure my belly button and spine have gelled.

'Come on then, those drinks.' He stops and lets out a moan. 'Okay, Adam, I'm starting to think you didn't think this through properly, mate,' he says more to himself as a rotund man in a three-piece suit approaches us.

'Adam. My boy!' he says as he puts his hand out for Adam to shake. He has one of those pocket watches on a chain dangling from his straining belt.

'Uncle Brian.' Adam shakes his hand.

'And who is this delightful young filly? They don't build them like you anymore,' he adds, looking me up and down.

I'd like to give Uncle Brian a swift kick in the balls.

Instead: 'Hi, I'm Lexie.' He stays focused on my chest for more than a moment too long, then jerks and leans his ear in close to me.

'Say again now, sweetheart?'

'We have to go chat to Frank!' Adam shifts me back down the bar.

'Aha! There yee are! Deb spilled wine over her, and she had a meltdown. 'Tis her,' the strong West of Ireland accent tells Adam.

The penny drops. He looks different without the cap. It's the guy from the flight that Annemarie had the row with who told the crappy joke. It's *that* Frank.

'You're with her?' He howls with laughter. 'She'll keep ya on yer toes anyways, Ads.'

'Oh . . .' I start.

Oh, please no. This is so embarrassing.

'Stop it. Come on, man.' Adam smiles but puts his hand on Frank's shoulder to step him back. 'What are you talking about?'

Adam looks at me, rolls his eyes.

'Hi!'

And there she is.

The woman in the double denim who spilled the wine does in fact step into the space beside Frank.

'Adam, you're late. Oh hello.' She clocks me.

'Oh . . . hi,' I manage.

'Would ya look who it is, Deb!' Frank laughs louder.

'Deb, this is Lexie.' Poor Adam is totally confused.

'Oh,' she replies but tilts her head to place me also.

'Hi,' I repeat and extend my hand.

'D'ya see who it is?' Frank waves his green bottle around again.

'Deb, what's this all about? Has Frank lost his mind? Mad cow disease or something?'

Frank's face immediately clouds. 'That's not even funny, Ads.'

'It's a joke. Sure, you enjoy a good joke, Frank, right, mate?' Adam kisses Deb on both cheeks. She looks fabulous in a plunging white satin V-neck dress, cut high at the thigh of one leg, and slingback white sandals. Her hair immaculate, a vibrant red lip.

'Listen, I'm so sorry about earlier today.' I have no choice.

'Oh don't be silly.' She stares at Adam, who seems to read her stare.

'Lexie! This is Lexie! Remember? The girl I met in Dublin? Who's staying with me for the weekend?' He winds his finger round and round.

We all stare at her beautiful face.

Registration dawns. She does a double take.

'Oh! You're Adam's . . . no way, oh okay.' She runs her index finger under her lip, always aware I'm guessing, that that deep matte red needs constant attention.

'Where's yer friend?' Frank drapes his arm around Deb, pulls her tight to him.

'Frank, I won't tell you again, shoo, will you!' Adam leans up against the bar.

'Ads!' Deb hisses at him.

'To be fair, she wasn't the worst one – it was her mate that was trouble, wasn't it?' Frank is enjoying this. He looks to Deb.

'Just leave it please, Frank.' Deb rests her head on his shoulder. 'It's not important.'

'Ah sure, I'm only havin' a laugh with Lexie here. Like a red setter the pal was.' Frank barks, laughs, looks around. 'Where is she?'

36

Dangerous Liaisons

I CAN FEEL MY CHEEKS BURN the colour of my dress. They're all looking at me. The headache that's been brewing after my row with Annemarie bursts into life behind my eyes and my mouth goes desert dry.

'She's in . . . her hotel.'

'So there was some accident with a spilled drink. Let it go. Who cares?' Adam pulls at his tie again; this time he opens the top button on his dress shirt. This seems to distract Deb more than the conversation. She leans across and fastens it as he tries to squirm from her.

'Well fine, just leave it.'

'Thank you,' he manages as she nearly cuts off his air supply doing the tie back up.

'Here, you'll like this one, Lexie.' Frank is off again, poking me now. 'Paddy Englishman, Paddy Irishman and Paddy Scottish man were –'

'Not now, darling. Really.' Deb stops him and steps closer to Adam. He elbows her from his space and reefs the tie down again.

'Now if you'll excuse us, we're going to get a drink.' He takes my hand again, but this time I slide right through, I'm that clammy. I wipe off on the sides of the dress and find it again.

'The centre of attention as always, Mr Cooper, hey?' A woman, late thirties I'm guessing, in a fitted black halterneck jumpsuit with thin gold-studded belt, sporting a sleek bob and waving a flute of champagne, joins the melée.

'Martha.' Adam heaves his shoulders and sighs out her name. Oh great, his ex-wife.

You've got to be kidding me?

Martha is – as I suspected from the glimpse of her I got under the fedora hat in the picture – all doe eyes, high cheekbones, full lips, like one of the sisters The Corrs must have had locked in the basement with a broom and talking to bluebirds because she was too beautiful.

'Aren't you going to introduce me?' She smiles brightly at me, crossing one strappy heel over the other. Perfectly aligned white teeth. If she's wearing make-up, I can't see it. Skin like porcelain. This woman is tiny, but every inch of her is toned to perfection.

Size six I'd guess. Her torso beautifully moulded. Breasts you could ski down.

My self-confidence is well and truly on trial. I feel as ungainly and hefty as Big Bird beside her.

'Lexie Byrne, you stand accused of tumbling self-esteem, am I correct?'

'Yes, Your Honour.'

My headache pounds. A desert storm continues to whip up sand in my mouth.

'Thanks for coming, Martha.' Deb and Martha air-kiss. 'And for all the help this morning setting up the room.'

'I wouldn't miss a Cooper family get-together for the world now, would I, sis?' Martha replies, catching my eye.

Sis, I think, just about stopping myself from rolling my eyes. That one was aimed directly at me – of that I have no doubt. Adam checks his watch as Deb stands in between Frank and Adam.

228

'Oh, hun, don't you look smart.' Martha kisses Adam on the cheek then raises her glass to her lips, crossing one leg over the other again.

We're all still standing around the bar and I'd give anything to sit down. Ideally outside with that pint and a cheeky Marlboro Light.

'I –' Adam starts but is interrupted.

'Have you seen Freya yet?' Martha asks Adam, who shakes his head.

Her voice is soft. Sexy. She's incredibly engaging.

'Oh, Adam, wait till you see her! She's been for her tea at the Campbells again, but she's wearing those adorable corduroy dungarees we bought her a few weeks ago in Castle Quay.' Martha is very expressive with her hands and the champagne flute. Her eyes seem to cower under ridiculously long eyelashes.

'We've only just walked in the door a few minutes ago.' Adam's face is giving nothing away now.

'Oh sorry, I thought I was late. Our bloody alarm is acting up again – you might look at it in the morning for me, if you can?' She turns her body slightly towards me. 'I'm Martha Cooper, by the way. Doesn't look like our Adam is going to introduce us.'

Her hands are white, perfect, not a single mark on them, but she still wears a silver band on her wedding finger, I notice as I take it. My hands, by contrast, feel large, unrefined, like a labourer's hands in comparison. We shake. I automatically conceal them, shoving my clutch bag under my arm and moving them behind my back. My hands, poor things, are mortified.

'Adam, there you are, son. I fear Mother is coming down with one of her migraines so we won't stay too long I shouldn't think.' Now his parents brush past and stand beside us.

'Hello, darling.' Adam's dad kisses Martha on both cheeks like they've just encountered each other on the banks of the Seine.

'Pops!' Martha coos at him.

'Martha, dear girl, don't you look lovely.' An older lady with incredible bone structure, in a soft red linen cardigan and pleated skirt combo, air-kisses her. It's immediately evident where Adam inherits his looks from.

'Heather,' Martha coos at her, 'don't say you're getting one of your migraines? Adam, did you speak to the doctors about us getting her another MRI?' Martha picks a hair or something from the bosom of Heather's cardigan, a very intimate gesture for an ex-daughter-in-law.

'She's fine. We've run every scan,' Adam says. I'm acutely aware I'm standing in the middle of all this yet to be introduced.

'Yes, it's a party – don't worry about me,' she flutters. 'Oh, Adam, don't you look smart . . . and, I say, hello there?' Heather clocks me finally.

'I'm sorry! Oh my word, my manners! Sorry! Mum, Dad this is her . . . this is Lexie.'

'You have such a pretty name!' Heather says.

'Hello there, Lexie,' Adam's dad says, and once again my second-class-citizen hands have to make an appearance. 'I'm Jeffrey.'

'Hi. It's so nice to meet you,' I manage.

'Oh, and you too, dear,' Heather says warmly. 'Adam told me you were coming to visit us. He had such a wonderful time in Ireland. I do hope he's been showing you around?'

'He has . . .' I flounder, unable to finish my sentence.

'Have him take you to Cerney House Gardens,' Heather says with a beaming smile for me.

'Do. It's like stepping into the pages of *The Secret Garden*,' Jeffrey says.

'It is magical. The house and gardens are stunning,' Heather insists.

'And they do the most delicious afternoon cream tea,' Jeffrey interjects again.

'Sounds wonderful,' I say inanely, then, 'It's so lovely to meet you all.' I'm really struggling here, a headache still pounding like a bass drum behind my eyes.

Boom!

Crash!

Boom!

Maybe me and Heather can go home together? Ingest pain-killers. Sit in matching comfy chairs, cooing over old photo albums of Adam as a baby. Maybe she still has the little name tag for round the baby's ankle like my mother saved?

'I'm sorry, Lexie, but how do you know our Adam again?' Jeffrey squints at me from behind his black-framed glasses, as though he can't quite place me.

'Adam met her in Ireland, dear, remember?' Heather smiles at me warmly again. I feel glad that she might perhaps be on my side.

'Lexie is over visiting me from Dublin, Dad.' Adam puts his arm around me, and I feel my headache start to leak out of my brain. If we can just get the hell out of this bloody room.

'Oh, don't let Uncle Brian near her.' Martha smiles and her face positively lights up.

We all stare at one other.

'Look maybe I'll just pop up to the room. I need to get . . . m-my . . . t-t-tablets.' Oh, why did I say tablets? FFS.

'Tablets?' Martha doesn't miss a beat. I catch her making eye contact with Heather, her eyebrows raised.

'J-Just non-prescription ones,' I croak, pulling at my dress. 'For . . . my cystitis.'

They all nod. Even Adam.

37

Clueless

THERE'S A TERRIBLE TIGHT KNOT IN MY STOMACH. Plus, this is all so incredibly uncomfortable I want to disappear. So I'll just quickly run upstairs, make up with Annemarie by sharing the gossip. She'll be all over this. Adam's awkward family can be my white flag. Wait until I tell her. A lump forms in my throat. I was so rude to her. *But she was rude to you too*, my numbskulls chime in. She was, in fairness. We both were.

'Up to the roo-hoo-hoooommmmmeeee.' Martha sounds out the word and does a sexy shoulder roll with her razor-sharp, toned shoulders. 'Oooh, you're staying here, at the Moritz?'

I nod, almost paralysed with fear of saying the wrong thing.

'Such a fine hotel.' Jeffrey nods too, then, 'Will you have a pot of camomile tea, dear, for your headache?'

'No, I'll take an elderflower, dear,' Heather says, pulling a tissue from her sleeve and wiping her nose. 'Where is our Freya by the way?'

'She's here somewhere already, with the Campbells again! She went across to them after gymnastics today. You know the way they always make their famous home-baked pizzas on a Friday?'

Everyone nods except me.

'Well, Freya is a big fan of them now, like our entire village, I know, but they got her eating chorizo. Oh the smell of that frying chorizo travels into all our houses, doesn't it?' More nodding. 'Anyway, they said they would bring her down after and take her back to our house at eleven.'

I can't help but think everything Martha says is aimed at me, all for the benefit of my outsider's ears. Then she does, in fact, turn directly to me.

'Sorry, Lexie, how rude of me. I'm sure Adam has told you our village is one big happy family, we all pull together, there's nothing we wouldn't do for one another. The Campbells are happy to have our daughter over because their children are grown up now.'

Martha's smile is as sickly sweet as the entire box of doughnuts Annemarie and I scoffed last week.

'I wouldn't call Linda Campbell grown up!' Heather sniffs and stuffs her tissue back up her sleeve again.

'At least she managed to keep her marriage together after all Niall's messing. We all make mistakes, Heather,' Martha says in a type of whispering child's voice, and Heather touches Martha's cheek with the palm of her hand and gives her an overegged look of sympathy.

'Aren't you going to your room?' Martha steps aside, directing her steady gaze to me once more.

'Em . . . in a minute,' I manage.

'If you'll excuse us.' Adam tries to move me.

'Do you like the function room, Lexie?' Martha asks, blocking our way. 'We all worked hard on it all morning.'

'It's beautiful. The hotel is just gorgeous.' Again swallow, dry mouth.

'You two go enjoy yourselves.' Heather looks at me kindly. 'I look forward to seeing you again, Lexie.'

But before we can make our escape: 'Evening all.' A thick-necked guy in a grey flat cap, holding a whiskey tumbler joins us.

'Dominic,' says Martha.

'Hello, Dominic,' Adam, Heather and Jeffrey say together.

'Howrya . . . D-Domin-i-ic,' I try, but my voice trails off. I actually recognise Dominic from the night I met Adam at the Brazen Head. He quite obviously does not recognise me. I feel like the largest invisible woman in the world.

'Dom, this is Lexie,' Adam says.

'Hello.' He shakes my hand. Yes, it still looks freakishly massive to me.

'Village news alert.' He takes a sip. They all immediately lean in. 'I heard from Dotty that Jane did in fact forget to play our lottery numbers on Saturday because she had to go collect Bob, who was at that thing in Devon with Charles Junior, and now we all have to pretend we don't know if our numbers come up.' Another sip.

'Poor Jane,' Martha says, her back slightly arched now so she's blocking me out somewhat.

'Why is Jane even still involved in our lotto?' Adam asks. I'm annoyed to see that he seems as invested as the rest of them. Would Dominic notice if I snatched that whiskey out his hand?

'You're so right, Adam. I keep telling her to leave it to me now! We really need to organise a village meeting next week. I'll cook some stuff, bring it over so we can all meet after work, eat and discuss? Do my lamb casserole everyone loves so much?' Martha takes a step closer to Adam.

'She should just come back here and go back to her old job,' Jeffrey says.

'Agreed,' Dominic says.

'Oh yes,' Martha murmurs, her body as close to Adam's as she can possibly angle it. 'The rooms were way better when she was here. Like, our wedding night – remember, Adam? – Jane scattered those rose petals all over our bed and the –'

Oh, beam me up, Scotty.

How long until this nightmare is over?

38
Overboard

Not now, Martha.' Adam moves a step back and takes me with him because his arm is still around me.

'Oh, Leddy doesn't mind in the slightest my reminiscing at a family occasion, do you, Leddy?' She opens her eyes wide.

She knows my name. She said it earlier. She's just trying to undermine me; I don't give her the satisfaction.

Adam does. 'It's Lexie.'

'Oh, I'm sorry, Lexie. Don't pay any attention to me. I say things without thinking! Most of my fondest memories happened in this hotel. All of ours really? Remember, Adam, that mad party we all had after we'd been to that Oasis gig on what's now Alex James from Blur's farm just down the road? Adam thought he was Liam Gallagher himself when he sashayed back into the Chill Out bar in his oversized parka singing "Live Forever"!' Martha giggles, puts her hand over her perfect mouth. 'Good times.'

'Thanks for that, Martha.' Adam's expression is neutral.

'And who is this, Adam?' Another man holding a pint of lager steps in.

'Uncle Charles, this is Lexie. But let's catch up properly later, shall we? We just have to attend to something – won't be long.'

Adam moves his hand up in between my shoulder blades and powers me out of there.

'Running away, Adam, most unlike you!' he jeers loudly after us.

Rude! But I bite my tongue, glad to be finally getting away.

We reach the double doors we came in through and exit the engagement party into the airy hotel lobby.

'Oh, man,' I gasp.

'I know. Ahh ... I mean, you know when you know your family are mad, but you're used to them and it's only when you see them through someone else's eyes that you think, shit, they really are totally bonkers? I'm so sorry. Are you okay?' he asks me, his eyes worried.

'Yeah, of course,' I say, taking a glass of water off a tray from a passing waiter heading into Deb and Frank's soiree.

'I'm actually dazed,' he says. 'That was bizarre about your friend on the plane? Where is she staying did you say?'

'I know ... what are the chances.'

Just tell him she's upstairs.

Won't he think that's weird?

The anxiety is adding to my headache. Then I remember I've two painkillers in my clutch bag. There is a God of horrific engagement parties after all! Halleluiah!

I see a couple striding towards us; the woman raises her hand in a wave to Adam. She is beautiful in a flowing, strapless maxi dress. Perfect peroxide pixie cut.

I turn to see Adam smile awkwardly and hold his hand up to wave back at her. His watch slips down his wrist. The guy stops to talk to someone as she approaches us.

She stares at me.

I stare at her.

'Hey! I wasn't sure you'd be off shift tonight since you had the week off. It was chaos last week.'

'Yeah.' He seems suddenly tense again.

She nods.

'I wasn't aware you were coming?' he says.

'Oh yeah, Deb and I are still friends. When she's home we go out, grab a bite, a few drinks.' She shifts from right to left on her high-heeled boots.

'Lexie, this is Jess,' Adam tells me quickly.

You what now? I nearly topple over.

'Jess, Lexie,' he says as Jess grabs my hand and shakes it vigorously.

'Hi! Oh, it's so lovely to meet you.'

'Likewise,' I manage.

'You aren't local then?' Her face is warm, eyes soft and kind.

'I'm Irish,' I tell her.

'Oh, no way? I adore Ireland! I've only ever been to Galway! We've been three times now! Shop Street is just my favourite street in the world! The buskers are incredible. The street artists amaze me. Keith's granny is from there . . . way out in Barna, but I want to do a proper tour of Ireland sometime. I heard that the Wild Atlantic Way is just spectacular!' She just has the kindest face and the most beautiful smile.

'Jess is a paediatric nurse at Cotswolds,' Adam goes on.

I remember. 'Oh wow . . . that can't be an easy job.'

Jess grins. 'They keep me on my toes all right!'

Up she goes on her toes.

'Ready, Jess?' The guy moves in beside her, still balancing an array of beautifully wrapped gifts in his arms.

'Oh, sorry, Keith. This is my boyfriend, Keith.' Adam and I exchange pleasantries.

'Right, we better go. Good to have a man to do the heavy lifting, eh? Hopefully see you later? It was so nice to meet you.' Jess winks at me and walks away.

237

Even though she was brilliantly friendly, I feel like I'm in a soap opera. 'Isn't her being here, like, *really* awkward for Martha?'

'No. Not anymore. It's old news. It's such a small village, there are a lot worse things going on for people to gossip about now. We're fish and chip wrapping now, thank goodness. And Martha doesn't hold grudges; she forgave Jess a long time ago, and they're friends. Well . . . so she says.' Adam narrows his eyes. I'm relieved to see he's not that delusional about his ex-wife.

Somehow, I think Martha's more cunning than forgiving.

'Excuse me, I just need to use the bathroom, won't be a second.'

I turn. I have no idea where the ladies is.

'Just under the staircase there. Push the door; it sticks – Freya can never push it open.' Adam points in the direction of the loos.

'Thank you.'

I see his face; he looks a little unsure, a tad deflated.

'Won't be long.' I smile at him and walk towards the toilets with the dress digging into me, cutting me sharply under the arms.

Keep it together – we'll be up in the room in no time, I think. Focus on that.

'Daddy says you're visiting from Ireland!' a sweet voice rings out. I jump and look around. I can't see anyone.

'I'm under here!'

I bend.

Two girls sit under the staircase. One smiles at me, the other has her head bent over a tablet. Both are wearing dungarees, both in white Converse.

'Hi there.' I smile back at her.

'I'm a big Niall Horan fan – do you know him?' she asks me excitedly. It's without doubt Freya, even more like Adam in the flesh. I get down on my honkers, praying the dress won't split.

'Well now, I don't know him personally, but I could try get you an autograph, eh?' I tell her. The other girl drops the tablet.

'W-What?' Her little round face lights up. 'I'm her BFF. Can I get one too?'

'Oh wow. That would be sooooo cool! We don't like One Direction now, they're sooooo cringe, just Niall.' Freya smiles at me, adjusts her baby pink cat ears.

'I'm Lexie by the way; nice to meet you.'

'I know. Daddy told me. Did he show you around?'

'He sure did.' I laugh.

'He's been super excited about you coming!'

'He has?'

'Sure. He never has anyone to visit us. I had to tidy all my Lego friends in the living room, clean out the fridge and wash Spangles . . . he even finished the last coat on the outhouse.'

I smile at her.

'But don't tell anyone you saw us, okay? We're playing Among Us, still trying to figure out who the imposter is and vote them out, but they'll try to take it off us. *Too much screen time* is Dad's favourite saying!' Freya crinkles her nose.

'I promise,' I say.

'Pinkie promise?' A little finger reaches out, and I link it.

'Pinkie promise,' I say as she pulls her finger back and curls up again beside her BFF, into the darkness, illuminated by the blue light.

39
Fools Rush In

I PUT MY SHOULDER TO THE DOOR of the ladies and push it open, glass of water in my other hand. My head still thumps. Mercifully, the place is empty.

It's one of those large old-fashioned bathrooms, with a shabby chic vanity table and chair that I hurl myself onto. The low temperature and quiet is bliss as I look at my reflection in the oval mirror: in fairness, I don't look anywhere near as bad as I feel. Nothing a mound of pan stick and a smoky eye won't fix. I lift my arms to smooth out my hair, brush through the high ponytail with my fingers and see two damp patches beginning to leak through into the red material. I can't let them become any more visible, so I pluck a few soft tissues from the square box on the table and stuff them under my pits and down my cleavage for now. Soakage – as Annemarie calls this trick I do with tissues when I get sweaty. I need to text her right away. Rummaging in my messy clutch for the loose pain relief, I tear open the squares, popping two round tables into my glass of water then lay my phone on the table.

'Oh, what do I say to you?' I say aloud. We've never had a fight like this one in all the years we've been friends. We need to work it out – I'll be devastated if we can't.

'Don't worry, you'll get used to us!' A high laugh from behind me as the door is pushed off the carpet and then pushed closed again.

Martha.

'Hi again,' I snap out. It's not my politest voice this time by any means.

'Calling someone?'

'No.'

'Sorry, this must be pretty awkward for you?' She leans against the vanity table. I pick up my glass and swirl it as the tablets hiss and fizz.

'Not really.' I look up at her.

She slides the gold zip across her slim black bag and removes a lipstick, rolls it up, leans in and perfectly rounds the colour out onto her voluptuous, natural lips. A nude beige I'd say. She smacks her lips. So she does wear make-up but it's almost invisible to the naked eye.

She clicks the lid back on and drops the lipstick back into her bag. 'I want him back.'

'I'm sure you do.' I lift the glass, swirl it again, determined to keep my cool.

'Woman to woman . . . He had an affair – I'm not sure if he told you?' she asks me, turning and perching on the vanity table, our eyes almost at equal level.

'You're too kind but that's really none of my business,' I say, putting the glass to my lips and draining it, the grainy powdered water sliding down my grateful throat.

'You're not his usual type.' She rolls her shoulders.

'Is that a fact?' I put the glass back down. Hold her gaze.

'I heard you were coming, but you weren't what I expected.'

'My horns?' I smirk at her, but she ignores it.

'I forgave him, but he still wanted a divorce.'

'Again, it's not my business.'

'I want us to be a family again.' She unzips and zips her bag back and forth while I wait. 'Does he talk about me?'

I shrug a little, aware of the damp tissues sticking to me. 'I really don't feel comfortable with this conversation.'

'I mean he chose to live across the road from us – that means something, right?' She stands and turns back to the mirror, runs a finger across the delicate, unlined skin under her eyes.

We both look into the mirror at the reflections of each other.

'I think you're asking the wrong person,' I say.

'I wish I knew what was actually going on in his head.'

'No one knows what's going on in anyone else's head.' I push the chair back. It sticks to the carpet – I have to lift it slightly. Then I stand up, aware that I'm towering over her.

In fairness, she doesn't flinch, just raises her eyes to me. 'I'm going to tell you exactly what I said to Jess: I won't let you stand in the way of our little family being together.'

'Martha, you need to talk to Adam, not to me.'

It could do with it, but this isn't the best moment for fixing my make-up.

'You have tissues in your' – she points to me – 'cleavage.'

'So I do.' I pull them all out, throw them in the small chrome bin then dump my phone back in my clutch. But it seems that Martha hasn't finished.

'Maybe just lose his number when you go back to Ireland?'

'Excuse me.' I brush past her.

Outside I walk across the lobby in search of Adam. He's by the revolving door, scrolling through his phone.

'There you are!' He smiles and extends his phone in his hand for me to look at. 'Freya eating pizza with the Campbells after school today.'

I see it was sent from Martha Cooper's phone. I look at the

little girl, tucking into a huge slice of pizza. I can't tell him I've met her – I pinkie promised. To be honest all I can really see is the pizza anyway – and it does look delicious.

'Mmmm, nice pizza!'

Nice pizza, I scream in my head. Why did I say that? I should have admired his daughter!

'She'd eat pizza for breakfast now if we let her. In fairness to Martha, she makes home-made pizza too, so she blends a load of hidden vegetables in the tomato sauce.'

Does she now.

'Come here,' he says, a vision of handsomeness in his sharp suit.

I don't move.

'You okay?'

'Yeah . . . I – I just really need a drink, Adam.'

'You got it!' He reaches for my hand once again and I walk in a daze across the lobby, away from the function room and down a long marble corridor into the not so aptly named Chill Out bar. A sandwich board with EIGHTIES NIGHT written in chalk sits inside the door. And, indeed, it's a pretty busy bar with eighties hits playing. My head is spinning. I'm the exact physical opposite of both his ex-mistress and ex-wife. It's literally like piggy in the middle. How did I feel so good earlier? I feel nothing of the sort now. This is all going very rapidly downhill. His family are so intense, it's all too much. I feel vulnerable, clumsy, idiotic. We don't say a word until we slide into a free booth.

'I'm really sorry again about all that inside,' he says, sitting opposite me.

'I-I'm not sure what's going on,' I manage.

'I mean, the fact you'd had a run-in with Deb and Frank on the flight over? You're right, what are the chances?' He reefs his arms out of his well-fitted suit jacket.

I meant Martha and Jess.

'Right.' I wipe my nose with the back of my hand. The earlier alcohol is wearing off, but the thumping in my head is improving. The woodpecker is slowing down. I've been solpo-saved.

'Welcome to our eighties night. Can I get some drinks for the table, Adam?' A waitress appears with two swinging high pony-tails tied in luminous neon ribbons, fingerless gloves, fishnet tights and a leather mini, a pristine white apron around her waist, pen and pad in hand.

'Please!' we say in unison, and I try to laugh. As I glance down, I see a light pinkish stain in the material under my arm.

'Can I get two large glasses of white wine please, Gracie?'

Of course, they know each other. It's like Toy Town around here. I feel like such an oddball that I don't even know one person in my whole apartment block. I hold my arms tight against my hot body. I shouldn't have let Martha get to me and gone ahead and fixed my make-up, put my arms under the hand dryer. I can't even raise them now with him sitting directly opposite me – I feel too self-conscious.

'Actually, let's take a look at the wine list. Maybe we'll get an expensive bottle after all that? I think we deserve it! What's with the ribbons?' He lifts the menu from the table.

'Eighties night. They're making us dress to the theme.' She sighs as he looks through the wine list. I feel for her – poor girl wasn't even born in the eighties.

I think back to how the night could have gone. Meeting his family like that, them all really liking me, fitting in like a glove. Not this.

This disaster.

This actual shit show.

In fairness, his mum and dad were nice to me, as was Jess, but the rest of them . . .

And my best friend, who's at her most vulnerable, is sitting on her own in a hotel room because she's always there for me and I've managed to treat her like total crap.

I have to tell him she's upstairs.

'A bottle of the Santa Margherita Pinot Grigio Alto Adige, please.' He smiles at Gracie.

'You okay?' he asks as she leaves.

'Define okay?' I sigh.

He takes my hands in his across the booth.

'Sorry about all that, Lexie. My family are a bit of a handful, I tried to warn –'

'No, listen –'

'Frank's a harmless idiot – thinks he's a comedian, lives his life through a series of cringeworthy jokes. Deb lives with him on his farm in Clare. We all secretly hoped she wouldn't go through with this wedding, but she seems to want him.' He holds his palms up.

'He's a gobshite all right, but I –'

'A what?'

'Gobshite – but I was –'

'Would you like to taste, Adam?' On-the-ball Gracie returns with a bottle in a bucket, Adam nods, and I watch the routine as I plan my next sentence. She pours a delicate drop into Adam's wine glass; he swirls, smells and tastes.

'Lovely, Gracie, thank you,' he tells her, sitting back and still not looking at me as she half fills both our glasses, settles the wine noisily back into the deep ice bucket and takes her leave. I glance through the mottled glass of the bar windows. Is that Martha peering in?

'So spit it out,' he says.

'What?' I reply. 'Oh, okay, well where do I begin?' I open my eyes wide, so he knows a shock is coming.

'You think Jess was too young for me?'

'What?'

'Jess.'

'No! I wanted to –'

'She's older than she looks –'

'Okay, but I didn't –'

'She's only a few years younger –'

'You really don't need to explain.'

'Then why do I feel like I do?' He lifts his glass by the stem, his eyes avoiding mine.

'I dunno.' I try to smile at him through my easing but still very present headache.

He drinks.

We look at one another.

'Adam, it's not about Jess. Or Frank . . . I have to tell you something. This is so ridiculous.' I lean my head in my hand. 'I told you I didn't come here on my own. I – well, Annemarie, my friend, was the one on the plane who had the argument with Frank, although I was rude to your sister, but it was only because of my white shirt.'

His face is unreadable.

I keep rambling: 'I'd planned my outfit so carefully and the shirt was ruined, and Annemarie gave me her hoody and she's here.' I point my index finger to the ceiling. 'She's staying in this hotel and we've just had a blazing row, and I was cheated on before, by my last boyfriend, Dermot. We lived together. I was with him for five years. It's been over for ten months now and I really don't want to go back into that engagement party because if I do I'll tell Frank and probably your pervy Uncle Brian and rude Uncle Charles what I think of them, and it won't be nice. I don't care what age Jess is – it's really none of my business; she seems lovely – but your ex-wife just warned me off you in the ladies and made it very clear she wants you back, and I feel like I'm some sort of outsider who no one wants here . . . and . . . and I just feel, I dunno, fat and awkward – and old!' I grab the glass and don't make eye contact with him.

He says nothing.

The sounds of a busy bar surround us.

Simon Le Bon warbles about Rio. Lucky her, I think, dancing on the sand.

Glasses clink, bottles fizz, tills ring, people talk loudly. I sense Adam's eyes on me, but I really can't look up.

40
As Good As It Gets

His dark eyes are intent on me. 'Where is Annemarie now?'

'Upstairs in her room.'

'She's sitting up in the room on her own?' He slides his elbows across the booth.

'Yes.' I want to sink my head in my hands; he likely thinks I'm a complete crackpot.

'But . . . w-why didn't you tell me she was here?' Confusion rains over him.

'You never asked.'

'I guess not. But you might have thought to tell me –'

'You never thought to tell me Martha desperately wants you back.' I try a rebuttal, pathetically.

Not sympathetically.

'I sorta did.'

'But you sorta didn't.'

'I had an affair; we got divorced.' He swirls his glass. 'Simple.'

'She lives virtually next door and she's still in love with you.'

'That's not my fault.'

'Are you still in love with her?'

'Hell no!'

His body is slightly slumped now. His tie undone, the first three buttons now open, he looks vulnerable, irresistible. All I want is to lean across and kiss him. Instead, I stand up. He jolts.

'Look, this is stupid, I shouldn't have brought you here. It's too much. It's no problem about your friend being booked in here – I get it, totally. You told me she was freaked about you coming here alone.'

I sit again, lean towards him. 'We had this big fight earlier, when I was getting ready. We said stuff that wasn't true, personal stuff like how I said I didn't –'

'Stop.' He raises his glass. 'Please. You don't owe me all this, Lexie. This is my fault . . . I went too far spilling my history to you so soon. I just wanted you to know how things are for me.' He begins to re-button his shirt, straightens his tie back and sits upright against the black padded wall of the booth, closing the very top button.

'No, you didn't go too far.'

'I did. You're right, I mean we don't even know each other, and I drag you over here, to this family fiasco. I'm not sure what I was thinking!' He shakes his head, bites on his bottom lip.

'I wanted to come,' I protest.

'I should never have asked you.' He removes the bottle from the bucket, lets the melted ice drip for a second and pours more into my glass.

'Don't say that.'

'I mean it. This is my sister's engagement party – I knew Martha would be here, and Jess and Deb have been friends since their horsey days. I should have thought it through! I just desperately wanted to see you again.'

'I did too – I really . . .' I catch the pleading tone in my voice and immediately stop myself.

'But you don't want to come back inside, or you're going to

have a fight with Frank and my Uncle Brian, Martha is there, Jess is in there, Freya is probably in there now too if the Campbells haven't taken her home by now and I haven't even seen her. Oh and Martha plays on the fact we still do things together, like shop for corduroy dungarees, eating her lamb casserole, or me going to her house to fix things, and she always brings these things up when I'm in a conversation with a woman. I don't react anymore . . . I try to ignore it but I – I'm tired of it all.'

I don't say anything, but I feel it. I feel him slipping away.

'But I *have* to go back in there,' he says quietly with finality to the sentence that makes me want to cry.

'I'll come –'

He raises his hand. 'No, seriously, please, it's not worth it. This is all . . .' He exhales heavily. 'Look, I'm glad your friend is here to be honest.'

We drink our wine. I can't quite believe this is where we are right now.

'I know I said it's no big deal, and it's not, but *were* you highly suspicious of me or something?'

'No! Not at all. Annemarie insisted . . . I told you –'

'Adam! There you are!' Deb stands, one hand on her protruding hip, waving at someone behind us. 'Sorry to interrupt but the photographer wants us all by the staircase.'

'I'll be there in a minute.' He's not bothering to hide just how pissed off he is now; he barely got to drink a drop of his wine.

'We're all standing out there waiting for *you*. It won't take a minute.' Deb makes no eye contact with me. Clearly, I'm not included.

'Okay.' Wearily he stands himself up as Deb glides away.

'Can we just park all this for a while until . . .' He points to the door.

'Yeah, sure.'

Have I hope left that he still likes me?

Oh, grow up, Lexie Byrne, I tell myself, *you sad cow*.

He's still standing over me and I realise he wants me to go with him.

'Really?' I mouth.

'Come on, please. One picture won't kill us.'

I slide out and we go around to the grand mahogany foyer, full of chatty, happy people arranged in tiers. I see Jess at the front kneeling down and Martha not far behind, beside her Freya in her corduroy dungarees, with her baby pink cat ears and two French braids trailing down her back.

'Daddy!' she calls, using her hands on either side of her mouth as though he was a million miles away. 'Up here!'

'Hello, sweetheart!' Adam beams at her, waving back as he shouts over the photographer issuing instructions at the gathering.

'We've saved you a spot!' Martha calls out. 'Squeeze in beside us, Adam!'

'Here's my brother now,' Deb calls over the raucous throng to the jerky photographer who makes a beeline for Adam and, hands on his shoulders, places him in at the side to the front.

'Where's his suit jacket?' Deb eyeballs me. I'm desperate not to catch her eye.

'Um, in the bar.'

'Up here, Daddy! Hurry!' Freya calls again.

'Could you possibly grab his jacket for me, do you think, Lexie?' Deb asks me, stress contorting her otherwise beautiful face. Her red lippy is in need of a slight touch-up.

'Oh . . . sure.' I slip back out to our booth and grab his jacket, glad of a moment to escape. Hashtag awkward.

41
The Pursuit of Happiness

ADAM'S MOVED. HE'S NOW STANDING beside Martha with Freya in front of them and both have a hand each on the little girl's shoulders.

The perfect family tableau.

'Lexie, come up!' he calls out as I return.

'I . . .' I start to say.

'Come on!' Adam calls again.

All eyes are on me as I squeeze through them all, trying to keep my arms tight by my side so my sweat patches aren't on show. I walk up the middle of the staircase and carefully hand him his suit jacket. He slips into it.

'I'll be in the bar, Adam – this is just for family and friends – if you don't mind?' I whisper, gesticulating to the bottom of the stairs.

'Oh, Lexie.' Adam reaches for me. But I'm having none of it. Again, the party splits to let me through, past the bouncing photographer who is still pulling people into positions.

Adam catches my eye, a look of horror sliding over his face, but I force myself to smile at him.

I shoot him a look that says: *don't say another word.*

The photographer shouts. 'Smile everyone! Say Coopers!'

They all shout and laugh merrily as flashes go off and the photographer bends and twists his body to get the right shots. From where I'm standing, Martha looks like she might shit herself with joy.

'We're the Coopers!' she squeals.

Fuck this lot.

I won't let them see how mortified I am. I straighten up in defiance of all the characters on those stairs.

I trudge back to the booth, with my matching red face and frock, perspiring profusely. Picking up my glass of wine, I glare at poor Gracie for no reason other than she's a part of this scene and I'm not. I skull it.

'Is this free?' two guys ask at the same time, one dressed as Like A Virgin Madonna, the other Papa Don't Preach Madonna, both holding large cocktails, with umbrellas and swizzle sticks.

'It is now,' I say, opening my clutch and putting two twenty-pound notes down for Gracie.

I've no idea how much the bottle of wine Adam ordered was, but I can't actually face any more embarrassment tonight, so I walk away hoping it can't be more than forty pounds and Gracie will get a good tip. In the lobby I have no choice but to watch them all.

The Calculating Coopers.

The Burned Byrne.

Although I smile brightly at Adam, and I flick my free hand as if to say, *Don't worry, I'm fine.*

Just breezy.

In fairness to him, he looks noticeably discomfited by this situ.

Freya is beaming, as is Martha. Another few rounds of pictures are shot off, and when they start to disperse, I see Adam take Freya into a bear hug and kiss her, then he fights his way through the crowd, shrugs Dominic off with ease, in behind Uncle Brian, dodging Charles, and straight down to me.

'I'm going up to the room, okay?' I say, smile still plastered across my face.

'Oh, please don't.' He tries to take my hands; I keep them by my side.

'I want to.'

'Okay, I'll walk you up so.' He looks so despondent yet still so sexy. I'm drawn to him like he's some sort of magnet.

'Thanks,' I say, giving Martha a rather elaborate wink as we walk past her on the last step. Admittedly, I wouldn't want to let him go if I were her, but I don't appreciate being cornered in the ladies as though I'd deliberately cheated on spin the bottle and snogged someone's fella in school.

'Where are you going now, Daddy?' Freya skips beside us, holding her cat ears in her small hands.

'Won't be long, sweetheart . . . just showing Lexie where . . . her room is.'

'Mummy says we're all sitting together for dinner! Yay! I'm having chicken goujons with skinny fries! And after it's hot fudge brownie and home-made vanilla ice cream. Do you like that?' She looks at me.

'Do I!' I smile and rub my tummy.

Adam laughs.

'Are you not eating your dinner?' she asks me, hopping up and down on the square patterns in the carpet.

'Oh, I've eaten already,' I fib.

'I ate pizza already but I'm hungry again.'

'Won't be long – stay out of trouble, sweetheart.' Adam takes her cat ears, puts them on himself, blows her a kiss and hands the ears back.

'I'm going to watch Roblox tutorials on my tablet. Mummy

says I can have an hour on it, so half now and half after dinner! Pops promised me he'd play Heads-Up. I'm going home with the Campbells and staying up till midnight tonight!'

'It was so nice to meet you, Freya.' I bend down and whisper into her ear, 'I'll report back to your dad about Niall Horan as soon as I can.'

She nods rapidly and skips off back to a beady-eyed Martha, who wraps her arm around her daughter as if she'd just been talking to Slugworth himself.

'This way.' Adam directs me to the lift, and I jab at the circular button several times, harder than is necessary.

'Deb's obsessed with her Instagram, but still she shouldn't have done that,' he says quietly. 'I'm mortified. I didn't think you wanted me to make a scene.'

'It's fine, don't . . . I mean, I didn't want you to make a scene – it was bad enough.' I try to laugh but it doesn't come out.

'Sorry you weren't in the pictures.'

'Don't be silly. I'm not family or a friend. I couldn't,' I say as breezily as I possibly can.

The gold door pings its arrival and slides open.

I get in.

He gets in.

The doors close.

We both turn around to face the door as the lift jerks into action. I burst into unexpected tears. I can't believe it. I haven't cried since I found old Ger, dead in her chair, watching *Judge Judy*, in Sir Patrick Dun's one Sunday morning.

'Oh, Lexie.' He covers his eyes with both hands but remains standing back against the mirror, leaning onto the gold bar behind him.

'I'm sorry,' I heave, holding up my hand. 'I have no idea why I'm so emotional!'

'Please, don't.' Still he makes no move.

'I'm sorry . . . I just don't want this to be over . . . already.' I ugly-cry some more.

The lift shudders. A ping sounds and the doors slowly open. We step out.

'Go! Please . . . you go down to dinner.'

'But.'

'No buts, Adam, seriously,' I sniff.

'I have to go back down, for Freya.'

Find your dignity, Lexie, I scream in my head. He's going back to them. I sniff, swallow my tears and gather myself.

'Of course you have to go. Listen, I get your sister doesn't trust me and thinks, ya know, I'm some mad, feisty Irishwoman, especially since she's meticulously planned every inch of her engagement party. Why would she want me in her photos?' I struggle to control my breathing. 'It's fine.'

He moves to me now and wipes my tears with the sleeve of his suit jacket.

'Please don't cry . . . I . . . this isn't . . .' he whispers, thrusts his hands deep in his trouser pockets, his voice cracking now. 'It's not over.'

'Okay.' My heart thumps.

It's not over.

Maybe my unexpected love story isn't over.

42
A Star Is Born

I'M STILL CATCHING MY BREATH as the lift doors close together. 'Do you hear that?'

'Hmm?' All I want now is for him to go back to the party, for me to get out of this bastard *little red dress* and go see Annemarie to tell her I'm so terribly sorry. Plus, I've so much to tell her that she will *have to* forgive me just to hear the goss. If I know Annemarie, and I do, she'll have a field day with all this drama, and maybe, just maybe, Adam will come back to the room tonight.

'What is that?' Adam moves a few steps across the plush carpet and stops dead, right outside room 128.

Annemarie's room.

I freeze, though I don't know why. He knows she's here.

There is definitely a weird sound coming from behind the door.

He drops his head, his brow furrowing in concentration.

'Is it . . . the TV?' I say.

'No.'

He steps closer to the door and leans his ear to it. The noise comes again and this time I drop the wine glass I'm still carrying. It bounces on the thick carpet.

It's Annemarie and she is howling.

'Fuck!' I bang on the door. 'Annemarie!'

'What?' He looks at me.

'It's my *Annemarie*! That's her room!' I bang harder. 'Are you all right in there? Open the door!'

'Lexie? Is that you? Oh, Lexie, help me!' she roars back.

'Open the door, Annemarie!'

'I can't . . . I can't move.' Her voice is jammed with pain.

'What? Why not?'

'Help me please, Lexie!' Jammed with intense pain.

'Quick, Adam! Please get someone to open the door!'

He turns and runs for the stairs.

'It's me, what is it? Please, you're scaring me – what's wrong? I'm so sorry.'

No answer.

'Please, Annemarie, don't let this be a . . . a joke?'

No answer.

I do that thing they do in the movies where I run at the door and shoulder it. I do it again. It doesn't budge obviously.

'Arrrgghhh!' Annemarie cries out.

'Please, what is it?' I call, trying to keep my voice steady, as my heart beats out of my chest.

'I don't know, I can't move . . . it's so sore . . . I'm . . . it's . . . Argggghhhhh! The baby!' she roars again. 'I'm losing my baby . . .'

'Move to the door!' I plead now, on my knees with not even a keyhole to look through as Adam trips at the top of the stairs and I see him stumble, but he keeps his balance and races up to me with a woman in hotel uniform not too far behind him.

'One two eight! It's room one two eight!' He points at me, though there's no need.

'Oh, hurry! Open the door!' I yell. 'Please!'

'Leeexxxiiiie!' Annemarie calls again.

'I'm here, love! We have a key, just hang on!'

'Is she epileptic? Medical history?' Adam asks me.

I shake my head.

'Drug user?'

'No!'

'Hello, this is housekeeping, are you okay?' She knocks.

Nothing now.

'She's not okay!' I shout at the poor woman.

'Just open the flipping door!' Adam shouts at her too.

'It's the law that I ask first.' She holds the white square card up against the door; it flickers red.

Oh, this cannot be happening! 'Annemarie!' I call again.

'I'm –' She sounds nearer to the door now.

'Here, let me try!' Adam takes it and holds it up; again it remains red.

'Arrrrrrrrrggggggggghhhhhhhhh!' Annemarie roars again.

'What's going on!' I look at the woman who ignores me and calmly tries the key card again. Adam puts his arm around me, pulls me close. This time green flashes up and I reef the gold handle down and push open the door, as gently as I can so I don't hit her.

She's on the floor.

'Annemarie.' I rush and drop to my knees beside her.

'Lexie.' Her face is wet with tears, her hair stuck to her face, pale as a ghost as she clutches her massive stomach.

'What's wrong?'

'W-When you left' – she creases over, grits her teeth – 'I got those pains again, t-that I had in the taxi . . . I thought they were just Braxton Hicks again.'

'Oh God.'

'I'm losing it . . . I'm losing my baby, aren't I?' She dry retches.

Adam throws his jacket across the room and gets down on his

knees beside me, looks into Annemarie's eyes, holds her steady with his gaze.

'Hi there, Annemarie, I'm Adam. I'm a nurse, okay. You're pregnant, yes? Can you tell me how far along?' He takes her wrist and places his finger over her veins, looks at his watch.

'Thirty-two weeks,' we say in unison.

He looks from me to Annemarie.

'Thirty-two weeks?' He continues to check his watch, releases her wrist. Puts his hand on her forehead.

'Have you been vomiting?'

She shakes her head.

'Will I call an ambulance?' the woman at the door asks.

'Immediately please,' Adam says as she wedges the door open with a doorstop.

He's so calm.

'Are you bleeding?' Adam asks, his hand now hovering over her stomach.

'I don't know . . . I can't look. I mean, I can't feel it gushing . . . like the last time. It's different. Arrrgghhh!' Again, Annemarie doubles over into the foetal position, clutching her stomach, her face whiter than I've ever seen.

'Annemarie, I'm going to have to look, okay?'

I see her flinch, terrified. 'Are you really a nurse?'

'I'm really a nurse,' he soothes her. 'Trust me, we're here now.'

She nods and I stroke the sweat-soaked hair from her face.

She's still in the dark navy hotel bathrobe so it's hard to see if there's any blood. The carpet is stained, but I see there's an upturned smoothie cup on the ground so I'm not sure if it's blood or spillage.

'Call Tom, Lexie, please.'

I nod.

'I will, I promise. Where's your phone?'

She turns her eyes to the desk where I see a green light, charging. I pull the connection out, look at her last calls and hit redial.

'Can you lie back for me, on these pillows here? That's great. You're going to be fine. That's it . . . well done, Annemarie.' Adam's calm voice steadies the room. With the phone pressed to my ear, I watch Adam open Annemarie's robe – she's just got green high-rise pants on and I look away. Then I look back as Tom answers and she wails again as Adam's hands feel around her belly.

'Oooohhhhh!'

'Hi, love! Missing me already?'

'Tom?'

'Yeah?'

'It's Lexie.'

'Huh?'

'Lexie Byrne.'

'What's going on? Why are you ringing me from Amo's phone?'

'It's Annemarie, she's – Oh, Tom,' I say, swallowing hard. 'The baby . . .'

'I'm going to examine you, Annemarie, is that okay?' Adam looks up to me and nods to the door. I take myself out to the corridor.

'I think she's losing the baby,' I whisper down the phone.

'Okay,' is what Tom says.

'Okay?' I say softly.

'I, eh . . . I don't know what else to say?' He sounds so shocked. I soften.

'Just get online and book a flight to Birmingham right now. Expedia it on the way to Dublin Airport – that way you'll also be available for stand-by seats to get over here. I'll text you the address of the hotel now, taxi rank outside arrivals. You'll need sterling.'

'I'm on the way,' he replies. 'Thank you, Lexie.'

'Okay.'

'Mind her for me, won't you, Lexie?' He tries to hold his voice steady.

'I promise, Tom,' I whisper as I hang up, then quickly google the Moritz, screengrab it, and WhatsApp it to him.

As I step back into the room, I see Adam out flat on the ground, down at Annemarie's nether regions. She's breathing like she has a straw perched between her teeth.

'There's no blood, Annemarie, but I think your waters have broken. We need to remove your pants, okay? I need to examine you.'

Jesus. Poor Annemarie.

'What can I do?' I ask him.

'Okay, that's okay, I'm sorry. Towels please, Lexie,' he orders me, and I run to the bathroom, grab one from beside the sink and hand it to him.

'Clean ones please, if you don't mind – as many as you can.' He hands it back to me, and I run back and grab the whole fluffy pile from the silver tiered rack above the bath and drop them beside him.

'Thank you,' he says. His hand is busy feeling around on her stomach for something.

Annemarie whimpers, her face gaunt with beads of sweat.

My heart breaks. 'I –'

He slides down her pants and covers her with a clean towel, then he moves his hands under the towel.

'Oh Jesus Christ, help me, what is going on? Lexie, can he really help me?' There's panic in her eyes.

'Shhhh. Of course he can!'

'I'm sorry about earlier, Lexie.'

'No! I'm so sorry, Annemarie.' The tears fall from my sore eyes again and I move behind her, unsure if I can physically touch her, really be there for her, I find Adam's eyes.

'That's it, Lexie, take her hands,' he says to me.

So I lean forward and take her cold hands in mine.

'I didn't mean it.' She gasps the words out.

'Neither did I,' I manage. 'Shhh now, it doesn't matter.'

'I knew I'd never keep my baby.' She pants the words through her pain.

'It's okay, you're going to be fine.' My voice trembles as I try and swallow down the tears. My head is saying she'll get pregnant again – I know she will.

'Okay . . . yeah . . . oh . . . oh . . . Okay. Now, Annemarie, listen to me closely.' Adam emerges from under the towel. 'Listen to me now. You are about to deliver your baby . . . and this baby is coming right now.'

'What?' I gasp.

'W-What?' she gasps.

'She can't be having a baby – she's only thirty-two weeks pregnant! It isn't time?'

Annemarie squeezes my hand so tight I think it's going to break.

'She can and she is. Baby's head is crowning. I have to scrub up. Just stay with her, keep her breathing steady, and do not let her push. The ambulance is on its way. Everything will be just fine, Annemarie.' He tugs at his tie for good reason this time and pulls it off over his head, rolling up his shirt sleeves as far as he can then disappears into the bathroom.

'W-What? What did he say?' She looks so alive that I'm frightened. Her green eyes are a shade I've never seen them before and almost popping out of their sockets, her skin so translucent I can nearly see through it.

'He says that the baby is coming now.'

'Arrrrrrgggggggghhhhhhhh!' She doubles over again. 'Oh Jesus . . . oh my God, is this a bad dream? Lexie!' She screams again. I squeeze her hands.

'He says . . . he says . . . he says he can see the baby's head.' I say the words catatonically like I'm a tragic voice in a Greek chorus.

My head spins. Flashbacks whizz behind my eyes: her weird cravings of the last week, her extreme tiredness, her erratic mood swings, the back ache, the stomach cramps today.

'Just look at me and listen to me now? Lexie, can you move back.' Adam is wiping his hands on a small white face cloth, smiling reassuringly all the time.

Extinguishing our worry as much as he can.

Annemarie puffs and pants as her whole body starts to shake.

'It's going to be fine. I'm an A&E nurse and I've delivered quite a few babies before, okay? But I need you to listen carefully to me, to tell me when you feel the next contraction. Lexie, get clean sheets or just grab the ones off the bed and a pillow, and can you find me some shoelaces?' He disposes of the facecloth in the small bin under the desk.

I push Annemarie's *Mother & Baby* magazine onto the floor, along with the heavy duvet, pull the sheet off and grab the pillow.

'Laces, laces?' I spin around.

'If no laces look for dental floss.'

Then I spot Annemarie's runners at the end of the bed and start to weave out the laces.

'Annemarie, I'm going to move you onto the sheet, all right? It's cleaner than this floor. We need to keep this as sterile as we can.' He's so in control it's amazing to watch. Ever so gently he moves my beloved friend onto the white sheet.

'How can this happen?' I say, thinking, Holy shit, this is all my fault. 'I mean she's on the floor in a hotel room?'

'Can you move for me, Annemarie? Can I get you onto all fours?' Adam tries to manoeuvre her gently, but she screams again.

'No! Please, no . . . don't!'

'That's no problem. We'll work this way, you and me.'

Adam places his hands behind her knees and bends her legs up, props the pillow behind her back.

'I'm sorry I said that about you not wanting babies, Lexie.' She cries out, grabs my shoulder and her fingers dig into my flesh. I let her; she can hold on to me as tight as she likes.

Before I can answer, Adam says gently: 'You've lost a pregnancy in the past?' I'd told him this. 'For this one, did you have your scans? Were they all okay?'

'Yes, yes I – I did.' Annemarie yells out in pain. 'It's coming again!'

'Okay, good, good. Let's do this. You can do this. Deep breaths, Annemarie.'

Adam manoeuvres her in some way, and she bellows like she's being stabbed.

'Great! That's great! Now when I say push, push down hard, from your bottom yeah? Like you are doing the biggest poo in the world. Keep your chin tucked in,' he tells her.

'*Now*!' he says.

'Arrrrrrrrrgggggggghhhhhh!' she cries, her hand deep into my shoulder. I think, stupidly, how glad I am that I'm not bony.

I hear muffled voices from outside and turn my eyes to see a crowd of people gathered at the open door.

'Door please, Lexie,' Adam instructs, so in control. I push out with my leg, kick the doorstop away and it slams in their faces.

'Stop! Stop! Great! Well done! You're doing so well. So well!'

'What's happening?' she begs, but he stays focused in nurse mode. 'I'm being split in two!'

'Can I do anything?' I say because I can't say nothing. No one answers. I don't expect them to.

'You have the laces? Or the dental floss?' he asks me, his eyes wide.

'I've laces.' I hold them up to him.

'Okay, on the off-chance baby's cord is around the neck, I need them immediately. Okay, Lexie?'

'Why?' I look at them in my hands, not exactly clean.

'I need them to tie to cut off the blood flow. Just keep them tight in your hands, okay?'

'Okay.' I grip them as instructed.

'And again,' he says to Annemarie.

'Arrrrrrgggggghhhhhhhhhhhhhhhhhhhhhhhh!' she grunts, more focused than I've ever seen a human face.

'Now just wait . . . deep breaths . . .' He is fully concentrated.

'Good-good-good, Annemarie.' I manage the words. 'Good girl.'

'Do you forgive me?' she pants; it's like she needs the distraction, so I go with her.

'Of course I do!'

'I only said that because . . .' She grinds her teeth, her face puce. 'Because I'm incredulous you don't feel this desperate craving that I do. Arrgghh!'

'Shhuusshh . . . that's enough now, Annemarie,' Adam says softly but with authority. 'I need you to focus for me.'

'Here it comes again!' She bears down and pushes with all her might.

'Well done! Keep that chin down.'

'It's coming. Oh God, help me pleassse! Arrgghhhhhaaaaahhh!' She howls, a purely primal sound.

And I watch as a small slick head emerges from under the towel that's covering some of Annemarie's modesty.

A perfect head, covered in damp reddish-brown hair.

'Good-good-good, Annemarie!' I croak again.

I feel like I might faint and literally kick myself to stop it happening.

'Well done, Annemarie! We have the head out. Shoulders next. Don't push again until I say, okay?' He's not sweating, there's not a trace of panic in his voice or eyes – he's just doing his job, I guess.

Will he be by my side as I give birth to our child?

Lexie Byrne! I bite the inside of my cheeks so hard I draw blood. *What the hell are you thinking?*

A whoosh of watery blood floods past the baby's head now, covering Adam. Unperturbed, he wipes himself with a fresh towel.

'Good-good-good, Annemarie!' Dumbstruck, I can only manage a whisper.

'And push push push push push push puuuuussssssssshhhhh! From your bottom, that's it. Keep pushing, keep pushing, keep pushing, keep pushing . . . oh well done!' he coaxes her, like a coach bringing a runner over the finish line, his voice in control all the time.

'Arrrrrghhhhhhhhh!'

Her face is turning purple, the veins in her neck the size of udon noodles. It will be a long time before I eat in Wagamama again, I think bizarrely, as I watch them pulsate, and then out comes a pair of tiny shoulders.

'Yes! That's baby's head and shoulders out now . . . that's the hardest part, Annemarie. You're doing so well. One more push. Come on – you've got this. Bear down, keep that chin right down into your neck, you're just there.' Adam smiles up at her poor purpler than purple face.

'Waaaaaaaaaaaaaaarrrrrrrrgggggggggghhhhhhhhhhhhhhhh!'

And, at last Annemarie pushes her baby out along with another gush of watery fluid. Tears are pouring down my face; my breath has gone all gulpy.

I look. The baby is covered in what I know is vernix caseosa, thanks to Annemarie's constant talk about childbirth. It's like it's been dipped in thick cream. Like it's dressed up as some kind of zombie baby for Halloween. The tiniest baby I have ever seen in my whole life, its beautifully shaped head no bigger than an apple.

'Oh Jesus!' Annemarie cries out, suddenly lucid. 'The experts don't tell you it hurts like that!' Her head falls back as Adam flips that baby upside down and rubs it hard on the back.

Nothing happens.

It's not moving.

'Good-good-good, Annemarie!' I stutter again, my eyes fixed on Adam.

'Stop saying that, Lexie!' she shouts. I know she's trying to listen.

No noise.

No cry.

I stare transfixed.

'What's happening? Is my baby okay?' Annemarie's face is distorted, wet with tears and sweat.

He flips it again.

The colour is changing.

The tiny baby is going from a pink to a purple.

'Please, is my baby all right? Tell me! Lexie! Adam!' she roars through a tumult of heavy sobs.

I'm still dumbstruck. It's like watching a car crash; I can do nothing but sit here on the floor and stare.

'Good-good-good, Annemarie.' I am barely audible.

'Hello there, baby ... welcome. Come on now, little one,' Adam murmurs to the tiny baby as he carefully strokes his hand down the little human's nose and mouth.

268

Nothing.

'Is my baby breathing?' Annemarie has steadied her voice – she sounds possessed.

Adam blows a few gentle breaths into the baby's mouth.

Nothing.

I watch him slap the bottom of the baby's feet.

Nothing.

'No . . . please God no.' Annemarie gulps for air. 'Don't do this to me.'

Adam puts his mouth over the baby's nose and mouth and sucks hard. Then he spits out some kind of yellow and black mucus.

'It's dead, isn't it? My baby is dead.' Annemarie sobs and sobs. I take her in my arms the best I can, terrified she's going to choke herself the tears are coming so fast and hard.

'Hey, come on . . .' I'm crouching by her side, trying to comfort her with my body.

The silence from the baby is deafening.

'Hey . . . hey . . .' I cradle her wet head, her legs covered in blood. I have no other words.

'That's it, that's it!' Adam's voice is lighter now. 'Come on now, precious one!'

Suddenly we hear it.

A cry.

The most joyous sound I've ever heard in my entire life. My heart swells fit to burst.

'Congratulations, Annemarie,' Adam says. 'You have a beautiful baby boy.'

The door bangs.

'Paramedics!' I hear a woman's strong voice as the door opens and a man and woman swing into the room.

'Wh-What?' Annemarie heaves as Adam gently places the tiny baby into her shaking arms.

269

'I've nothing to cut the cord with so be careful.' He turns to the paramedics.

'Oh, sweet Jesus, thank you.' Annemarie gasps for a breath.

The baby cries and cries, and I cry and Annemarie cries.

'Mother needs attention and delivery of the placenta; he's very prem,' Adam tells the paramedics. 'Thirty-two weeks. His airways were blocked. I think we get them in ASAP, yeah?' He's controlled but direct as we all stare down at this precious bundle.

'What the hell, Annemarie?' I say eventually as the female paramedic cuts the cord and takes the tiny bundle from Annemarie.

'My baby?' she cries, still shaking uncontrollably, still terrified. 'What are you doing?'

'We need to do a few checks on your little man, wrap him up warm before we take you both down to the hospital,' she informs her with a friendly grin. Annemarie nods, immediately reassured.

'What the hell, Lexie?' She looks back at me and I almost laugh at the state of her. I should take a photo, capture the moment, but she'd kill me.

'How did this happen?'

'How did this happen?'

'Stop saying everything I say.'

'You stop saying everything I say.'

'Adam, Adam,' she calls out to him. He's writing something on a long pink form that the paramedics have handed him.

He turns to her. 'Hi, well done.'

'I don't know what to say.'

'Well we'll never forget the first time we met, that's for sure!' He winks kindly at her.

'Thank you, thank you so much!'

'My pleasure and congratulations,' he says warmly. 'Happy to help!'

'I'm so sorry – I ruined this for Lexie.' Her cries come uncontrollably again.

'Would you shut up, you mad thing. You've just had a baby!' I lean over, kiss her face.

Adam laughs, the same warm sexy laugh I first heard that night in the Brazen Head

His white dress shirt is blood-stained, his face splattered – not quite as bad as Annemarie, but it's like he's been in a war zone too.

'Kinda – looks – like – you – are a painter and decorator now though?' She's still struggling to catch her breath but delivers me a watery smile.

'Right?' He looks down, unbuttons his shirt and pulls it off.

Now listen, I know Annemarie has just delivered a baby on the floor of a hotel room in the Cotswolds *but* like all close friends she gives me the secret look that says, *Holy shit, he is a ride all right.*

'*I* may well have been secretly jealous.' She turns to me, the colour edging back into her face. 'Now can someone get something resembling clothes *on* me please?'

We both start to giggle like a pair of naughty kids.

'Ouch, stop, it hurts,' she says. 'And I might well wet myself.'

43
Against All Odds

'D O YOU WANT TO HOLD HIM?' the paramedic asks as they fuss around Annemarie.

Do I?

'Yes. If you're sure.'

She smiles at me as she passes him over oh so carefully, wrapped in a soft silver sheet.

I'm a little scared to hold him but I take his tiny body into the crook of my arm, his dark eyes wide just looking at me. His perfect button nose, his creased skin, his pocket-sized hands and feet, and his smell.

I inhale him. This miracle. This new life. He coos at me.

'Hello. Hi there. Welcome. I'm your auntie Lexie.' Softly I rub my nose against his, and I'm not sure why exactly but my eyes start to water and heavy tears fall as I look down at Annemarie's newborn baby.

'Oh, Lexie, what's wrong?' Annemarie asks me tenderly.

I pinch my nose and hold my hand up to her.

'Okay, miss, we have to get you and baby to hospital now.' The ambulance man opens out a wheelchair and a wincing Annemarie is hoisted into it. I hand her the baby, who's started roaring at the top of his lungs.

I can't believe he's here. I can't take my eyes off him. So small, yet so perfect.

'Lexie, are you okay?'

'I'm fine honestly; I'm just emotional that's all.'

'I know. Can you pack some of my things up for me?' She winces again as they settle her and cover her in a red woollen blanket.

I nod and gather up her pyjamas, her brush, her magazine and locate her handbag on the desk.

'You are a living *Woman's Weekly* cover story,' I tell her. 'Sexy nurse delivered my baby on a hotel bedroom floor.'

'I know.'

'Will you try to feed? It will help you expel the placenta.'

I watch Annemarie slide down the new navy robe housekeeping dropped up to us as she offers her breast to her son. After a few attempts, he latches on and the crying stops, and the room falls silent. But a very different silence this time – a joyful, thankful silence.

'Oh my God, I haven't called Tom!' she says.

'I did.'

'But not to say he has a son – not to say he's a father?'

'No . . .' I smile.

The paramedic hands me a large yellow plastic bag and I drop all of Annemarie's stuff into it.

They wheel her out and I walk alongside her.

'Call Tom now, though – tell him we have a son. I have to go.' Annemarie doesn't look up at me. She's staring down at her suckling son, his two minute pink fists curled up tight.

'He's already on his way,' I assure her.

Relief floods her face. 'Oh, thank God.'

We arrive at the lift.

'Is he coming here now?'

'Yes, love. Honestly, Tom is on his way.'

The doors open and I go to get in.

'What are you doing?' she says.

'I'm coming with you.'

'No. No, you're not.'

'Huh?'

'I want you to go back to Adam – go back to the party.'

'Annemarie! Are you on drugs?'

'Soon I hope?' She winces again and looks at the paramedic, and she nods in agreement.

'That party's not for me,' I confess. 'It was a nightmare. His family hate me, his ex-wife cornered me in the toilets to tell me she still loves him and . . .' *Shut up, Lexie,* my numbskulls tell me. 'And you've just had a baby!' It hits me like a hammer over the head. It seems to hit us both.

'I did. I really did.'

We both look down at this miraculous bundle.

'I'm a mammy, Lexie.' She sniffs.

'You sure are, Annemarie.' I choke up.

'They really need to get them into the ambulance, Lexie.' Adam walks up towards the lift. 'Now. Go on – I'll follow you.'

'I'm coming with you. That's final,' I tell her.

'Period,' she says.

'Period.' I do a slash-like movement with my arm.

'I'm no longer afraid to say the word period – it's so liberating!' she says as the lift takes us down.

When it opens, the lobby of the Moritz is heaving. As is the case when an ambulance pulls up, sirens blaring, people gather to wait and see what's happening. Half of the engagement party are in the lobby as we push out past them from the open lift.

'Would ya look! That's her! There in the wheelchair!' Unmistakably Frank's accent.

'Shush!' someone shushes him.

'Is she dead?' Uncle Brian squints as I walk past them.

'I'll meet you at the hospital?' Adam must have sprinted down the stairs two at a time – he's sweating now, panting, and still half naked. I can't help but blush at the sight of him. Maybe I should give *ER* another shot – all this medical emergency lust suddenly makes sense.

'Coops! What the hell happened, mate?' Dominic shouts from the back of the crowd.

'What on earth, Adam!' Deb asks, standing right at the reception desk, holding a miniature bottle of Moët with a slim black straw. 'Are *you* all right?'

'Adam!' Martha shrieks. 'What's happened to you?'

A rush of *Adam* murmurs around the lobby as I turn to face him, even though the whole place is also staring at me.

'Thanks again, seriously. A million times over. You were incredible.'

'Lexie, I just –' He's still breathing hard, body bent, his hands resting on his knees as if the whole intensity of the past – hour? I literally have no clue – has just caught up with him.

'You really don't have to,' I start, acutely aware of the massed ranks of the Coopers' eyes on me.

'Lexie's friend delivered a baby, early,' he informs them all over my shoulder. 'I'm fine.'

'All in a day's work, eh? I've delivered a fair few premature calves meself. Fair play, boyo.' Again, I recognise Frank's voice as he turns to head back into the bar.

At which moment I take my eyes off Adam for a second and see myself reflected in the wall mirror in front of me.

Oh, sweet Jesus no.

My dress is stained and covered in sweat patches, my hair sticking up, mascara running into the smudged eyeliner that's halfway down my cheeks, my face blotched, roaring red. It wasn't me who just had the bloody baby – why do *I* look so bad?

'I just want to.' He walks towards me, ignoring his approaching sister.

Annemarie is almost out the door to the open doors of the waiting ambulance.

'Oh my goodness, is everyone okay?' Deb moves through the crowd and stops directly in front of me.

'Yes, thank you, bit of a shock, but they're both fine. Adam was amazing,' I tell her.

'That's wonderful. I – well my dinner is being served, so if you're sure . . .' She trails off looking directly at Adam now.

It suddenly occurs to me that the miracle of birth is irrelevant here. This woman is controlling all right. And nothing else matters to her other than that I'm totally ruining her engagement party.

'Please let me take you to the hospital?' he offers.

'Adam, really,' Deb interjects. 'I'm not quite sure what exactly happened upstairs, but honestly, you can't leave.'

'In a cab, please – I want to. I –'

I see he's almost buckling under the full force of all these eyes on him, but however much of a bloodied, exhausted mess he is I can't take him away from them.

'It's okay, Adam, honestly, there really is no need. I'll go with Annemarie, but thanks. Please go and enjoy the evening. Have a wash first, eh? But your sister is right – the food is about to be served.' Never have I wanted to leave a party so desperately.

'She should definitely just go with her friend!' Martha declares, pushing herself through to the front of the crowd. 'Adam, you need to make yourself presentable, darling. You simply can't go to your place of work like that. You know your friend will be in safe hands with our team at Cotswolds.' She puts her hand on his bare shoulder.

'Absolutely,' I say.

'Guys, seriously, I get that someone's just had a baby, but let's keep this show on the road. The meal is sitting, the roast beef is tender, but it's all going cold,' Deb repeats, and I can see that she's desperate not to let the night slip away from her.

'Adam, please, this isn't your drama,' Martha chimes in. 'Our daughter – who hasn't seen her father all day – is seated and starving, waiting for you to join her.'

She slaps down her trump card. Reveals her winner's hand.

'You'll come back? Here? To me? To the hotel after?' he asks quietly as the crowd disperses.

'No, I doubt it; Annemarie and her baby are my priority now,' I answer honestly as I turn my back and spin through the revolving door, finally leaving the Moritz.

44

The Age of Innocence

I'd been waiting for him but I'm still more than surprised to see him standing in the hospital corridor as I carry two paper cups of lukewarm tea from the vending machine. You know the way it is? Seeing someone in the flesh where they aren't supposed to be is weird. You see them differently, in another light, like right now. His figure is somewhat surprisingly comforting.

'Tom!'

'Lexie!' He drops his brown backpack and stands there like a little boy lost in his hoody, pale skinny jeans, angular glasses and beanie hat, holding an 'It's a Boy' balloon.

It's as if I'm seeing him for the very first time. I suddenly realise he's actually very handsome in a cute, quirky kinda way.

'God am I pleased to see you! The only reason I made that flight was because you called when you did – by the skin of my teeth too! I bought this balloon in the hospital shop just as it was closing. Where is she?'

'They.'

'They,' he corrects himself, picking his bag up off the floor.

'This way.' I lead him down to the special care unit where Annemarie sits in a high-backed hospital chair beside her son's incubator.

*

There was a lot of rushing when we arrived at the hospital. Things hadn't been as uncomplicated as Adam wanted Annemarie to believe. Bless him, he'd kept the drama to an absolute minimum. Annemarie had doubled over again in the ambulance where they'd had to deliver her placenta and the baby, now off the breast, screamed the whole way. I'd sat, terrified, in the ambulance, staring out the back doors at the blue and red spinning lights.

'Hello there, new mum! Congratulations! Let's get a look, shall we? All right, he looks pretty prem, let's get you guys up onto the ward,' was the first thing the nurse said as we arrived at A&E. They weighed him – only four pounds, three ounces, measuring at 16.9 inches long – and rushed him straight up to the special care unit. It really was like being in an episode of *ER*.

'We need to attend to Annemarie medically – she might need some stitches and maybe a catheter inserted, so perhaps you'd like to wait in the café on the third floor. Have you the price of a cup of tea?' the kind nurse, Adam's colleague, asked.

'Yes.' I'd held my clutch bag up and she'd smiled again, then they'd wheeled Annemarie towards a blue plastic door that flapped and flapped as she passed through and eventually shut in my face and, as I stood there all alone, I'd bawled my eyes out.

*

'Tom! Oh, Tom!' Annemarie calls as she sees him now. He runs to her and holds her tight, her pale purple hospital gown coming loose at the back.

279

I rest the cups on the window ledge and tie it up for her.

'Is he . . .?' he asks, his eyes wide as he takes his first look at his tiny, wriggling son, who is attached to various tubes in his incubator, a dinky little woolly hat on his head.

'He's fine, Tom, they've checked him over thoroughly. A little over four pounds, his head circumference is eleven inches, but they say he's all good. Our little warrior. Still awaiting some results from standard tests, and they have to keep him here a few weeks obviously, so . . .' Annemarie starts to gently weep again.

'Don't worry, Amo, shush now. He's our boy; all will be fine.'

'I can't believe he's here, Tom; I can't believe he's finally ours. I'm the luckiest woman in the world! But . . . you missed the birth. I'm so sorry I wasn't at home with you.' She sobs heavily now.

'Don't be silly. Nothing else matters, only that you're safe and so is our baby. The rest isn't important. I thought you didn't look right, didn't I say? And every night those back aches I tried to massage, but I never dreamed of this. God works in mysterious ways,' Tom soothes softly. 'Are you sure *you're* all right?' He turns to her, strokes her face.

'Oh, Tom, I'm fine. It was terrifying, and intensely painful, I won't lie, but now I'm worried about everything else – work . . . the mortgage . . . where will we stay here? They don't know how long we'll be in for,' she sniffles.

'I'm sure the hospital can help us with everything.' He rubs her hands in his as if to warm them. 'And we'll sleep on the floor here if we have to. Don't worry, Amo, promise? Oh, my darling, I'm so proud of you. You wanted to stay home with our baby anyway – that's what we'd agreed, right? I promised you I'd make that happen. *If* you were. *When* we were. Well now we *are* . . . we are parents, Annemarie Rafter – we did it!' Tom stands over his son now, staring in pure amazement and love. 'This boy here is why I started the sailing lessons business.' Tom bends, kisses her sweetly on the head.

'But you still need to get back to the shop?'

'No, Donnacha Cantwell's happy to hold the fort while we focus on our little man. When Lexie called to say I was a dad, I'd just landed, I had to ask her to repeat herself several times, didn't I, Lexie?'

I nod.

'I immediately called our folks, then Donnacha, and he was genuinely thrilled for us – said to take all the time in the world.'

'But not everyone's as kind as him.' She looks at me steadily now. 'Will June sack me if I can't go back?'

'She can't.' I'm not so sure; I really wouldn't put anything past her, especially now August is on the payroll. 'But I'll fly home first thing, so if you give me your house keys, I'll pack stuff for you, send it over, and I'll go see June – she's in Saturdays after lunch. I'll fix up the rota. I'll do double shifts to cover you if I have to.' I'm rambling now, so when my phone beeps I pathetically grab for it, hoping it's Adam.

'No. You don't have to do that,' Annemarie says. 'You're here until Sunday.'

I'm wrong.

'It's Jackie.' I turn the phone to Annemarie to show her Jackie riding on a camel in the desert with the entirely predictable caption: *First decent hump since I got here.*

We can't help it. We both laugh. I tuck it away.

'I'll pop into Teeny-Tiny Hands and pick up some Babygros for him. I'm sure Samantha will give me a good discount if I smile nicely. Eh, is your little bundle of joy getting a name by the way? Everyone will be asking me!'

'Soon,' she says.

'We have some picked out, don't we, Amo?' Tom cannot take his eyes off his newborn son; the man is melting with pure love.

'What about Adam?'

'As a name?' I say, trying not to be taken aback.

'No! As in the man who seems to make you happier than I've ever seen you before in the entire decade and more I've known you!'

'I – I'll talk to him.' I nod a few too many times.

'You must. He was amazing!' She turns to Tom, wincing a little. 'Our baby wouldn't be here without Adam.' Then, to me, her eyes steely: 'And tell June I know my rights – she can't sack me for having a baby! But, knowing her, she'll try to issue me with a second warning to get rid of me that way.'

'Never mind her now,' Tom soothes. 'We don't care what she does.'

'But I have to care, Tom. All these anxieties are with me. Can I really afford to give up work? What about your trips away and pints at weekends?'

A sense of guilt starts in my toes. Tom looks at me; I look at the ground.

'I've researched this for some time now, Amo – we'll be fine.' He pulls his hat off; his hair is a mess. I've never seen Tom not all coiffed and I like it. 'I don't care about cricket and the lads; all I care about is you and our son. This is our new life, the three of us.'

'Oh, Tom.' Annemarie gives him a look of total adoration. 'Okay, you're right. And so are you, Lexie – I've no idea how I'm going to feel about work in a few months' time. I'll make my decision then.' She winces again and I nod.

'There's no rush,' I say softly.

'Exactly. Whatever you want to do, darling,' Tom reassures her.

'Lexie's been incredible, Tom. I don't know what I'd have

done without her, and Adam her . . . her . . . her nurse friend who delivered our baby was our saviour. Literally. I don't know what would have happened without him.'

And that's when it hits me.

She is so right. I don't know Adam. He's *no one* to me. Maybe I do need a *someone* after all.

Maybe I need a Tom. A safe, steady bet.

Shut up.

Shut up.

Shut up.

My inner Lexie is screaming at me. *That's not who you are.*

This moment is overpowering: a new baby, a loved-up couple who have triumphed against the odds. A picture-perfect tableau. I'm smart enough to know it's only picture perfect now. Next comes sleepless nights, and the life journey of parental worry begins – and yes, I'm aware that the joy of having a baby will be way more powerful than any of the negatives I can ever imagine, but I can't paint myself into this lonely painting in my head. I've done the work on myself.

I've read the books.

I've been positivity-ified.

I have the tools for this situation. I recheck myself. I only need me. I will not settle. The mantras are all on hand:

Love yourself, Lexie Byrne!

Believe in yourself, Lexie Byrne!

You are all you need, Lexie Byrne!

45
Braveheart

TOM KISSES ANNEMARIE ON THE LIPS and holds her head in close to his body, his fingers massaging the back of it.

Then he pulls away to take me into a bear hug. 'Listen, thanks again, Lexie – I owe you one.'

When he releases me, he puts his index finger in through the small hole in the incubator, flutters it into his son's tiny hand.

'No worries, Tom,' I reply, my voice quiet.

'Tom, sorry, I never took my morphine tablet yet. Could you go get me a glass of water? There's a cooler by the nurses' station outside,' Annemarie says.

'Lexie?' he offers.

'No, I'm fine for morphine thanks; I've a wrap of coke in my bag.' I wink at him and, in fairness, he laughs.

When he's gone, she shifts in the chair to face me.

'I want to say something to you.' She flinches as she tries to adjust her position on the rubber ring set in the chair. 'I didn't settle for Tom. I knew exactly what I was looking for. He might not provide the electricity of Adam, but I don't want that. I adore him, so thank you for getting him here – it means so much.'

'I'm such a cow.' I just realise.

How dare I question her choices?

'You're not at all! I am! Let me admit I was terrified when you told me about Adam. I could tell this was something special . . . and you see, his living here put the fear of God into me that I'd lose you! I wasn't thinking of your happiness; I was thinking of mine! I've been so selfish, so preoccupied with my pregnancy.' She chokes up and I'm immediately choked up too. 'I'm so sorry.'

'I'm sorry too.'

'I want to say something before Tom comes back. You mean everything to me, Lexie. I don't know what I'd do if I didn't have you . . . Tom is the love of my life, and my new baby too now, but you are the light of my life.' She nods to the door just as Tom walks back in, water in hand in a clear plastic cup.

A lump the size of a coconut sits in my throat. I can't speak.

'You, Lexie Byrne, you need something different to me. You *need* that drama and passion and excitement, and I don't ever want you to settle for anything less. You deserve that life, so go get it! Do you hear me?' Her clear green eyes are brimful of tears.

I swallow the lump down.

'Yeah.' I have to look away from her. 'Yeah, I hear you.' I make circles shapes on the hospital floor with the toe of my boot.

'We're all different. If you never want to get married or have babies or any of those things, that's totally fine. *Obvs.* I'm blessed to have you.'

She takes my hand, looks up at me. I can see that she's just slightly delirious with happiness.

'I love you, Lexie,' she says.

'I love you too, Annemarie.'

'Everything all right?' Tom gives us an odd look.

'Fine,' I say, composing myself, making my eyes wide. 'I'm hoping I get the gig?'

'The gig?' Tom says.

'The gig is yours!' Annemarie nods in agreement.

'What gig?' Tom asks again.

'My godmother gig.' I nudge him with my elbow. 'I will be an epic godmother – birthday cards and play dough, steady hand on the head at confirmation, all that stuff.'

'Oh right,' Tom says. Then with a killer grin: 'The job's yours.'

'And congratulations, you two. I'm so happy for you both, I truly am. He's a miracle.'

We all stare in at his sleeping face. Perfect. Like a tightly curled up ball of beauty. Annemarie gratefully gulps down her pain relief, and Tom turns to me.

'You might come for Sunday dinner when we get him home and settled? Maybe you and me can combine our culinary skills? Leave Annemarie a day off? Help me pick a godfather from one of the lads?' He pushes his glasses up his nose.

'I'd like that,' I say, and that's when I know it's time for me to take my leave.

I take up my clutch and fold it under my arm. I've no place here anymore as their baby boy wakes with a cry, and the nurse arrives on soft white plimsolls. This is Annemarie's family, and as I slip out of the room she calls after me: 'Lexie!'

I turn back, stand in the almost darkness of the doorway.

'Yeah?'

'You know what you have to do.'

'Do I?'

'Oh, come on. You know the scene? The soundtrack is probably playing in your head right now.' Annemarie smiles brightly.

'Huh?'

'If *I'm* imagining it, I know you must be!' She laughs out loud now, a strange sound in that room. The first authentic laugh I've heard from her in so long. Her face shines and her freckles dance under the blue lights of the special care unit.

I lean against the doorframe.

I think.

I stand up straight.

I do know it. Of course I know it. She watches me, willing me on. I take a slow, deep breath in. *'But most of all I'm scared of walking out of this room and never feeling the rest of my whole life, the way I feel when I'm with you . . .'* I whisper to her dramatically.

'There you go. Now go get him,' she says as I laugh, spin on my heels and walk through the special care unit and down the long hospital corridor with 'Cry to Me' scratching out on that record player in my head.

46
Reversal of Fortune

THERE IS SOMETHING ABOUT BEING in a hospital in the still of
night that makes you grateful for everything you have; it's a
humbling place to be. An involuntary shiver hits me even though
it must be twenty-five degrees. Annemarie is right. I have to fight
for him. I just need to figure out the right moves. The right shots
to pick out. There are some strong opponents lined up against
me in this fight.

'Goodnight,' I say easily to a patient taking a late-night stroll
with his drip.

'Night,' he replies, his rubber-soled slippers squeaking on the
corridor floor.

Still a sorry, sweaty, crumpled sight in my party dress, I take
the stairs as fast as I can in the too-tight fabric to ground floor,
and just as I approach the exit, I see a row of cabs lined up. For
some reason I turn and take one last look back at Adam's place
of work, think of my friend and her family safe in its maze of
rooms. I have a feeling that my life is about to change.

*

Even though it's the early hours of the morning, the Moritz is still lit up like a Christmas tree. I pay the driver, run my hand along the side of Adam's parked car and step in through the revolving doors. Music and laughter spill from both the Chill Out bar and the function room. I head straight for the lift and up to our room. Out of politeness I knock, but then I open my clutch, hold my key card to the door. It stays red. My heart starts to race – he's probably fast asleep; it's been a long day – then I hold it up again. Green flashes and I push the heavy door open.

It's cool and dark inside. I can hardly see and lean against the wall to listen. It sounds deathly quiet.

'Adam?' I whisper.

No reply.

'Adam, are you awake?'

Nothing.

'Adam, it's me, Lexie?'

I dip the key card into the slot on the wall and the lights come blazing on. I see the vacant bed. It doesn't look like he's been back here at all. Not even to find a clean shirt? My make-up bag is still where I left it on the bed after my fight with Annemarie, my case spilling open on the floor. I could call him but it's so late. What if he just went home and is sound asleep?

Or what if the party is still in full swing and he's downstairs? Or – my paranoid brain probes – what if he's with her? Martha.

'Go back down.' The words leave my mouth without my brain processing them.

'You can't.'

'You can.'

'You can't.'

'You have to.'

I step into the bathroom, lean on the marble sink counter and stare at my reflection in the mirror. It feels suddenly airless, so

289

I heave at the red dress, reef it up over my head – nearly taking my ears with it – and sigh with the greatest relief as I toss it to the floor. I sit on the cold toilet seat as my thoughts come fast, flurrying, mulling my options.

He must be still here. I have to go down. He's the entire reason I'm here, in the Cotswolds. How can I hide away up here if he's downstairs?

I have to see him.

I need to see him.

I long to see him.

But how will I emerge on the other side of this situation?

The bathroom feels still, silent, but I can pick out the beat of the bass as music comes up through the hotel. I can't get into bed – I'm far too awake.

I'm going to go back down.

I stand up and take a long deep breath.

I stare at my reflection again in the mirror, the overhead lighting doing strange things to my features. In this split moment I fully recognise who I am.

I am me, Lexie Byrne.

I can only ever be me.

Whatever is coming back at me is the thing I've been scared of.

Myself. My worth when it came to a true relationship. My desperate desire to wait for true love. But this *is* me. The almost forty-year-old Lexie Byrne. And in this strange hotel, with people I don't know, I've tested who I think am and I am more than good enough. I was afraid that simply being me wasn't enough to keep a guy like Adam, but in its emerging outline I'm not afraid at all anymore. I don't have to squint to see it.

I don't *need* him. But I *want* him.

I embrace the difference.

The realisation calms me, and I strut out to the bedroom.

Kneeling by my case, I drag out my leaving outfit, pull it on. Turned-up jeans, long-sleeved grey cotton top with a V-neck, invisible socks and white runners. Back in the bathroom, I brush out my tangled ponytail, pull my hair back into a sleek bun, clean off my face with warm water on cotton pads and brush my teeth.

'Well,' I say with a grin to my cleansed, brightened reflection, 'nobody puts Lexie in the corner, right?'

47
Back to the Future

I EMERGE FROM THE LIFT WITH MORE than a spring in my step. Could be the sheer comfort of my runners after the suffocating dress and high wedges, I'm not sure. I see the flickering pattern on the carpet from the fairy lights through the open doors of the function room as I approach.

'Just be yourself,' I whisper.

As I reach the doors, my eye is drawn to the packed dance floor.

And there he is.

Adam.

And there she is.

Martha.

Adam and Martha holding hands.

Adam and Martha dancing close. Intimate.

I'm not sure if I'm prepped for this.

She whispers something into his ear, and although they're in a circle of people, all dancing and holding hands, my heart plunges. Sliding in, I stand at the back bar, observing for a moment. There isn't an inch of space on the dance floor with everyone in the circle. As I squint, I see oh so unsurprisingly that Deb and Frank have some pre-prepared dance routine that they're performing in the centre of the circle.

'Go on, Lexie,' I say out loud as I push myself into action and walk slowly in Adam's direction. He notices me first. He's not quite sure if it's me or not; he looks away and then does a double take, looks back then drops Martha's hand like a hot potato. My heart jumps as his face lights up and he turns to me. More handsome than ever, now in a black T-shirt and jeans.

He calls my name. 'Lexie!'

'Hey.' I raise a hand, stand in front of them.

'Oh. Oh hi.' Martha reaches for his hand but misses it as he steps further away from her.

'Come.' He points to a table at the back.

I follow him.

Martha follows me.

'I didn't think you were coming back,' he starts as we reach a round table scattered with party detritus. I notice Freya's cat ears abandoned in the middle. He's wringing his hands and stumbling over his words ever so slightly.

'Yeah, well, my stuff is here,' I tell him. 'Plus I wanted to talk to you?' I treat Martha to my brightest smile. She doesn't smile back. She looks positively fuming.

We sit.

She sits beside us, tucks her legs up beneath her like a deranged Little Mermaid.

'Can we have a moment please, Martha?' he asks her, fidgeting with the silver feather on his tight chain.

'Go ahead. I needed to sit down anyway. Don't mind me, Leddy . . . sorry, Lexie!' Smoke's still coming out her ears, but she tries hard to smile.

With a wave, he stands and takes my hand, pulls me up.

'But . . . the fireworks are being set off outside any minute now.'

He doesn't answer her, and we walk away. In the busy lobby, a free seat sits under the bay window and we head for it.

'Um . . .' His eyes are a little bloodshot.

'How are you doing?' I say because it seems the right thing to ask.

'Well that was all a bit mental.' He's not rat-arsed by any means – he's dog-tired, a little punch-drunk maybe. 'If I may be so bold as to say mental?'

'You may.' I sit, crossing my legs as I spy Martha now standing beside the lift, staring over at us. She's barefoot, I just notice.

'How long have you been here, Lexie?' I immediately wonder if I might have seen something he doesn't want me to have seen.

'Five minutes.'

'I honestly didn't expect you to come back. But I'm so glad you did. Jesus, you've no idea how glad I am.' He sits beside me. 'You look beautiful.' Then, as if worried he's overstepped the mark: 'Perhaps that dress was about ready for the bin after – after . . .'

'Annemarie and the baby are doing well,' I tell him awkwardly.

'Oh, I know . . . I checked in a few times with neonatal and the gang up there. Sounds like Annemarie's doing great, just a few little repairs, and the baby's early all right, but they'll be fine. He's a strong little Irish lad. I won't call him Conor McGregor . . .'

'Oh, please don't!'

He's struggling to make the easy eye contact we had before, I notice.

'They have test results to come back still.' I'm keeping up the chat about my friend and her baby, but I'm scarcely able to believe he's beside me again and that I feel the exact same way about him.

Worse.

I feel more attracted to him than ever and I would never have thought that was humanly possible.

'All routine I assure you.' He pushes his dark hair out of his eyes with both hands. 'You must be famished, Lexie?'

We are talking about everything but.

'Not really.'

'I – I'm not sure what to do here?' He breaks the small-talk ice.

'You don't have to do anything else, Adam. You saved Annemarie and her precious baby – I'm in total awe.' I lick my lips, jumpy with nerves, aware that how I play this situation can make or break everything for me.

'All part of the service, Lexie Byrne.' He bows and nearly falls off the seat.

I laugh.

He laughs.

'I'm just shattered . . . and emotionally drained. I could do with a glass of water.'

He rests his hand on my thigh, suddenly more relaxed with me. 'I followed you to the hospital by the way, did you know that?'

'No? You did? How?'

'A member of staff gave me a lift. Annemarie was in theatre and I couldn't see you, so I left. I didn't feel it was my place to be around anymore. The hotel knows, obviously – they tidied the rest of her things up and will look after them. The manager wants to treat Annemarie – and Tom and the new baby – to a luxury long weekend whenever she's able to return.'

'You couldn't make this shit up, right?' I brush down my fringe with the palm of my free hand, feel the roundness of my tight bun.

'That's for sure,' he says, his eyes meeting mine now.

'I'm glad it didn't ruin your sister's party – at least not too much?' I only half care, I have to be honest.

He shrugs.

I tie the lace on my runner even though it's in no danger of coming undone.

'They all hated me, Adam.'

That didn't take me long.

I shut my eyes, but we are inches apart. I can smell the same mint shower gel from earlier off his body. It's hard to believe the life-changing event that has happened in between those two hot showers. It's hard to believe Annemarie is a mammy at long last.

'They don't.' He bows his head as I open my eyes. 'Mum and Dad loved you. That's the way the others go on – it's always chaotic. I ignore it most of the time. It's such a small place – everyone has their nose in someone else's ass.'

'Nasty.' I crinkle my own nose.

'The only person I cared about liking you was Freya, and she was too busy playing Heads-Up with my dad, eating chicken goujons and hot fudge brownies to notice a damn thing.'

I can't break my pinkie promise, but I feel like we did click nicely with each other when we talked.

'But your ex-wife wants you back,' I blurt as the cold air from the revolving door blows in with people starting to leave for home.

He drapes his strong arm around my shoulders, pulls me close. 'It's never going to happen. I can't believe she cornered you like that. We are divorced for good reason, and honestly it's not just because of the affair.'

'I can't believe you cheated on her.' I shrug. 'It is a shit thing to do.'

'I know. I'm sorry, and I'm sorry that Dermot cheated on you. I don't want to sound like a hypocrite. But I would never cheat on you, Lexie – you know that, don't you? I'm not that guy.' He looks at me with his big brown eyes and my heart turns somersaults, scoring that perfect ten from the judges once again.

'She's still staring at us from by the reception desk,' I say through gritted teeth.

'Let her stare. She'll give up one day. If we didn't have Freya, I'd be far less polite, but I can't say nasty things to my daughter's mother. Freya is my priority.'

I'm so glad he's just said that his daughter is his priority. Exactly as it should be – makes him the man I hope he is.

'As she should be.'

'And always will be.' It's a loaded answer and he awaits my reaction.

'Good for you, Adam.'

We let that settle for a moment, both knowing where we stand now.

'At least you didn't have a boring night,' he tries.

'Ahhh, I wouldn't say that.'

He laughs as I lean my head on his taut shoulder. He tightens his arm around me. I feel his bicep against my head. I've already forgotten what it's like to be wrapped in his arms, to feel the vibration of his laughter in his chest. *Bull by the horns Lexie*, I say in my head. Be honest. Tell him what you want.

My reverie is interrupted by the sound of my own name.

'Lexie?' Martha moves in and looks at me.

'Yes?' I say as she holds her teeny-tiny strappy heels in her teeny-tiny hands, but just like that I'm no longer even the teeniest-tiniest bit threatened.

'I think Adam's had a lot to drink.' Her mouth is slightly pinched. 'I should drive him home.'

'Should you?' I ask her.

'Yeah . . . I only have one glass of champagne nowadays. I don't really drink.'

'Course you don't,' I say.

Then I feel a shift. It happens all of a sudden.

297

My mouth moves before my brain tells it to. 'Actually, Martha . . .'

I take my self-respect into my own hands. Actually, now that I look down at them, pretty nice hands – hands that serve me well, thank you very much!

'Adam is coming up to bed with me. I leave tomorrow. After that . . . who knows?'

'You don't leave tomorrow; you leave Sunday!' He turns in to me.

'No, I have to go tomorrow – I need to sort out stuff for Annemarie and Tom and the baby and for Máiréad Farrell, a woman who needs me.'

'But you'll be back?' The hope in his voice raises his tone more than a few octaves.

'No, I'll just express post the baby stuff back. Like I said, I have things I need to do . . . not to mention Jimmy.'

'Jimmy?' Martha's on it like a flash.

Nice try. 'My pot plant,' I say and stand up.

'Adam, I really think you need to get home and sleep. Perhaps you can stop by on your way to the airport to say goodbye? The Campbells need to go home now – they've been in our house since eleven.' She tries to take him by the elbow; he fudges her off carefully.

'Stop this, Martha, please – you have to stop,' he tells her quietly but sternly. 'I make my own decisions.'

'Life can be cruel, Martha; it doesn't always give second chances.' My tone is light but layered with hidden meaning and I think, well, she deserves that. Mother of his child or not, she's giving me a pain in the hole.

'Adam, we should discuss this in private.' She glares at him.

'Goodnight, Martha. Safe home.' He stands up now. 'Though she's right, I am a little drunk . . . it's just that I like you,

Lexie . . . *so* much.' He groans, drops his head into his hands.

'Adam! Y-You really should go back to Rosehill Cottage, but fine . . . up to you,' she snaps. 'Good luck with your *decisions*.'

I'd say her head is spinning on Adam's words as she bends and slips on her shoes, and while my brain searches for a smart reply, she simply says, 'Safe flight back to Ireland.'

And off she goes.

We stand side by side.

'You said you needed water.'

'I do.'

'Follow me, Nurse Cooper.'

He does.

In the Chill Out bar, the eighties hits still ring loud, a few stragglers still partying the night away. A booth with a messy table is free and once again we slide in as Spandau Ballet find it hard to write the next line.

48
Dirty Dancing

GRACIE LOOKS SHATTERED. Her apron stained, her ribbons loose.

'Two pints of tap water please, with ice,' Adam says.

'Long shift?' I sympathise, and she nods and rubs her eyes.

'These locals never want to go home! I was warned; I should've taken the job in Cerney House Gardens serving the cream teas. Thanks for the really generous tip earlier by the way.'

'My pleasure, Gracie,' I tell her as she leaves.

Adam sits, slightly slumped, staring straight at me.

But it's with *those* eyes.

Oh, come on, you know the ones.

Those eyes we've all seen women get from their men, from partners, from husbands, the ones we've witnessed from across the room and all thought wow, he really loves her. The he-only-has-eyes-for-her truth.

Well Adam's looking at me in that way. I can't tell you how reassuring it is to know, to really feel, that he gets me. It's like being shot through the heart with cupid's arrow itself. The authenticity of us is one hundred per cent real. Empowered is the only word to describe how amazing I feel.

'I fell hard . . .' he starts.

'As did I.'

'Now it's late, and you said I could ask the burning question later, remember? What is it Lexie Byrne is looking for?' he blurts out.

I smile. 'So I did.'

What am I looking for? I know the answer.

True love.

A good man, one who I'm madly attracted to. Someone to go to dinner with, to take long weekend breaks with, to share my life – laughter, Garfield, messy tears, the good and the bad days, everything – with.

The One.

'I didn't want to ever just settle again. I found out I'm actually fine on my own. Better than fine, I'm happy. So I held out for *it*. Refused to settle. Because I knew exactly what I was looking for.'

'And that is?' he urges.

Go on, Lexie. Be honest.

'You.'

'Really?' The relief in his voice is evident.

He leans his elbows on the damp table, rests his chin in his cupped hands, gazes adoringly at me. 'I can't tell you how relieved I am to hear you say that. I know I made a mammoth mistake. I should never have cheated – it's inexcusable; it's not who I am. But we're here now and I think we were meant for one another. I just . . . feel it.'

Melting.

'I do too, but . . .'

'Don't but me, Lexie Byrne, please no *but*!' He leans back, brings both hands up and draws them down his face.

'*But* your life is complicated, Adam. I don't want to add to your list. I want to ease it, so here's what I'm proposing . . .'

'You're proposing? I do!' He lifts my left hand and kisses my ring finger. I giggle.

'I think we should just meet up whenever we can – no pressure, no expectations. Let this all evolve naturally.'

There I've said it.

'W-What? Whenever we can? That's *all* you want?' There's a dumbfounded look on his face.

Our pints of water arrive.

'That's all I want *right now*. That's not all I want forever! But you have so much going on, so many responsibilities. I don't want to be another responsibility; I want to be a possibility. I want to be your future.'

'I . . . I . . . oh.' Then he stops abruptly. I can see his mind whirring and he seems to digest what I've said. He twists the feather around his neck, downs his water in one.

'Does that make sense?' I urge.

'If it means we get to keep seeing one another, I'll do whatever you want! No rush.'

'No rush.' I exhale. I'm happy with my honesty.

'No labels,' he says.

'No labels,' I agree.

'No rules?'

'Well . . . some rules.' I tilt my head at him, and he laughs, nods in understanding and reaches for my hands across the table. They are no longer clammy, thank the lord. I hold his tight.

He doesn't need to spell it out. I can see it. He really is in love with me. It's true. Love at first sight is an actual thing.

Now would be a perfect time for Deb and Frank to set off their fireworks.

I take a look around the bar. Toy Town was an unfair comparison, and I take it back. I was overwhelmed and hassled. But Adam and Freya's home is a small, close-knit village, and I can hazard a guess at what it will take to be accepted here, which is something I need time to prepare myself for. But one day, some day, I can see myself settled here in this beautiful part of the world.

'I feel the same. And I'm totally enamoured with where you live, but I'm realistic. I'm not moving over any time soon and you're not moving to Dublin with an eleven-year-old daughter, who by the way if I haven't said yet, is a *total* dote.' I clutch my chest and he beams.

'Isn't she?'

'I can't wait to get to know her properly.'

'Can I ask you something?'

'Anything?'

'What about kids?'

I was waiting. Hoping, trusting he was the type of man who would ask me that question. Which is why I already have my answer prepared.

'You know I always presumed I'd have kids, then I was okay with not having them, but when I saw that tiny baby in Anne-marie's arms, it made me realise quite how wonderful a baby would be.' I raise my shoulders. 'If it's to be for me.'

He nods.

'Does that change things for you?'

'Yes. It makes me love you even more. The thought of us having our own baby one day.'

'Hold on. Let's try to get this relationship up and running first.' I laugh and relief floods through my veins like the bubbles in champagne.

'We're only a couple of hours away on a flight?' He sits forward, taking this all in. 'All those adventures to look forward to!'

'I know!'

'Exotic weekend breaks!'

'I know!'

'Rome?' he says.

'Venice!' I enthuse.

'But someday soon I want to carry you over the threshold of Rosehill Cottage?'

See Annemarie, my being-lifted-into-his-arms days aren't over, I think.

'On one condition.' I lean in, my eyes serious.

'Anything.'

'We are not having our wedding at the goddamn Moritz hotel!'

He throws back his head and roars laughing. 'Agreed.'

'Something small and tasteful in Nerja maybe, where my parents live? The El Salvador church on the Balcon is something very special,' I say, blushing slightly at how I'm getting ahead of myself. But he nods, his handsome face as happy as I've seen it. He lets go of my hands and stands out of the booth.

'One moment please.' He holds his index finger up to me.

I can't take my eyes off him as he walks across the empty floor and I see him at the DJ box. The DJ removes one covered pad of his headphones and nods. As Adam walks back, the two Madonnas' heads turn, but his eyes only connect with mine. Once again, I'm intoxicated by him. Floored. Adam is the antithesis of me settling. He reaches the booth, leans down and puts his cold lips on mine and we kiss softly.

'What was that about?' I ask.

And then it starts.

The opening bars I know so well.

'Would you like to dance?' Adam pulls himself up tall, extends his hand.

Now I've had the time of my life.

'No?' My hand flies to cover my open mouth. 'You didn't?'

'I get the feeling it's your favourite film, right? I thought this could be our song?' He can't keep the massive grin off his face.

I'm speechless as I take his hand and he leads me onto the empty dance floor. The music washes over me. I put my hand around the back of his head, twist his messy hair, not so gently, in between my fingers, pull him in close. We are oblivious to the last remaining punters watching us as Adam spins me now and I throw my head back and laugh, giving a few moves from the famous last dance of the film. I dance across the floor to where he stands and he lifts me off my feet, his arms tight around my waist as I kiss him with everything I feel inside. When we part, we're breathless. I lean my head on his shoulder as we listen. The heavy certainty of our future, like a smooth Cotswolds stone in my jeans pocket. I've never felt this happy in my entire life.

I say, 'Shall we go to bed, Adam?' and take his hand in my other hand, and he follows me out of the bar as the last of the crowd gives us a cheer.

We walk across the lobby to the lift. The doors part, we step in, and as they close, I look into his eyes, stopping inches from his mouth, and in time with the music, I whisper: 'And I owe it all to you . . .'

Nine Months Later ...

O H, YOU DIDN'T!' My mouth drops as I beckon four delivery
men into the games room at Sir Patrick Dun's. It's a dark,
sleeting Christmas Eve morning. I cradle the phone under my
chin. It's my boyfriend, Adam, on the line. Oh, hark at me!

'I hope it fits! I saw it online, just outside Dublin, and took the
chance. Merry Christmas,' he tells me.

The delivery men are carrying a brand-new pool table that
Adam has had delivered.

'Margaret! Paul! Look!' Máiréad, hardly recognisable in her
smart skirt and cardigan combo, her hair set into neat pin curls,
trots behind them in her comfortable slippers, Garfield close at
her heels. Ever since Máiréad took residence, Garfield hasn't left
her side. I'm happy he's happy and he has company all day when
I'm at work, not to mention the endless treats.

'Oh, Adam! You shouldn't have, it's far too much, but I'm so
glad you did! This is the best Christmas present I could have
asked for!' I tell him excitedly.

'I gotta go, I'm in Gloucester Quays, last-minute shopping
with Freya. Here, hang on, she wants you – she's pulling the
phone out of my hand.'

'Lexie!'

'Hi, sweetheart.' I beam at her sweet voice.

'Hi! We got you other presents too, so don't worry! They are under the tree for when you come over next week. Daddy wrapped them all himself. He never wraps!'

'And I have a few things for you too.' A few, I think, laughing. I'll need a second suitcase with all the stuff I've bought for her. The most special being a signed photo of Niall Horan I got through a collector on eBay.

'Okay, Dad wants you back. Bu'bye.'

'I love you, Lexie. Can't wait to see you.'

'I love you too, Adam!' I say as all the residents slowly gather in the games room beside the pine-scented Christmas tree. Happy, well-lived faces all round. I sign a docket as the delivery men take their leave.

'Now then, I had a surprise for you all this morning, but this was not it!' I tell them.

'I bagsy first break!' Máiréad says.

'You're on!' Paul Buckland leans on his Zimmer frame, removes his waistcoat and rolls up his sleeves. He looks suddenly taller.

'Hello?'

I hear her voice and I spin round. It's Annemarie, Tom and baby Ben.

'Aha, here they are!'

Instantly I reach out for Ben, and his chubby arms tighten around my neck and I breathe him in. He's dressed today in the red and green Elf outfit I bought for him in Teeny-Tiny Hands in Silverside, complete with bobble hat and booties.

'Oh, there he is! Hello, my boy. Oh, who's a beautiful boy then? Who is? Ben is, that's who is.' I plant butterfly kisses all over his chubby cheeks.

'Seriously, Lexie, you know he'll bawl when I try to take him off you. He's obsessed with his fairy godmother.'

Annemarie, munching on a chocolate croissant, takes a seat

by the fire. She looks like my old Annemarie again. A sense of fulfilment echoes around her very being and she's filled out, put back on much-needed weight. She smells of contentment, if contentment had a smell.

'I'll go grab us some coffees – won't be a tick,' Tom says as he leaves the room.

'Cream and sugar please, Tom,' Annemarie requests.

Things have been so much better between us all; we've found a new common ground. That is Ben. I babysit regularly while they go out for dinner or to the cinema during the week.

I ease myself gently into a cosy armchair by the side of the fire and pop Ben, facing out, on my bouncing knee. All the residents, men and women equally, come to coo over him as Kevin, the owner, pops his head in.

'Shall I play some music over the intercom before lunch?'

'Yeah lovely,' I say.

'What is it?' Máiréad asks, sitting into a high-backed leather armchair as Garfield climbs up on her knee. She strokes him lovingly.

'Oxtail soup, followed by bacon and cabbage, finished off with a sherry trifle. That suit you, Máiréad?' Kevin winks at her. She rolls her tongue around her mouth, settles her teeth in place, smacks her lips.

'Gorgeous,' she says and smacks again. I catch Annemarie's eye and we smile.

'I'll miss you not being around Silverside when I go back to work part-time, Máiréad,' Annemarie tells her warmly.

I watch as Paul sets up the pool table, settling the coloured balls perfectly into the triangle. Máiréad chalks her cue expertly. Bing Crosby's soothing voice comes over us as he croons the first bars of 'White Christmas'. Ben starts to cry gently, and I stand up.

'He's not due a feed for another while,' Annemarie says.

My phone beeps, and I check it. It's from Jackie:

'C'mere, would ya look who's come to visit me in Dubai! And he's wearing flip-flops so he doesn't need socks!!'

It's a picture of Nnamdi, the barista from Café Tree, in three-quarter-length khaki shorts, a sleeveless T-shirt and luminous flip-flops, his arm draped around Jackie, both beaming in front of the Burj Al Arab hotel.

Ben cries harder. I slide my phone into my back pocket and get up with him. Down the long corridor, through the hall and into the conservatory we go. I gently bounce him in my arms and he stops crying, just whimpers, then nestles deeper into my shoulder. His warm, sweet breath on my neck. The sleet turns to a light snow and the skies darken. Looking out, I take a slow, deep breath, armed with the wondrous knowledge that it's not what we have in life but who we have in our life that matters.

'But most of all, I'm scared of walking out of this room and never feeling the rest of my whole life the way I feel when I'm with you.'

Frances 'Baby' Houseman,
Dirty Dancing